# IRIS

## BIRTH OF THE
## IMMORTALS

## O. BOGOSIAN

First paperback edition September 2023

Book cover and interior design: Kelly M. Carter

ISBN 979-8-35092-672-9 (paperback)

ISBN 979-8-35092-673-6 (ebook)

www.thefallenangelseries.com

*To God who has never left me,*

*to my family and friends who kept*

*pushing me to follow my dreams.*

*Thank you from the bottom of my heart.*

# CONTENTS

# PROLOGUE

I the first Realm of Seven, ethereal beings created by divine fire stood together and watched over the fallen children of Adam. These celestial spirits, known as the Gregori, originated when a single mortal man and woman were formed from the clay of Earth. As commanded by the sole Creator of all things, the Gregori's purpose was to protect and guide humans into a prosperous existence.

Their charge was only to observe the mortals and help when commanded by the Seventh Realm. They could not interfere with the choices made by the man and woman nor attach themselves as a protector to any offspring. From the fall of man inside the great Garden of Eden, free will was given to mortals, and it was to remain as such until death.

For hundreds of years, the vigilant Gregori stood guard over the mortals, watching them in their daily struggles of labor, grief, pain, and inevitable death. But throughout all their trials, the people's spirits did not diminish from their light. Instead, they grew stronger, smarter, and their children more beautiful with each new generation. Easily enchanted by the Gregori, the daughters of Adam's beauty and grace almost matched the unearthly allure of the Gregori themselves until they slowly seduced every Gregori that watched over them.

The Gregori's lust for the mortal women rose so great that they soon disregarded their duties as Watchers of Earth and willingly gave themselves to the powers of self-enlightenment. Unaware of their gradual morphing, the glorious celestial beings fell. The conveyer of this dangerous rebellion was ever so pleased to see his intricate web of deceit and lies come together so naturally by the sworn protectors of mortals. Tainting as many Gregori as possible was done effortlessly, for once the dark seed of lust had taken root in their souls, it was impossible to remove.

As the one who proclaimed proper illumination through knowledge and declared himself a true sovereign deity, Samayaza had already begun what he thought would lead him back to the Seventh Realm. There, he would deliver immeasurable retribution to the one he once called Lord for exiling him from all seven realms. The dark prince might have lost the first battle of the realms, but he managed to influence a few before being banished.

Samayaza, who had lacked the vigor to fight alongside the dark prince, now ironically became an ally. As one of two appointed commanders among the two hundred Gregori of the First Realm, Samayaza had accomplished more than expected of him, for all two hundred beings of virtue had become enamored with the idea of taking on human forms and marrying mortal brides.

With immense pleasure, the Dark Prince would lead his new legion to corrupt and defile the Holy One's precious humans. By distorting truth and morality, he would wipe out hope, and by invoking fear, he would weaken their cornerstones. Block by block, he would crush them with the weight of their sins until only darkness prevailed throughout the entire Earth. And in the end, he would sit on a throne made of their weak and pathetic bones.

# CHAPTER ONE

## IN THE BEGINNING

Majestic beings gathered around their newly chosen leader, patiently awaiting orders for their most rebellious and disobedient act yet. With no remorse or second thoughts, the Gregori were ready to follow Samayaza into possible damnation as they readied themselves to take an oath that would seal their fates forever.

Clad in dark robes of gray, they stood magnificently grand and beautiful. Made by divine fire and strength, they could not look anything less than magnificent and enchanting. Now, they stood in opposition to their original purpose; all had given permission and allegiance to the one leader they had chosen. In doing so, they relinquished their fate along with their pure white robes that were fashioned for them by their Creator, and in return, they now wore dark garments that promised power and god-like worship from the ones they were to protect.

Their chosen commander, Samayaza, stood before the Altar of Oath, arrogant and proud in a dark robe of black Altar. They stood silent in the sacred Third Realm and waited on their leader. Samayaza had successfully enticed and influenced them into complete submission of their fiery souls. He had been able to wield and maneuver their minds ever so smoothly and cast them into the mold that would bring the absolute power to him and the one he served. Samayaza knew it would be easy to sway his brethren into error, primarily when the most effective tool was already provided for them and had been in front of them for hundreds of years—lust.

The need for power was an insatiable hunger within them, and the allure of lust called to each feverishly. Eager were these beings to take on mortal form and consummate their crime through the daughters of Eve. All had one purpose now: to complete their vows and begin to conquer the realm they'd once protected—Earth and all who dwelled in it. This act was only the beginning of the great victories preceding their descending. Knowledge and titles would be granted to those following their rule without question and a softening of earthly life's burdens and toils. And all this would prove that the Gregori were worthy of worship and were actual deities greater than the one who created them. Their presence alone would be enough to gain adoration among the docile species below, but to feed them small quantities of knowledge and watch them battle for every morsel would be a sumptuous feast of entertainment.

Samayaza was ready to begin the oath but noticed his brother, Daniel, was not in their midst. Interesting. He knew Daniel would come, but he wanted to make a point by having them all wait on him. Samayaza raised an eyebrow and thought about how clever his fellow brother was. Daniel was the first Gregori; thus, he demanded obedience and respect. Following another and falling from "grace" was not in his design. His discipline to follow his genetic code was solid. Directly embedded into his very essence, it was not easy to break.

But Samayaza knew something the others did not. He knew weakness had been plaguing Daniel for some time now. Though powerful in his purpose, Daniel was still susceptible to the same emotions that had infected the rest of the Gregori. It took Daniel longer to break since he was their true commander of the First Realm.

Samayaza did not worry at all about his brother's actions. Instead, he began to chant a very soft and sweet melody. A light wind came forth and brought with it the presence of a beautiful, fragile flower. Fluttering long blue petals with yellow veins, it landed and sat perfectly in Samayaza's palm. He looked at it and smiled, then turned to the Altar of Oath again and gently placed the flower in the middle. Samayaza knew that if anything were causing Daniel's hesitation, it would flee when he heard Samayaza bind himself to this flower.

For you see, this flower was not just some fleeting creation of nature. No, it was a very fragile yet mystical flower only found in the sacred Garden of Eden. It held beauty, strength, and the essence of purity lost to the mortals in their great fall from grace.

Called the Iris, this delicate flower had a unique and special meaning to Daniel. One that Samayaza would be quick to use if Daniel was hesitant in his pledge to descend.

This flower was the most beautiful in the Garden of Eden, and just like above, it grew below on Earth. The name also belonged to the most beautiful of all the daughters of Eve, whom Daniel had been appointed Watcher of since her conception. He had protected her and watched her grow into the most charming and appealing of females on Earth. He had become attached without even realizing it, going against his purpose by coveting. Samayaza knew this little secret of Daniel's and planned to use it accordingly, should his soon-to-be-former commander fail to appear.

All the Gregori knew of Iris' beauty and strength but kept silent and veiled their interests until opportune. They had all coveted her and were ready to battle it out, even with each other, once they descended, but they feared Daniel's wrath. But Daniel was not one to bring down so quickly. So, they would wait—something they all knew how to do best. Being the first Gregori created had its advantages, and Daniel made sure they all knew he would use those advantages against his brethren if they even thought of claiming Iris as their mate. Even though he would not claim her in the way they were planning once they descended, he knew that Samayaza would already have claimed her if he did not comply before any of his brethren could get near her. Daniel didn't want to see Iris's soul broken and defiled by Samayaza, so he agreed to take the oath and relinquish his command if Samayaza would take on the total penalty for their actions.

Samayaza agreed. And thus, Daniel would pass his leadership on and become second in command once they descended to Earth.

Clouds departed, slowly clearing a path through the two hundred Gregori. Soon enough, Daniel stood in front of the Altar of Oath. Clad in a deep forest green robe, he looked straight at Samayaza in a challenging yet solemn stance. His presence demanded obedience, and though he glanced at no one, all who were present slightly bowed their heads in respect. This action irked Samayaza. But knowing he would be in command soon, he kept himself calm.

Daniel's gaze shot directly at the fragile flower in the center of the Altar, and the bloom disappeared in a blink of an eye.

Samayaza only smiled and raised his eyebrows. "Blame me not for what you would have done, brother."

A small flame of fire swirled in Daniels's eyes. "Assume not my judgment on you, brother, for you will be disappointed."

Samayaza nodded slightly, presenting his truce in the matter for now. There was never a conquest that Samayaza would relinquish, but for this moment and purpose, he would release his grip on the subject.

Samayaza ignited the cauldrons surrounding the Altar with a simple command and looked at Daniel. "Let us begin, brothers."

But not once did he look around at his brethren. Instead, with malice in his eyes, he looked upon Daniel in an almost mocking, challenging gaze. Power began to transfer to him through the Altar. If Daniel hesitated to relinquish those powers, Samayaza would be happy to bind himself to Iris before Daniel could blink him into oblivion. Once attached, she could never be free.

Silent message heard, Daniel reluctantly placed his hand on the Altar, and a measuring scale appeared above his hand. Samayaza placed his own hand on the Altar opposite Daniel's, continuing to chant with the rest of the Gregori. Light beamed out of Daniel and hit the scale with speed and force. The scale was a bright light that reflected Daniel's strength and power. The Gregori, while chanting, stood in awe at this display of power. They knew of Daniel's strength and willpower, but to see it in raw form was a treat. The bright, burning scale shifted to where the side leaning toward Samayaza was greater in weight, and suddenly, the power shot straight into Samayaza. His eyes closed, his mouth wavered, and a slight hiss escaped him at the magnitude of strength overflowing in his fiery body. He reveled in the new power, raised his hands to his brethren, and continued to chant louder and louder until all the Gregori began to glow, and then all turned into light.

# CHAPTER TWO

The night air was cool and crisp, drastically changed from the afternoon heat. The heavens were clear of clouds and bright stars for my sister and me to gaze upon from the humble rooftop of our family's home. We had been sleeping most of the night away peacefully until Boria began speaking in her sleep and woke me from my restful slumber. I would have been angry, but she was troubled and weeping. I softly awakened her to release her of whatever dream haunted her, and of course, neither of us could fall back to sleep. So, we did what any two sisters would. We shared secrets, complained about our chores, imagined how our future husbands would be, and stared at the luminous night sky.

"Have you ever seen so many stars? I do not believe we couldn't find a patch of the night sky even if we tried!"

My sister's light laughter warmed my heart. She was the most graceful and caring sister anyone could wish for.

"Hmm...there does seem to be quite a number of stars," I answered as I looked up curiously. "I wonder if Grandfather Enok has taken notice of them." He constantly monitored the heavens and told us what he believed the changes meant.

Boria shifted her weight onto her other elbow and rolled her eyes at me. "Iris, there's nothing amiss. Just look at them, and if you are to have thoughts, it should be whether gods sit upon each one and stare down at us as we stare up at them."

Now it was my turn to roll my eyes at her. I could not help but laugh and shake my head at her nonsense. "Boria, only you would think of vanity by looking at the heavens."

She smiled back, accepting my accusation with no objection. She knew she was beautiful and always looked for things that were the same as her. I, on the other hand, could not care less if beauty resided upon one's exterior, but I would mind if they were ugly in nature. Explaining this way of thinking to Boria would be as foreign as teaching swine to be clean. My thoughts always lingered on the artistry all around us. My family, our village, and our life-giving river, the Euphrates. No amount of heat could dry its flow. I believed the sun's heat was always quenched by it, and our lands flourished with its calm waters. It was our source of life, including the lives of our animals and grains. I could not imagine another place thriving as much as ours.

Hearing it now instantly brought peace. Our attention returned to the magnificently lit sky, with so many stars that it dimmed the moon. The moon could have rested, allowing the stars to shine in their place. It was lovely but unusual. But I decided not to think much of it and followed my sister's advice to enjoy the moment. Everything was clear, like she had said. All seemed calm. Even the breeze was tender in its caress, bringing the fresh scent of the river.

More than anything, I wanted to enjoy this moment for what it was, but I could sense her trouble and could not ignore it. In the morning, my beautiful sister would be promised to a man who was not of her choosing. A man who was not from our village, nor even our side of the river, but a man who descended from Cain.

"Boria, I know you are tormented by what is to be when the sun rises. I beg of you to speak and not keep it hidden." I hoped I had not ruined this moment with my simple plea, but I couldn't just sit there while I knew deep inside, she was hurting.

She closed her eyes, brows furrowed in sadness as she inhaled deeply. I felt uneasy about disturbing her peace, but I did not want her to feel as though she was alone. I waited for an eternity as she shifted slightly and pushed back her long black hair, revealing beautiful blue eyes filled with tears. My heart ached instantly for her.

"Nothing troubles me, Iris. I am happy to fulfill my destiny." She lied as tears stained her cheeks.

"Then why are you crying?"

Taking a deep breath, she said, "I am not crying. I am just...."

"Just frightened of becoming a wife to a man from Grandfather Turian's village?"

"No," she replied softly as she continued to look down at her hand.

It hurt my heart to know she did not speak the truth. We had trusted each other so much, yet her stubbornness over carrying this weight on her own was silly. Not knowing what more to say, I held her hand and hoped that would be enough to let her know how much I cared for her. She still did not look at me but continued to look down in despair. She inhaled deeply and laid her head down upon my lap. She began to cry, at which point tears overflowed from my eyes as well.

This dilemma needed to be corrected. It felt wrong; Boria was a pure, joyful, and clean soul. Though her stubbornness was strong, her heart always thought of helping others. She was my friend, confidant, and the one I always yearned to be like. Yet, she would endure a lifetime of unhappiness for her kindness because of a promise made by another many years ago. How could it be right to give her away to a depraved village just because of some old oath?

A fate not of her choosing. A marriage not of her desire and a man not worthy of her spirit. He would never truly love her but would only sully her soul and tarnish her light, a man who wished to have her only because he lusted after her external essence. He cared nothing for who she was and what she cared about. He did not deserve her, and yet, no one was trying to stop this unholy bond from taking place.

Her tears continued rolling down my hands, and I felt helpless. Even though she was not speaking of her pain, she was showing it, and that was enough for me. Anger stirred within me. My beloved sister, my only sibling, protected and taught me so much, from shielding me from bees when gathering honey to rampaging sheep when I was young. She had taught me how to swim in the river's calm waters and see the beauty in almost everything that surrounded us, including animals that frightened me, like scorpions and serpents. I was not going to watch her spirit be crushed like this. Now, it was my turn to be stubborn, whether she wanted my help or not.

"Boria, I will speak to Mother and Father. I will make them change their agreement somehow." I felt her stir as I continued to speak. "Maybe we can give them all our trades for a summer and our sheep?"

Rising beside me, she smiled and wiped tears from her fragile face. Her eyes were red and swollen; she calmly said, "And if they agree, how will we survive without any source of food and trade within our village? Do you even think of anyone other than yourself!" she snapped, irritated.

"I am thinking of others, of you!" How could she even say such a thing?

"You cannot escape fate, Iris! This fate is mine, so allow me to fulfill it in peace, knowing at least that you, Mother, and Father will be all right when I am gone." Her tone was defeated, and she looked at me with sadness.

I could no longer hold in what was bursting to come out. "I cannot lose you!" I cried as I threw myself upon her, wrapping my arms tightly around her waist, wishing with every bit of my soul that this was not real, that no one would take her from me when the sun rose. She belonged here with her family until she chose a man worthy of her heart.

Her comforting voice gently soothed my restless spirit. "You will never lose me, Iris. I will always find my way to you, no matter what happens. We are sisters and always will be."

Both of us were crying. We knew what was to come, and we had no way to stop it. We held each other for a long time and didn't let go, even though we knew morning's light was getting closer. For now, the night was ours, and we would watch the stars and moon until they disappeared.

Our eyes now dry and empty of tears, Boria and I remained

huddled together. My soul still cried, but I knew I had to show courage, not despair. It was my turn to show her strength, as she had always shown me. I would not be useless to her by giving in to my sorrow.

I lifted my face to the stars, the many, many beautiful stars that shined down upon our restless and heavy hearts. Closing my eyes, I made a last and final desperate plea to our Creator. Please hear me, anyone who will listen to me, take away this fate that is to come to Boria and place it upon me in her stead. Do not let her take this path that will lead to her destruction; instead, give her one worthy of her heart.

I breathed forth my silent prayer into the night sky and hoped that maybe Boria was right and angels were sitting upon the stars who would hear my prayer and take it to the grand Creator. Upon that final thought, I opened my eyes and stared at the sky while holding Boria.

I was expecting the stars to continue shining in the ever-vast night sky, but to my utter amazement, something extraordinary was happening. I could not believe what I was witnessing. The stars were moving!

"Boria!" My voice came out in a rasp of excitement. "Boria, look up. Look at the sky!"

Without casting my gaze from the moving stars, I felt her slowly release me. She, too, was silenced by what we were seeing.

The stars swirled and twisted into a beautiful array of lights, dancing to a silent melody I wished I could hear. They left streaks of light behind them as they drew apart, then came together again with colors I did not recognize, yet they were so beautiful I would remember them for all eternity. All thought ceased, and every emotion fled. Only awe remained, and I had never felt so at peace. It was as though I was being lifted into their dance and cradled by the warmth of their light. All around us, stars continued to sway and illuminate the darkness. They gathered close, and in one beautiful swirl of color, swiftly fled to the east toward Mt. Hermon.

Excitement within my heart, I turned to Boria. Her mouth hung agape, and her eyes stared at the night sky. I knew we had both witnessed something incredible, and I hadn't just imagined it all.

"Is this a dream?" Boria asked as she slowly turned to look at me.

I shook my head and stared at her in disbelief. Had we just now witnessed a heavenly event?

"We have to wake Mother and Father." Boria frantically stood and began to make her way down the rooftop.

My mind racing with questions, I quickly followed her, leaving behind our blanket and plate of dates. I couldn't explain what we had seen, but I knew Grandfather Enok would know if Father and Mother did not. Grandfather Enok had vast knowledge of the stars or anything divine. He would know precisely what we had just witnessed.

Boria was speedy for someone who wasn't that tall, and it was such a short distance that I struggled to keep pace. Once we both made it down, we quickly came around the side of the house and burst through the front door.

Trailing behind Boria, I did not miss a step and followed her closely, a bit too close as she abruptly stopped, and I didn't. I bumped her forward, but she didn't get as angry as usual. A candle burned, which meant Father or Mother was not asleep as they should be. I slowly made my way around her to see what the matter was.

"We must leave now!" Father said as he swung a satchel onto his back.

"What?" Boria asked, confused.

Mother approached us and grabbed Boria's hand. "We will not let them have our firstborn or second." She looked at me. "For as long as there is breath in your Father and me, we will not allow them to take either of you. No oath or pact will ever separate us." Her eyes filled with tears but did not spill over. She was a strong woman, and we rarely saw Mother cry.

As Mother held Boria's hands, reassuring her protection, I looked at Father. He smiled at me, and I knew he would never let them take her.

"Hurry now; we have very little time to leave the village before they start making their way for Boria. We must pass the road leading them here before they do." Father handed me a smaller satchel. "Keep this safe; it is our family's right to everything we own. And a loaf of bread for the short journey to Grandfather Enok's."

Surprised, I looked at him. "Father." I hesitated a moment, "Are you sure I should be the one to carry this?"

"Are you not a part of this family?" he asked thoughtfully.

"Yes," I stated the obvious.

"Then, you must take the responsibility this family gives you." Without another word, he ordered us to hurry and pack the few personal items we didn't want to leave behind. I accepted what he said without question. He was right. I might be only sixteen summers, but I was no less part of this family than Boria. She was a mere summer ahead of me and received more responsibilities than I did.

I quickly went for what I knew I couldn't leave behind. Running to my cot, I reached under the many blankets and grabbed the little dried flower between two small pieces of sheep's skin bound with twine. I figured we would be gone for a while, and who knew what they would do with our belongings? I would not have them find this and destroy it! It was the only one of its kind and so beautiful when I first found it by the river. The colors of the petals were vibrant and soft. The shape was unusual, too. It had some long petals that flowed out of the center with another lively color that darted through the middle of each petal but barely touched the end. Now it just looked frail, but it still held its beautiful colors. It was all I had left of that unusual yet alluring flower.

"Iris, we must leave now!" Mother cried as she stood by the door, motioning with her hand to hurry.

Mesmerized by my flower, I had not noticed that Father and Boria had already left. I quickly put it in my satchel and ran toward the door.

"Quickly, child, we do not have much time! The sun will soon rise."

Hastily, the four of us made our way out of the village without alerting our neighbors. The only person who saw us leave was my Father's friend. He nodded and looked away as he returned to his home. Which meant sunrise was close. He was a farmer by trade and woke just a bit before the sun would rise. We only had a little time left.

Father must have also realized this since his steps quickened along the path that led out of our village. We followed earnestly, almost running in fear of being caught. I wondered what would happen if we did get caught, but I guessed it would not be good.

My mother's father wasn't one to take mercy on anyone, not even his kin. Mother had told us stories of him and how he had his brother killed for disobeying the laws of his temple. Mother had said she covered Boria's eyes at the time to shield her from that horror. But I knew by the loss of color from Boria's face that she had seen more than she would let on. Mother had said he had been sliced from belly to throat and bled over an altar to his gods.

That was the last time Mother ever took her to see her father. He was ruthless and cunning. I thanked the heavens Mother was nothing like him. She was more like her own mother. But her mother died in childbirth, along with what would have been an only male sibling.

"Shh!" Father crouched and pulled us all in close.

Stuck deep in my thoughts again, I hadn't noticed we were already past the village and on the road that led to Grandfather Enok's. It was mountainous, full of big rocks and scattered bushes here and there. I heard footsteps and the sound of men coming closer.

I looked over to Father and saw him cradling Mother closer. Boria moved into their huddle, as did I. This was the company coming for Boria! It sounded large and with many men! Why would they have so many? It was not like she had a large dowry that needed so many people to carry.

And then I heard a voice that caused my skin to rise in bumps. It was rough in tone yet slightly frail and aged. There was no doubt this had to be Mother's father. The lack of mercy in his voice was chilling. I could only imagine how terrifying he would be face to face. It was said Grandfather Turian was born under a malevolent moon where many died in sacrifice to be birthed into this world. Mother never spoke of the details regarding that tale, and I did not care to ask.

I peered over the side of the rock and saw many men dressed in Grandfather Turian's temple colors. Of course, he would bring his show of power to our village. Mother said he lived off intimidating others, especially those he viewed as blasphemous worms. According to him, this was everyone in our village because we did not believe in his teachings. Mostly we thought like my Grandfather Enok; one God, one way.

Boria shivered next to me. I put my arm around her tiny waist and squeezed closer. Father looked over to us in silent reassurance that everything would be all right. I half smiled, letting him know I had Boria. Nodding, he turned his attention to Mother, who was just as scared as Boria. I could not blame her; the man making her family uproot and run was her cruel father.

The sounds of the small legion that followed our grandfather and Boria's suitor began to fade when we heard footsteps approaching where we were hiding.

"If I do not relieve myself, I will end up leaving a trail leading into this forsaken village!" a guard spoke roughly.

Our hearts stopped, and I looked over to Father, as did Mother and Boria. We were going to be exposed! He would not miss us if he came around the rock to relieve himself by the tree.

My Father pushed my mother toward us, and I saw him reach for something from his cloak. A sharp pointed rock tied to a stick came out, and the guard was staring at us before I could say anything. Father leaped to his feet and struck him on his head, knocking the surprised guard to the ground with a loud thud.

The sound alerted his companions, and we heard them approaching us. Boria and Mother panicked, as did I. The yells warned more of the others as they charged toward us. Mother grabbed rocks and handed them to us, but it was too late. More of Grandfather's guards overtook Father. I tried to jump forward to protect him, but Mother pushed me back, as did Boria, to protect me.

Everything happened at such a pace that I could not keep up.

"Run, Iris!" Mother yelled at me and then at Boria, but Boria refused to move, and so did I.

Guards moved in as Mother plunged forward with a rock in hand. Boria followed suit, but both became subdued instantly, as they were no match for Grandfather's guards.

I could see more men turning and making their way toward us. Fear exploded deep within my belly. Mother yelled and demanded to be released while a guard roughly pushed Father against the boulder we hid behind. Boria did her best to pull away from the guards but failed miserably. Her petite frame was no match for their powerful grip.

Two guards came straight toward me with wicked smiles on their faces. I knew it was over, and our chance to rescue Boria had ended. I took a few steps back from the tree I stood next to. I could hear Father and Mother yelling, but all I could understand was that we had been caught fleeing, and who knew what punishment would be now?

A large crackling sound came from above. The tree that stood perfectly upright toppled over directly on the guards.

"Run, Iris, run to Grandfather Enok and tell him what has happened!" Father yelled.

I started to back away but couldn't run and leave them. I could hear men yelling and running toward the fallen tree. I had to go now but found myself immobile.

"Run, Iris!" Mother yelled.

Though my heart told me to stay, my feet began to move. I started to back away but could not run and leave them. "NO!" I cried out, "I am not going to leave you!"

Losing his patience, Father yelled, "GO! NOW, IRIS!"

Without looking back and satchel still in hand, I ran. I ran faster than I had ever run before. Blood rushed into my face, and heat stirred everywhere in my body. I could hear the sounds of men behind me, but I didn't look back. I kept running until I couldn't hear anything except for the loud beating of my heart, echoing throughout my entire body. Tears had dried the moment they had come down my face as I kept running. I did not want to stop; something kept pushing me to continue. But my ears rang loudly, and I knew I had to stop before I collapsed and lost consciousness.

I saw the small oasis of trees we would always see right before Grandfather Enok's hut. I had to make it and tell him what was happening to us. But I had to rest. My breaths were short and quick, and my heart felt like it was about to leap out of my chest! I had to stop.

All that was on my mind was my family and how I had to get them help. Only Grandfather Enok could command the men in the village and have the courage to confront my mother's father. I could not stop; I must keep moving.

I finally made it to the trees and fell to the ground. My vision turned black, and heat enveloped my body. Struggling to breathe, I dared not keep my eyes closed for too long. I slowly forced myself to sit against the tree and rested my arm on the small rocks beside it. The shade was lovely, but the desert heat blew in my face, making it harder to catch my breath. My hands drooped to my sides, lifeless and sweaty. I felt so tired and weak.

Still heaving and trying to collect myself, I felt something move next to me. Halfway opening my eye, I saw something thin, black, and long slither down the side of my leg. I grew stiff in fear. A cleverly hidden serpent was among the rocks I leaned upon. It came out so quickly and quietly that I had no time to think about what to do.

Fear gripped me, and before I could even think to move, I felt a sharp pierce against my ankle and the furious burn that followed. I could not believe my luck. It had bitten me and slithered away into the desert, leaving me behind to die. There was no one near me to take the poison out, and I could not bend my ankle toward my mouth that way. I had to try and make it to Grandfather Enok; that was my only chance.

Still heaving from my run, tired, and scared for my family, I got up and began to walk toward his home. I could already feel the burn in my ankle, and I was barely halfway there. But I had to keep moving. I couldn't stop; it would mean the end for my family and myself.

I tried to ignore the burn that had made its way up throughout my leg, and every step became heavier than the one before. There wasn't much time left, I could feel my strength draining as I pushed myself for one more step, but I collapsed in the desert sun. The poison burned as it made its way up my body, and I couldn't move. I felt helpless and useless. I had failed my family, and now, I was going to perish alone.

Visions of my family floated into my head, of Boria and I playing by the river when we were younger, and climbing onto the rooftop of our home for the first time, and remembering how scared I had been and how Boria had comforted me as I climbed back down. I needed her now, and she needed me. But

I had failed.

My whole body burned, and all I could hear was the slow beat of my heart. I turned over onto my belly. Tears and sand mixed as I tried to crawl, but it was useless. Face down in the dirt, I stretched my hand in a futile attempt to reach the direction of my grandfather's hut. Through the pain and hopelessness deep within my soul, I felt a cool hand touch my burning one. I didn't even bother to open my eyes as the effort was too much and most likely my imagination.

"Iris," whispered a sweet unearthly voice.

Yes, it had to be the venom creating this final illusion. I tried raising my head but whimpered in pain instead. Defeated, I allowed whatever fate to befall me. Anything was better than the pain I felt. I allowed myself to fall into the cool darkness without hesitation. Not knowing if I would wake again but hoping the pain would stop.

My last waking moment was trying to utter a small prayer for my family and their forgiveness, as I had failed them.

# CHAPTER THREE

A cool yet calm, reviving breeze caressed my face as I awoke with lush grass beneath my hands and feet. Healthy, abundant bushes and trees I had never seen encircled me—delicate flowers with the most dazzling colors and petals interlaced between brush and trees. The air smelled fresh and crisp. Not even the night air that carried the river's incredible scent at home could compare to how restoring the air was here, wherever here was.

Where could I be? I knew this was not anywhere in my village nor anywhere surrounding my village. Where was this place? Nothing was this beautiful and untouched by the sun's heat. Truly refreshed, I began to rise and instantly felt an ache in my leg. I touched my ankle with my finger and felt the bite of the snake. I looked down, and there it was—two tiny pricks where the fangs had injected poison into my body.

Suddenly everything came back to me. My family! The soldiers and my evil grandfather! I was going to Grandfather Enok, but a snake bit me.

As everything returned to me, I looked around and wondered where I was again. How had I gotten here? Despite the pain, I slowly rose and began to limp along. My leg felt weak, but I did not care. My curiosity burned more potent than the pain.

I wandered between and around the trees and bushes as I began walking. I found no one. Only more wonderous, green plants and colorful flowers. I did step in a small cool stream of water that trickled down between beautiful blooms, blue petals with white tongues to them.

My eyes grew wide as I recognized the flower. It was the same that I had held so tightly under my cot, the one I had seen once by our river. So beautiful to see so many in one area. It was truly breathtaking.

But where was I? Should I not be dead after the serpent's bite?

Curiosity beckoned, and I left my beautiful flowers behind as I continued toward a clearing. Soft sunlight peeked through the trees as I pushed past unusual and extraordinary green bushes with large leaves I had never seen before.

With a final step out of the lush forest, I stopped, shivering as I stared at a grand temple. It stood before me as though out of a dream. Wide beautiful steps led to a more extensive set of doors with unfamiliar carved images of great symbols upon them. Fire pits surrounded every enormous pillar that stood on the outer edge. Forgetting my aches, I began walking toward it.

As I got closer, I noticed a small stream of water flowing around the temple, with rocks that shimmered as the sun shone from within them. But in all different colors. It was most pleasing to the eyes and very enchanting.

My heart fell momentarily as I remembered something my mother had told me about a beautiful temple. Could this be my evil grandfather's temple? Rumors of its glory were spread all over our village. Of how grand and magnificent it was and how great a tribute it was for the gods. And how many men had sacrificed their lives building it?

But how could this be? How could I have gotten to his temple while dying in the sand from a snake bite?

Beautiful flowers and dark green grass surrounded me like a dream. This could be a dream. Or was I already dead?

I brought my hand to my face, and I could feel it. I reached for my hair and slightly pulled on it; I was alive. I could feel the tug. Yet I did not feel discomfort. Scowling, I pulled again. I felt the pull, but again, no pain. I pinched myself and came to the same conclusion. I felt the pressure but no pain. Like my leg, the slight ache was there, but no deep pain like before. Should I go in and seek help, or would I walk right into my grandfather's trap? If it even was my grandfather's temple. I could not imagine someone so ugly in nature could produce something so alluring as this.

I swallowed hard and walked toward the doors. Maybe I would see my family or be reunited with them. Either way, I had to keep moving, and with that thought in mind, I walked toward the stairs made of white and shiny rocks. The closer I got, the brighter they glowed. Even the ones in the water were turning into a magnificent array of colors, so beguiling I wanted to touch them. I would have done so if it had not been for the large doors opening, but the temple called for my attention.

I continued to make my way toward the final steps and stood before the open doors. They were magnificent, with intricate carvings and symbols of what appeared to be men but with wings like a bird. Some held objects in their hands, while others were just large with vast wings behind them. But they all looked large, powerful, and unearthly.

"Iris." A voice echoed through the dimly lit temple.

My eyes grew wide in fear at the sound of that voice, and I stopped where I was. One foot was already in the temple—did I dare continue?

"Do not fear me," it coaxed.

The voice was not my grandfather's, that I was sure of. But then, to whom did it belong?

Following the gently spoken command, I fully stepped into the temple. Wherever I was, it had to be safer than I had initially thought. My grandfather would have already had me shackled and offered as a sacrifice to his gods by now.

"Come." Again, the voice murmured in my ear.

Startled, I looked around me but saw no one. The voice was that of a man; strong yet gentle as he called to me.I noticed a large entryway up ahead, where a large white veil swayed in the warm breeze, revealing a man standing behind it.

I stopped.

How strange this was, indeed.

"Come to me, Iris," the voice commanded again, and this time without any hesitation, I continued toward him. Whomever this man was, he looked colossal in height and size as I drew near. His back was bare, with more muscles than I had ever seen on a man. His legs were defined by a tightly knit cloth that looked as smooth as the skin on his back. His arms were mighty in size but in perfect unison with the rest of his body. His hair was as black as burned wood, and his neck perfectly matched the magnitude of his tall stature. He looked as though he was a grand warrior.

Terrified and excited at the same time, I stood just a few steps away from him. I felt small and insignificant.

His head slightly turned. "Your will has never been weak, Iris."

I saw his strong jawline move slightly and shivered at the sight. Not because I was scared but because he looked familiar. This moment felt very strange, yet I wanted to move closer. The scent of his skin spurred my senses, and I inhaled sharply. It was exhilarating and exquisite, like the flowers by the small stream in the forest. Like river and flower met to produce this sweet and tantalizing aroma of rapture. But could such a being as this indeed be real? Was it a carving of a man? Without further thought, I curiously reached out and gently grazed the back of it.

A slight hiss escaped him; he was real.

His skin was smooth but solid, resilient yet delicately soft. Somehow, this all felt clannish, and that was alarming to me. Unwed maidens were never to touch a man's back, let alone a man's bare back. It would ruin her chances of having a good family, as she would be considered sullied. Yet, there I was, standing behind an exquisite form I could not stop from touching. My palm flattened against his back, and suddenly, a sharp pain shot through my ankle, dropping me to my knees. I screamed and looked up and only saw a bright flash of light instead of the man that had stood there seconds ago. Confused and in pain, I closed my eyes in hopes of relief.

I could hear loud spoken words filling the air around me through each labored breath.

"She must not know of you!" a sharp, angry voice chided.

I sensed hands on my feet, and my body held down by some

unforeseen force. The pain continued to shoot through my leg and into my stomach. I screamed again! My entire insides feel as though they were being pushed out through my skin! I wanted to open my eyes but could not!

"She already knows who I am, Enok," said a familiar, soft, commandeering voice.

"She has not been initiated! She belongs to no one until then!" Grandfather yelled.

Ah, Grandfather Enok was beside me. But his voice was not as comforting as I had hoped. Sweat ran down my face—or was it tears? My body extremely warm, and my heart pleading for reprieve I could not grant. The pain was unbearable, and my head was ready to burst.

I must speak and say something. But it took all my effort to keep breathing. My eyelids were so heavy that I could not open them to plead for help; I licked my dry lips and built enough strength to beg for relief. "P-please, Grandfather... pain i-is...." Gasping for air, I exhaled, "Please!"

Cool air flowed by my ear, and I heard a soft and comforting voice, "Allow me."

My heart jumped at the promised relief!

"Never!" said Grandfather Enok.

And in a mere second, my heart sank. Here I was, in the most pain I had ever been in, and all I wanted was for Grandfather Enoch to allow the familiar voice to help me.

"She will perish. I must finish the healing now!" The voice now became tinged with anger and urgency.

My breathing felt slow, and my heartbeat thumped weakly in my head. Images of my sister on the rooftop, staring at the night sky, came to my vision. Stars danced across the sky, and fascinating temples with enormous pillars, fire pits, and rocks shone as the sun danced in my mind.

"You wish to be healed?" asked the voice once more.

With what little strength I had left, I whispered back, "Yes."

"It is done." said the voice.

A calm breeze surrounded me, and every fiber of my being began to push the pain out.

As I heard my grandfather's disapproving voice, I feared losing this newfound relief, but to my great surprise and pleasure, it did not stop. I began to breathe easier. The incredible smell of the river returned and drenched my senses. I felt my body soak up every bit of energy it gave. I was being restored to peace I thought I would never feel again.

"This is against protocol, and your actions will have ramifications."

My grandfather's stern reprimand against the soft voice was unpleasant to hear, and I wanted to say something in defense of whomever it was that offered me relief. But all I could do was take in the healing air around me. My eyes remained closed as I inhaled for the first time without pain and was rewarded with the sweet smell of flowers.

"Protocol is always bound to be bent. To break it takes more than what you believe I have done." The soft voice was calm again.

"Being here is wrong! You do not belong in this realm!"

I could hear everything, but nothing said made any sense. I just wanted to continue this rapture of serenity and healing forever.

"Had I not been here, SHE would no longer be in this realm!"

I waited to hear more of the comforting voice. Had they both stopped speaking or had I gone deaf? I had to open my eyes and see what was happening. But my eyelids felt like they were heavy stones. Fear filled me at the thought of not having any control. I tried to move my hand to my eyes, but the second I moved, the pain began. I whimpered.

"Do not move, little one. Sleep," commanded the soft voice.

I had no choice but to obey. My fear vanished and was replaced by another cool breeze. It felt wonderful and soothing. Sleep was calling me with its ever-tempting peace, and I was only too happy to find it.

"She is not yours to command!"

Warm, inviting dreams were calling me.

"She has always been mine."

With those final soft-spoken words, I fell into slumber's soft, dark caress—no promise of what was to come but only of what was now.

# CHAPTER FOUR

A beautiful, serene, white landscape was all around me. From what I wore to what I stood upon. A soft, cushioned, white mass was under my bare feet. A delicate white cloth covered me, and a thin, beautiful, yellow-colored rope gently encircled my waist. The air was warm, and the fragrance of sweet flowers inundated the senses, bringing a familiar comfort. But strangely, not a single flower was in sight.

I stepped forward, and the ground under my feet molded to support my every step. It felt soft and supple yet held my weight. Remarkable place it was, as I felt no pain.

Pain.

I remembered pain and voices. Grandfather Enok! And another voice. A quick chill ran down my back, and I shivered though there was no breeze.

Who was the voice, and more importantly, where was I?

"You are with me," a calm, masculine tone emanated.

Looking from side to side, I saw only a vast area of endless white. "Who are you?" I asked as I spun around, looking for the owner of the voice. I saw no one. "Show yourself."

A light beamed to my right, a soft, welcoming glow. I saw a man's figure in a robe coming forth from it. But the closer it got, the more distorted the shape became, especially the face. Squinting my eyes to make out the face of this being was in vain.

Was this the man who had been with Grandfather Enoch? It felt so similar in essence, but the voice wasn't the same. This voice had a soft honeyed tone when it said my name. Whereas the other was firm and strict. But both had this penetrating quality that demanded attention. It was not because I was threatened or commanded but because my soul yearned to hear more of it. It felt like I was hearing a song, distinctively one note at a time.

The light intensified. "Open your hand, Iris."

Upon his word, I did so. And not a second later, I felt something soft, light, and delicate in my hand. As I raised it to see what it was, I barely saw my flower by the river before the light and the man disappeared. My vision became unclear, and my feet sank into the soft ground.

"Iris! Wake up, child!"

Grandfather Enok?

What was happening? Everything was strange. I tried to move but couldn't. I was sinking farther into the ground.

"By god, wake up, child!"

My eyes opened, and I shot straight up, taking a large breath.

"Grandfather!" I threw my arms around him as he stood motionless. I began to cry and clung to him tight. His arms tightened around me in a comforting embrace.

"Oh, my child." Patting my back, he exhaled, as did I, letting out a breath of relief.

Tears kept falling, soaking his shoulder where I buried my face. My entire world was falling apart, and I could not even figure out where the seams that broke were.

"Iris, there is much to say and little time to tell you all you need to know." He straightened me, meeting my tear-stained eyes. "You must listen to everything I say and remember what I tell you as the only truth you will hear. It will be up to you to discern truth from lie once you leave."

Wiping the tears from my face, I looked at him, distressed. "Leave? I just arrived and have much to tell you of what happened to Father, Mother, and—"

He hushed my concern and assured me they were all right for now and that I needed to heed every word he said. "You have been marked by the fallen one, and he will not let you go easily. He will come for you if you do not go to him willingly of your own free will."

He reached his hand out for me to hold, and once I did, he led us to the small supper room. He grabbed a piece of bread and some cheese, and water. He handed it to me and ordered me to eat before he continued speaking.

I did as he said since it was the only thing I could understand and make sense of. My stomach grumbled as I grabbed the bread and placed some cheese on it. I had not realized how hungry I was. Swiftly, I put it in my mouth then followed it with some water he had just poured for me.

"Easy, child," Grandfather said. "Nourishment is a small portion of survival. Heed my words instead. For the words I speak are true."

He pulled out a small wooden crate and sat before me as I quickly devoured the rest of my bread and cheese. I knew if I did not finish it before he started speaking, he would take it away like he always did.

"Remember the stories of creation I told you as a young child? Of how the Most High has winged beings watching over us all?"

"Yes, I remember." Of course, I remembered. I was fascinated beyond anything and was obsessed with them.

"Those beings have now descended and are here in our realm. Against the laws of the universe set by the Most High, they have disobeyed and entered our world."

"Are they not always with us, Grandfather?" I did not understand. He used to tell us they were always watching over us, so how were they here only now if they were always with us?

He grabbed my hands and came closer to me. "They have come for a purpose that is not what it seems." His eyes held worry and concern I had not seen before.

It made me uneasy to see him like this. "Are they not meant to protect us? Is it, not a good thing that they are here?" An idea raced in my head, and it came out before I could stop it. "Grandfather! They can help us rescue Father, Mother, and Boria!" Excited, I leaped from my seat too quickly, and a rush of darkness clouded my vision momentarily.

Grandfather caught me and placed me back where I was sitting. He sighed as he said, "You are weaker than I thought." He kneeled and checked my ankle where the bite was.

"It has healed. You should be able to walk now." Standing, he reached his arm toward me and instructed, "Grab my hands and begin to rise slowly."

I did as he said and slowly stood. My legs felt sore, as though I had been out in the fields gathering, but I did not feel the pain of the bite on my ankle. I reached down to see for myself. There was no fresh mark, nor was there a healing mark, just two small scars that I could barely see. How could this be? It should have taken many sunsets for this to heal.

"It has completely healed," I whispered in astonishment.

He heard. "Yes, it has, but at a cost, my child." Grandfather stated gravely, "You are now bound to one of these beings in a way that cannot be reversed. He is of great strength, and though he will protect you with all his powers, now that he has given his breath for your life, he cannot undo his disobedience that has taken place in the heavenly realms." He sighed as he saw tears swelling in my eyes

"Had he not given part of his essence to you, you would have perished from the poison. But the repercussions of this are yet to be discovered. I am unsure how it will fully affect you or if it has altered you. He is not of this Earth and was never meant to be upon it as a mortal."

I was bewildered by it all. How did my existence turn the stories meant for lessons and amusement into reality? Earnestly, I looked at him, and he knew I was scared. Pulling me into his embrace, he comforted me momentarily before he sat me back down.

"Iris, precious granddaughter. You have a fate that is meant for greatness. You will set the precipice of human limitations that will be told of until the end of this age. But you must not crumble and lean entirely upon your own understanding. You have great purpose because there is great strength and courage within you. The Creator of all things is with you."

I lunged forward and embraced him again. Tears escaped this time. I had no courage. I didn't know what he spoke of, yet he gently patted my back as though I had expressed my thoughts aloud.

"What is written must come to pass. And this is only the beginning, my child. There will be many that will come after you for purposes that are not honorable. Trials great and small will constantly be upon you, but you must seek higher ground where the waters cannot reach when you decide to come close to its edge."

I closed my eyes and wished I could be home with my family. I wanted nothing of these unfamiliar and strange occurrences. I did not even care about the angels being here. I just wanted to be home. I sighed deeply and opened my eyes. I wasn't home. The feeling of being lost had not disappeared. And I was still in my grandfather's arms.

He spoke as though I had no choice, and if there were any chance of seeing my family again, I would need to be stronger. He continued to remind me of the old stories he would tell us and how they were not made for our amusement, but rather, he had been gently introducing us to what was to come.

He spoke of how the angels were created, how they were given a single purpose, and how they had now disobeyed and descended against the laws that bound them to their realm. He told me how they were there for something even they didn't know quite yet but would soon find out. Some things made sense, while others I couldn't understand. His voice was full of urgency, and I dared not interrupt. I just listened and prayed I could remember all that was said.

He reached into his pocket and pulled out a stone. It was solid black. No lines, no other colors. Just pure black with a tiny hole where a leather string was inserted, making it into a neck adornment. He held it in his palm and asked me to turn it over. I did.

The other side held a blue stone in the middle, to my amazement. Astonishing! I had never seen such a thing; a stone in a rock!

He saw my wonderment.

"May I hold it?" I asked.

He nodded and handed me the unusual rock. It was smooth and cool to the touch—no sharp edge, just round and thin. I had never seen anything like it anywhere.

"Where did you get this, Grandfather?" I asked as I continued examining it.

"From a garden, not of this realm. Yet once it was."

In riddles, he spoke again. His green eyes were waiting when I looked at him, bewildered.

"And now, the one they have chosen as their leader calls you for his temple. His brethren wait for you outside."

And as though on command, three huge men came in, bowing their heads to avoid hitting the frame as they entered the door. They wore what could only be described as armor. The silver against the black breastplate shined like the moon in the dead of night. I couldn't tell if it was their stature, armor, or a combination of both, but a shiver went down my spine at their splendor.

Their somber faces and towering height made me feel insignificant. I felt like a mouse in a field of lions. They spoke to my grandfather in a language I had never heard, and surprisingly, my grandfather answered them in this strange new tongue. They carried energy around them that I had never encountered before. I should have been afraid, yet I wasn't.

I felt strangely calm.

Something about them brought a sense of wonder and security that I couldn't explain. Thoughts of fear seemed to disappear, and admiration remained, even though they had done nothing admirable that I had witnessed.

"Iris."

Their eyes were colors I had never seen before. One was green, the other a dark blue, and the being in front of them had the warmest shade of honey I had ever seen. All three had hair the color of the sun, and it fell down their broad shoulders, resting right on top of their armor; moon and sun collided.

"Iris, my child." Grandfather's voice broke my gaze from the three unearthly beings.

He leaned in close and said, "Go in peace. Remember, divine judgment has no escape, and the Creator will impose a sentence." He quickly tied the small stone around my neck. He turned it to the side without the blue stone. "Not all is what it seems." Then he turned it to where the stone lay in the middle. At first glance, it shined as bright as the sun, then in a blink, it paled to just a clear dark stone.

He embraced me once more, whispering in my ear, "Light gives life; life becomes light."

I knew not what he meant but felt I should remember it. I repeated what he said a few times so I wouldn't forget.

"Will you be safe, Grandfather?" I asked worriedly.

He smiled, and the wrinkles on his face multiplied. "Fear not for my safety, child; no one can alter my destiny. I will see you again. Until then, take heed of all I have taught you." He handed me my satchel as he gently caressed my head.

As though on cue, a dominantly harsh voice called my name. It was the one with honey eyes. I hesitantly followed my grandfather's direction and walked toward this giant of a man. One powerful arm extended, pushing the door open as he signaled for me to walk out. With each step I took, I knew I was walking away from everything familiar and into territory I knew nothing about.

Who were these grand men, and why were they here? Were they angels, as Grandfather said? How did they know my grandfather, or better yet, how did my grandfather seem to know them and the language they spoke?

I should stop asking myself these questions as I didn't know their answers. Jarred from my thoughts, I was lifted by one strong arm and hoisted onto a magnificent beast of a horse. It was beautiful and powerful, brown in color with white patches across its body. It snorted loudly and reared its head back as Honey Eyes hoisted himself upon it and settled right behind me.

His arms came around on both sides of me and grabbed the rope reins. Pushing up behind me as he tugged it into motion, I could only feel a solid mass, almost like rock but with ridges. I felt like a tiny child compared to his size. Never had a man sat this close behind me; it was out of protocol for a young woman in our village. It rejected modesty and purity. Such rights were allowed to the one who would court you and make you his wife.

The giant horse began to move so abruptly that, had it not been for his massive arms to hold onto, I would have fallen. He began to pick up speed, and I barely had time to turn around for one last look at Grandfather. With my hair blowing in my face and with the speed of the horse, all I could see was the back side of his hut. We had already traveled far enough around the hill that I couldn't see the entrance to his home. My heart sank as I had no idea when I would lay eyes upon him again.

We rode very fast for what seemed like a day. Honey Eyes and I rode with the other two giants flanking either side of us. The night sky and wind arrived too quickly, and I shivered from the breeze and how cold the air had gotten. Though the days were hot with the sun, the moon brought with it the cool winds of the desert.

I should be fearful, as Grandfather Enok had mentioned how threatening the beings could be, but whenever I felt anxious, a warm wind blew my way and calmed my heart. It was most strange at night, yet I welcomed it as I didn't know how to grapple with the fear within my heart.

He shifted and positioned the reins in one hand. He placed his other hand on my stomach, to my utter shock. I understood his reason for sitting behind me once I realized the height, force, and speed the horse would take, but such liberties wasn't going to be allowed. I was not going to be his in any way, no matter how magnificent he might look.

As I tried to push his hand off, I noticed something strange the second I touched it. His hand was warm and slightly glowing like a flame. He was instantly warming my whole body.

What kind of divination was this? Who could do such a thing except those made by heavenly fire? Grandfather's words repeated in my mind. I knew these men were not mere mortals but rather beings that reigned in realms beyond our own.

"Do not fight the comfort I grace you with," he warned ominously.

I could not have fought his hand off even if I'd wanted to. Looking at the size of his hand and mine, it was not hard to see who the winner would be. So, I let it be. I needed the warmth, and after realizing this was no average man, I had no choice but to go with them, just as my grandfather had advised.

We rode through the night, steady and strong, without any rest. My eyes grew heavy, and my head kept leaning toward his arms for rest.

I would not say I liked that, but I had no control over keeping my eyes open anymore. Sleep was taking over no matter how hard I tried to stay awake. I tried to think of everything Grandfather Enok said, but nothing made much sense. Not the dream, not the snake bite that should have killed me, not why my other grandfather was holding my parents and sister captive. Why was it so important to him that Boria be married into his tribe?

As much as I tried, I could not get my thoughts to go any further than those questions. I was tired, and my entire body ached. I was comfortable, though; Honey Eyes continued holding me with one warm hand. I do not know how it was possible, but I was grateful. I knew I could not hold out much longer; my eyes began to close, and my head lolled to one side. Honey Eyes shifted his arm, so it became more suitable to rest my head against. I did not ponder it twice this time when it came to propriety. I needed to sleep, and his arm, though hard with muscle, was all I had at that moment. It was enough to allow me some much-needed rest.

I sent my love to my father, mother, and sister, wishing they knew how much I missed them and that I would find my way to them soon. And with that promise, I allowed myself to slumber against the warm, strong being that cradled me as we continued to ride through the night. Where we went did not matter. That challenge could wait until daybreak.

# CHAPTER FIVE

W arm rays of light gently danced across my eyes and awakened me. The morning air was crisp and fresh, but the promise of warmth was already beginning as the sun made its way out of slumber. The pace of the beasts was slow yet steady. My hair was beautifully laid on my shoulders and arms, as though it was cleaned and brushed. I thought nothing of it since the wind while riding could have done that. I still felt the warmth of Honey Eyes behind me and around me. Though his hand wasn't upon my stomach, his body still radiated heat and cocooned me.

Taking a deep breath, I straightened myself and ensured he knew I was awake. My head barely reached the top of his chest; if I turned up to look at him, it would be considered very indecent. I decided to pull my hair back behind me, showing him

I was wide awake. As I lifted my hair, I noticed how soft and smooth it felt; someone had brushed it for a while. It smelled sweet of honey.

I heard a deep inhale behind me when I pushed my hair back. I looked up at him and witnessed a deep glow; like the sun's rays swirling within the depth of his eyes, it instantly disappeared when we locked gazes.

It was so stunning and unusual. "How did you do that?"

His eyes were the previous humble shade of honey now. He stared at me as though thinking of answering but decided against it and turned his focus ahead to the road, leaving me to follow his gaze. I understood that he would not answer. So, I focused my gaze on what was ahead of us. The land around us was sparse in trees but surrounded by tall grass and a river. A river that was on the opposite side of where my village would be. This landscape was precisely how Mother would describe it in the stories of her youth. And judging by the position of where the sun was rising, I knew now where we were on our way to that unforsaken place. It was a place I never wanted to see, yet it was the only place I wanted to go to now; my mother's birth village.

Where her father was holding her, Father, and Boria against their will, just the thought of him causing harm to my family released a rage inside of me that I had never known. I had survived and not wholly failed them as I had thought.

Without looking up at Honey Eyes, I said, "I know where we are and where you are taking me."

He made no response.

It didn't matter.

"I hope for the sake of all that my family is safe and unharmed." My threat was empty, but I wanted him to know I wasn't weak in spirit.

I felt a puff of air at the top of my head and a slight vibration of his body behind me. He chuckled at my threat. I felt little but still held my head high in defiance of his laughter.

We moved forward, going into the city, the sun still partly blinding me as we descended the hill. I slowly started seeing more of the town my mother had told me so little about.

I noticed bright colors our village didn't have, colors that clothed the homes and water vessels, along with other pottery I had never seen the likes of. There were many different-sized potteries on the sides and within the windows. Some were the color of the river, some of the grass, and others the colors of the sun. It was beautiful, and I felt angry at myself for thinking so.

How could I think anything was beautiful in this horrid village? It was ruled by a tyrant who murdered at the command of his false gods. Who cared nothing for the welfare of his child because she wasn't the son he'd waited for.

Honey Eyes kept the horse at a slow and steady pace as if he wanted me to see everything—or maybe for everyone to see us? As men and women started to come out of their homes, I noticed their curiosity. Ever so slightly, as though trying to pay as little attention as possible, they watched us as we made our way past. I could feel their stares and hear whispers of words I couldn't make out.

I chose not to care what might be said. Instead, I looked right back at them in the same manner as they did to me, at their clothing and the strange materials adorning the heads of the woman. Some had a round, thin material that went all around the top of their head and slightly covered their forehead, while others had some cloth as bright as the sun wrapped within their hair.

The men wore tunics like those in our village, but whatever they had made theirs from looked more vital, and some ended at their shoulders, exposing their arms completely. Some pebbles or pits lined up the two edges of these tunics in the middle of their chest and bellies. Very unusual design, but it was appealing to the eyes. It revealed much that was foreign and scandalous to me.

As the sun rose higher, I could see everything more clearly. This place was so different compared to our humble little village. The homes here had multiple levels with colors; we would only know when the sun rested or rose. And now, with the sun rising, it added vibrancy. Even upon the faces of the woman were these specific colors. Their eyelids held them, and it was fair to look upon.

This new revelation took me aback. I didn't know what to make of it. It looked so fierce, beautiful, and captivating. I realized I was fixated in curiosity, almost making me forget how much I should hate everything about this village. But I kept staring at each one as we passed home after home, woman after woman. Each woman had different colors on their eyelids and a dark, almost black, color outlining their eyes. Even some men seemed to have a fragile line underneath their eyes.

As the horse began to pick up speed, it jarred my attention back to my current dilemma. We passed by homes that were twice, if not three times, the size of mine. I noticed more people coming out and staring as we rode past. Interestingly, they all kept staring at me rather than the unearthly man that rode a giant horse through their village.

"You will be prepared before you enter his presence," Honey Eyes firmly ordered. "Once ready, I will escort you to the temple."

Before I could think of what he'd just said, the horse stopped, and I was carried down swiftly with him and handed over like some sack of grain to a group of colorfully adorned women. They, in turn, quickly ushered me away from him and to what I recognized as a large bathing room. The largest I had ever seen or ever imagined! The air smelled of foreign oils, yet the scent appealed to me. I could see a large pool of water ahead of us, and as we got closer, I noticed petals floating on top, almost covering it completely.

They barely said anything to me as they escorted me to the large bath. I did overhear them quietly, whispering to each other that I stunk and needed a bath. I grimaced and didn't argue with them as I knew the smell of the horse was on me. Feeling slightly ashamed, I fruitlessly ran my fingers through my hair, thinking it would make me presentable and clean. It didn't work, as they kept pinching their noses when they neared me. I reached for the stone tied around my neck that Grandfather Enok had given me. I wished it would give me the wisdom to figure out what was happening and where my family was. And why I was enjoying the scent in this bath chamber so much!

They continued speaking, cleaning me as though I wasn't there. One of the women mentioned something about scrubbing me down with wool from a sheep. That was enough to scare me to leave. "I would just like to clean myself and find my family. If you could allow—"

Before I could finish, an older woman came out of nowhere and shoved me closer to the water while trying to remove my clothing.

I slapped her hands away from me angrily but didn't realize how I was at the edge of the bathing pool and fell in! Warm water covered my entire being as I was submerged in a bath unwillingly. I quickly pushed myself up from the water while clinging to the rock my grandfather had given me.

All the women laughed as I scowled at them and began to make my way out.

"Stay within the water; it will provide a bearable scent than the one you arrived in," she said disdainfully.

Feeling slightly ashamed of my uncleanliness, I obeyed. Something else was strange about this woman, more about her tone. It reminded me of Grandfather Enok, hence my instinct to submit quickly.

She bellowed orders to the laughing woman, and they quickly quieted and scattered to the assigned tasks. She ordered two women to come to help me bathe. One started to pull at my stone necklace, and I slapped her hand away. She looked at me sharply and reached for it again, but before she could touch it, the stern female voice ordered, "Leave it!"

She obeyed but gave me a venomous look before trying to help me bathe again. I refused her help, along with the quieter one in the water with me. They waited while I scrubbed all the dirt and smell of the horse off me. It took a while as I combed through my hair and allowed it to soak in the bath water until the beastly smell was gone. At this point, I wasn't shy about being exposed. I took off my clothing as if it was like a bath in my village, just at a much grander level. I continued to scrub myself and used the oils they handed to me. I didn't want to take them, but the smell was so divine that I couldn't resist.

The water smelled lovely compared to our village bath water and had a softness that I had never experienced before. It lingered on my skin as though caressing it as it slid off and returned to the bath. It was pleasantly warm with light steam that carried the sweet scent around the bathing house.

I noticed the older woman just stood there watching every-one, including myself. She wasn't a large woman; she was slender and about my height. She had long hair like most women, but it was tied upon her head as it cascaded down her back. Her face held slight softness, but her frown made it difficult to imagine her with a pleasant smile. Her voice was forceful and demand-ing, but her eyes didn't look cruel. Maybe that was what stirred up such similarities between her and Grandfather Enok?

I finally felt clean after washing my hair and body. It took longer than I had anticipated, but making sure the smell of the horse and the journey were completely gone took some time. One of the women handed me a very soft cloth-like material and directed me to use it to dry myself and my hair. I didn't mind this; it was incredibly smooth and comforting.

"Azazzel!" The older woman's loud reprimand shook me out of my calm.

All the women gasped as two women quickly shielded my na-kedness. I looked between them and noticed it was Hone Eyes. And he was staring directly at me! Ignoring the older woman's reprimand, he just stood there with an amused grin.

I couldn't help but sink farther behind the two women and hide myself as much as possible. His actions are so shameful, and I was glad that these two decided to protect my modesty. Even though I should be furious that Honey Eyes would dare come into the woman's bath, I felt my face reddening at seeing him. It was a most unwelcoming feeling.

"It is forbidden to be here!" yelled the old woman. "Even for you, Azazzel."

He didn't once look at her but stared directly at me. I saw his bright swirling honey eyes right before he turned and walked away without a word. My body shivered with a sensation I had never felt before. I had to remind myself to focus on finding my family and getting out of the controlling hands of these women and the honey-eyed man whose name I now knew—Azazzel. How strange and foreign it sounds.

Azazzel. I kept saying the name as I allowed the two women to help me dry myself. I continually held on to the stone necklace Grandfather Enok had given me. I asked for my old clothing back once dry, but they raised their eyebrows and handed me a dress that looked very similar to what they were wearing. I looked at it, and though it was lovely with the dark color of night and specks that shined like little stars, I wanted the familiarity of the clothing from my village, not theirs.

I needed to wear the clothing of my village when I met my evil grandfather. I wanted to show as much defiance as possible when I enquired about my family's whereabouts, and fear could not be a factor as it would mean instant defeat. I glanced around as much as possible as they prepared to help me dress, but I saw no trace of my old clothing. Slightly defeated, I let them finish dressing me in their unusual yet delicate garments.

"Now sit; you will need adornments for your face and hair," said one of the two women dressing me.

"I am already dressed and prepared," I answered. How much more could one prepare themselves had it not been evident that I was not from this village?

I didn't want to sit and wait; the bath had already taken too long. I turned to walk away, but the older woman stood in my way. She looked at me and raised an eyebrow like I was a child not obeying my elders. It was true, but I wasn't a babe, and in my current situation, it didn't matter who I disobeyed. They had my family somewhere in this forsaken village!

My patience is slightly gone; I looked at the old woman and said, "I am clean and in the clothes of your village. What more can I possibly need to have an audience with your lord!" I was exasperated and wanted to leave already, "I need to leave now and find my family." I tried to go around her and leave, but she just stretched out her arm and blocked me.

"Let the girls prepare you, and you can see your family. I assure you they are well and alive."

My eyes widened at her admission! "You know where they are? Please tell me. I need to see them!" I begged.

She grabbed me by the shoulders and turned toward the women waiting for me. "Go now, and let them prepare you. Once they have finished their task, you may have your requested audience. The less you comply, the longer you will be here."

She directed me again to a sitting area where one woman began to brush and pull at my hair while another started smearing things on my face and eyes. They applied fragrant oils again; they smelled heavenly. It was the only thing I didn't protest as the smell calmed my senses.

As I sat there while they continued to adorn my hair and face, I was relieved to know my family was alive and that I would see them soon. I needed to tell them everything Grandfather Enok had said and figure out how to return to our village unharmed.

"Ow." One of the women tugged on my hair too hard. I looked up to see who it was, and of course, it was the one who'd tried to pull on my stone necklace. She gave me a half-snarl and half-smile and continued brushing. They continued pulling and tugging at my hair while one with golden hair kept telling me to close my eyes as I felt her smearing something upon my eyelids. I knew what they were doing now; I would look like one of them. It wasn'twasn't right to make me wear their colors! I wasn'twasn't from their village, and I didn't want to be a part of it in any way. All my anger and frustration were boiling over, and I knew if I tried to leave, the older woman would appear and tell me to sit back down as she had instructed. My options were limited, so I didn't move and reminded myself to be patient.

Finally, after what seemed like an eternity, they announced I was done and called for the older woman. I reached up to feel my hair; they had woven it into a braid with little flowers. It looked beautiful, and the color of my dark hair and the blue flowers complimented each other very well. Boria would love this! I couldn't help but think of how Boria had never considered adding flowers to our braids. It made me smile to think of her, and I could not wait to see her!

I heard shuffling feet all around me again. I looked around and noticed all the women lined up to one side of the room with their heads bowed as Honey Eyes, or Azezzel, was walking past them directly toward me.

His unwavering eyes focused on me as he passed by all the women. I felt the rush of heat reach my cheeks again. This emotion was not appropriate in the least. I momentarily closed my eyes and tried to remember everything Grandfather Enok had said about them and how I should always be wary. My heart felt calm for a moment, but once I opened my eyes, I noticed how close he stood; the feeling returned.

I looked up as he towered over me and noticed the golden swirls in his eyes beginning to glow brighter. It was unreal and mesmerizing. Never had I seen such eyes. I wanted to look away

53

but had difficulty convincing my head to obey. I was, again, trying to control my actions, but I Could not. Nor should I not be this close or stare back so intently, but executing the thought was not coming to fruition.

"She is to go directly to the temple as he waits for her now. Do not stall, as he will know your intentions," said a dry and stern voice that belonged to the old woman. And for the first time, since I had met her, I was happy to hear her speak and free me from his gaze.

He turned toward the older woman slowly, as though she didn't have the right to speak to him.

The woman kept her stance and didn't back away. She continued to stare back at him unyieldingly.

I felt a slight chill in the air around me, which was strange as we were in a bathhouse with steam that emanated from the water. Suddenly, out of nowhere, ripples in the air flew from Honey Eyes to the woman. A loud sound emerged as whatever that energy was passed from him to her with force, but it hit something before it even had a chance to reach her.

Bravely, the woman didn't even flinch. Instead, a slight grin emerged as she turned around and began to walk away. But only after Azazzel gave her a warning. "He will not always protect you." She paused for a brief second, then continued her way.

I had no idea what had just transpired before me, but I knew it wasn't suitable for the older woman. Azazzel, for sure, preferred to avoid being given orders. And now, according to the older woman, I was to be escorted to my evil grandfather within his temple. Azazzel looked at me, and I noticed those golden swirls were gone from his eyes. His face was hardened like when I'd first seen him at Grandfather Enok's.

"Come."

I didn't hesitate to follow. Whatever he had just tried to do with those strange ripples in the air sent chills down my back. I feared his temper was very short. If he could try to harm an older woman just because she was repeating an order, then I better than to test him.

I followed him quietly and quickly. His one step was two of mine, and he wasn'twasn't showing any signs of slowing down for me, which was fine as the new sandals on my feet were soft and fitted, making it easier to keep up.

Once outside, I noticed the morning sun was almost gone. Before I could contemplate the time lost in the bathhouse, strong arms lifted me on the horse again. Interestingly, the horse didn't smell as awful as I remembered this time. Or maybe all the oils in the bath water penetrated my skin so well that all I could smell were the oils. Either way, I was not going to complain; I was headed to my family finally and inwardly readied myself to face this man with no soul, my grandfather Tuarian, to tell him I wouldn't allow him to direct my family in such a manner.

Each time I gathered strength in my mind, I felt Azazzel wrap me deeper into his embrace. It kept distracting me from the tiny bit of courage I was collecting before I had to confront a tyrant. But nothing helped to stop the nervousness. Everything here was foreign to me, including all my clothing and adornments.

People again stared at us as we steadily went through the paths to what I could see now was a vast temple! Mother had said her father was a high priest to the gods and that the men of his village would work both during the day and at night to complete the massive tribute to the gods. She had never seen it completed because she married my father and vowed never to return. But of course, her father put a condition to her marriage, and without question, they accepted and left. Hoping that whatever the situation was, it would never come to fruition; sadly, they were mistaken.

The closer we got to this temple, the more I was amazed by the sheer size of it. Never had I seen such a massive, grand temple. It not only exuberated nobility but was beguilingly beautiful. With night approaching, it was as though the temple illuminated itself. How could a monster create such a beautiful temple? The massive stones that rested upon one another shined bright like a star. As we got closer, I saw wide steps leading up to the entrance. It had pillars encircling the temple, and the doors were just as imposing as the structure itself. The steps to the temple door glimmered in the moonlight, revealing stones within them.

The horse stopped as we neared the temple steps, and Honey Eyes tightened his grip around my waist and effortlessly hoisted me down along with him. With a half smirk, he spoke, "If you lose your path, call upon me, and I will arrive before my name leaves your lips." His eyes swirled again momentarily as he gestured toward the temple doors.

I watched as he led the horse away, leaving me standing there staring at the massive steps that belonged to this enormous temple. I pondered the words Azazzel had left me with. It was as though everyone had begun to speak like Grandfather Enok, and it was starting to make my head hurt.

I started to make my way to the steps. With each step I took, I could see the beautiful colorful stones embedded within them. The colors of the rocks glistened within the moonlight, creating an array of light that was so very beautiful! I couldn't help but be mesmerized as I walked up to the temple doors. Large Images adorned the two enormous doors at this entrance. As I neared, I couldn't help but trace the beautiful cravings with my fingertips. So smooth and delicately carved. Flowers and strange creatures were centered on the doors, while the edges had foreign symbols that flowed harmoniously in design. I pondered how such beauty could exist in a place that held so much fear. How did Grandfather Turian design such wondrous things yet have such a dark heart?

I remembered how he came for us and the last time I saw my family before I ran to Grandfather Enok. Sweat warmed the palm of my hands as I moved to the center of the doors. I had mere minutes to gather as much courage as I could. From everything my mother told me about her father, he wasn't one to give mercy and wouldn't hesitate to punish his family.

I suddenly felt fear within my heart and felt very small standing in front of the grand temple doors. The amount of courage I hoped to find wasn't enough. I felt irrelevant. How was I supposed to match or surpass my evil grandfather's intelligence? He was much more competent than I assumed. I felt defeated before I even began the battle. My heart sank deep within my soul.

I took a deep breath and took the only choice I had. With unsteady hands, I reached out, placed them on either side of the enormous doors, and pushed them open with every bit of strength. They moved instantly and effortlessly. Quietly, barely making a sound, they turned inward to reveal a large entrance. I took a few cautious steps inside and waited, knowing guards should be present, but there was no one. Where were they? I knew that he knew I was here since I'd been escorted by one of his strange beings. But I saw not a soul at this large entrance.

I took a few more steps and noticed large pillars like the ones on the outside, with smaller vessels with fire within them. They delicately lit up a path that I assumed I was to follow. A sweet-smelling breeze flowed around me and brought calmness to my soul. The excitement in the pit of my stomach vanished, my hands ceased shaking, and my heart was calm.

I didn't know what beguilement this was, but I began walking into the temple and stood amazed at how magnificent it was; these mighty pillars held the highest ceiling I had ever seen, as sheer fabric swayed in between. Fire vessels were behind the swaying material, creating a shadow of the wee-sized dancing flames. With the emitting sweet breeze, I almost didn't notice the two men that stood on either side of another set of doors ahead of me.

Noticing their size, they were his standard faithful protectors as I remembered their clothing from watching them behind those rocks back in my village. They stood there with narrowed eyes, looking straight at me as I slowly approached. That calm and serene feeling I felt a moment ago was quickly replaced with apprehension as I noticed rope, coiled and hanging on one side of a guard.

I stopped where I was.

They noticed and took a step forward.

I was about to turn around and run, but they turned toward the doors and pushed them open, revealing a bright, majestic room. This had to be the throne room. And if it was, I knew who would be waiting for me within it.

Fear dripped slowly back into my soul, and I shivered at the thought of him. I felt weak in my hands and feet. My stomach turned, almost making me sick, and my mind went into a frenzy of thoughts. I remembered Azazzel's offer to call upon his name if in need, but I couldn't bear the thought of calling upon a being that I feared slightly less than my evil grandfather.

Taking a few deep breaths, I tried to calm my heart as I reached for the stone around my neck, hoping it would restore the courage I'd had a moment ago. The cool and smooth surface immediately calmed my fears and relaxed my breathing. I still felt my stomach turn, but I could manage. With a step forward, I walked into the room, passing the two glaring guards.

My steps were slow, but my heart was racing. I squeezed the stone tighter. It was solid, exactly how I should be right now.

I kept walking.

I turned and saw the light from the room spilling over the entrance as I furthered my way in. I noticed the floor was like one excellent river rock, smooth and without seams. I could hear water flowing, almost as if a river was close by. No other guards were present. Similar pillars lined up on either side of me, making a path that led toward my left. But these pillars somehow illuminated the room like the outside of the temple was illuminating the night. It was otherworldly. How could they glow like this? Curiosity overtook fear, and I couldn't help but want to touch one.

"Bow to your lord when you enter his throne room!" A booming voice echoed throughout the room.

I jumped back in fear.

"Petulant child, like your mother!" Turian snarled and began walking toward me, stopping only a few short steps from reaching me.

My heart raced in fear as the palm of my hands began to sweat, and I knew I was in trouble.

"Did your mother not teach you proper protocol when in the presence of your lord!" He raised one hand in a gesture of waiting for my reply.

I opened my mouth to respond, but he began to chide me again. "Have you not been taught to obey and respect your ruler?"

I felt fear, but I also felt hatred as he continued berating my mother.

He took another few steps and came closer to where I could now see his wrinkled evil face, which was exactly as I had envisioned it. His cold, black, lifeless eyes had the same dark line on top and below his eyelids as the rest of the men in this village. His eyebrows were dark, and I could tell they, too, were colored and outlined to look fuller than they probably were. His skin was so wrinkled by his neck that all you saw was folds of skin on top of another. He seemed very old and weathered. But strangely, his stature was bigger than I expected and seemed more robust than what should be for his age. Or could it be an illusion created by the thick robes he wore? I couldn't remember if Mother had mentioned anything about his stature, it was always about how cruel he was.

"Bow," he demanded as he took two more steps and stood at arm's reach.

A pungent smell that was very unpleasant radiated off him and settled around me. I should have expected his evil soul to give out such a malodorous stench.

Looking at his merciless eyes, I found myself frozen, unmoving. I felt an uncontrollable fear that I had never felt, not even when Azazzel had summoned that strange wind to hit that older woman.

"Did you not hear me? I said bow to your master!" His voice

crackled with malice and anger. And the smell of his wretched breath flooded my senses, almost making me heave.

I felt trapped again. My mind felt like it was on the verge of leaving me, and I had no choice but to allow it. Everything was beginning to take a toll on me in a way I never thought possible. I'd come here to rescue my family; instead, I'd started to fail again. Where was this courage my grandfather Enok spoke of that I had? I reached for my stone again and closed my palm hard around it, hoping it would provide the reprieve I needed.

I felt nothing.

I was doomed.

I could see the impatience in his black eyes as I stood there, quiet and unmoving. His spiteful hand reached high, and I knew what was coming.

Instinctively, I stepped back, closing my eyes in anticipation of his hand colliding with the side of my face.

But it never did.

I slowly opened my eyes and saw him just standing as he was with his hand halfway down toward me, but he was frozen. He looked at me with rage but could neither move nor speak.

"Turian, did you forget who your master is again?" said a nonchalant bold voice. "And what your master commanded of you?"

I looked around, searching for the person who spoke.

"I suppose in your ripe age, you tend to forget now and again," the voice teasingly said.

My evil grandfather was still frozen in place, but the venom in his eyes disappeared; instead, he looked fearful. Who owned the voice that brought fear into this evil man's eyes?

I heard footsteps coming toward us from behind my evil grandfather. Slowly, the figure revealed himself as he came upon us. He dwarfed my evil grandfather when he stood behind him. He stood at least a head taller and had impeccable and unearthly features, just like Azazzel. Except this being had straight black hair that went behind his broad, commanding shoulders, a strong jawline with perfectly drawn lips, and dark prominent eyebrows that arched and created the perfect space for the most beautiful blue eyes I had ever seen.

He stepped around my grandfather and came to stand in front of him. He looked down upon me with intrigue. It warmed my face, and I knew I would have crimson cheeks. His demeanor was instantly alluring. Fear had vanished, and unexpected admiration had taken me over. Gone was any shame I should have felt for staring back upon the most heavenly blue eyes ever created. His long dark eyelashes only added to the ethereal beauty of his face. But his eyes were what held me captive. The inner blue of his irises was like many small stones encircled with a thin black line. It was otherworldly and fascinating. They shined like stars.

"Iris." His voice was deep in timbre and dripped with honey as he said my name. I was enthralled and comforted at the same time.

Without lifting his gaze, he spoke words I didn't recognize, and out from behind the bright pillars appeared six beings of his kind. Now I broke my gaze from him as I looked at these newly arrived beings. All had long hair, some tied freely about their shoulders, and all looked different yet extremely enchanting in their physical features. I felt ashamed to look upon them continually, but they were all so unusually alluring as their presence demanded adoration. In my village, women were beautiful, not men, and here I was, gawking at men with no shame. If Mother had been there, she would have chastised me for such bold and unabashed staring.

At the thought, I looked away but locked eyes again with the one who'd just saved me from my evil grandfather's hand. He was still watching me with an amused expression. Instantly, I felt my face turn red again. He must be like Azazzel and could somehow sense my thoughts.

"Azazzel is more like me than I am of him," he answered, confirming what I assumed.

Though I didn't understand what that meant, I felt it would not be easy to control my emotions around them. One glance into their eyes, and all I could do was stare in admiration without a thought in my head other than how I could continue to keep their gaze upon me. This thought was frightening and terrible. If anyone were to see me like this, especially Grandfather Enok, they would all be very disappointed.

Light burst behind him and broke my gaze, thankfully, but as I looked past him, I noticed no one was there anymore. My evil grandfather and those six beings had vanished. Who were these beings that held this type of wonder, and how powerful were they?

Aghast, I walked around him with no fear. "Where did they go?" I whispered.

"To a place where your grandfather can rest and reassess his duties to me and my kingdom."

"Your kingdom?" I repeated as I turned around.

He smiled as though I acknowledged it rather than questioned it. These beings were so large and opulent that they made me feeble in responses. But with a trembling yet determined voice, I asked, "Where is my family?"

"Here," he replied with a slight tilt of his head.

Was he toying with me? And why did I feel so brazen in my response to him?

"Where?" I asked again.

"Behind you, my sweet Iris." His voice sounded like a song as he spoke, relinquishing any leftover fear I had left within me. I should have been trembling at this unknown being, but instead, my heart felt happy and cheerful.

"Iris!" A voice I longed to hear called my name.

I turned to see Boria running to me from behind one of the illuminated pillars. I couldn't believe my eyes. I was finally going to hold my sister again! I ran towards her and crashed into each other's arms, almost taking my breath away. I squeezed her tight as I cherished the moment.

"You're all right. I thought you were imprisoned or...." I couldn't bear the thought and teared up.

"Oh, Iris, my worrisome little sister. I am fine, and so are Father and Mother," she said reassuringly. "They await us now. Come, let me take you to them!"

I felt so relieved and happy now that I knew everyone was alive and well. I sighed in relief. My heart was whole and at ease; I made it safely to my family.

She grabbed my hand to lead us away, but not before she turned to him. "My gratitude, Lord Samayaza, for returning my sister to us," she said as she bowed.

Lord Samayaza? How was he a lord? And what another strange name—Samayaza?

He gently nodded, thus dismissing us.

I glanced at him as we left, and he returned the stare with those piercing blue eyes. I felt a shiver run down my back, but it wasn't of fear. My cheeks flamed, and I turned away in hopes he didn't see my crimson cheeks again.

"Iris, come! Father and Mother are eager to see you!"

His one-sided smile and churning blue eyes brought forth emotions I had never known. It was all so foreign and inappropriate at the same time. I needed to see Mother. She would set me straight and on the right path. Turning to Boria, I allowed her to lead me to our family while ignoring the tingle that still lingered in my belly.

# AMONG ANGELS 1

"You dared to touch her," an angry, reserved voice accused.

Samayaza smiled as he turned toward the familiar voice he knew all too well. Just as he had expected, Daniel did not miss the last sensation he threw at Iris before her sister whisked her away. He could sense the rage crackle within Daniel even though he had not yet made himself physically present.

"Technically, I didn't lay a single mortal finger on her," he coyly answered.

Daniel manifested from behind the throne chair and walked forward, revealing himself. His heavenly, hooded robe softly swayed as he approached Samayaza with disdain.

Samayaza sensed his contempt but ignored it. He knew what he had done and how Daniel would have easily felt the threat to his guarded woman. He was still her guardian, and for some depraved reason, Samayaza found humor in toying with Daniel's temper. It brought him some cynical pleasure that feathered his ego to no extent.

Daniel lowered his hood, revealing the anger in his eyes as he stared at his brother. Merciless green eyes collided with the fierce blue storm. "Take heed of my warning, brother; she lays under my protection and mine alone."

The threat in Daniel's voice would have made any mortal quiver in fear and beg for mercy. But these were not ordinary mortals. These were beings made of holy fire and now encased in magnified and perfected semi-mortal bodies. Their physical capabilities surpassed any mortals by twenty-fold, and their appearance compared was hypnotizing to the mere mortal eye. They were large with tremendously defined muscle, endurance, intellect, and strength. And though they had certain similarities, each had a unique appearance that would allure any mortal, man or woman, to obey and follow as they commanded.

Samayaza was not pleased with Daniel's tone. Daniel had authority over him for too long, and now it seemed he had forgotten who reigned supreme. "And remember, your allegiance lies with me, Daniel." Calmly, he continued, looking straight into Daniel's swirling green eyes. "I am the head of this realm, and you should do well not to forget that!"

The air around them instantly cooled at his admonishment. The illuminated pillars quickly dimmed, allowing the shallow cauldrons with fire to compensate for the lost radiance. A sense of potent tension radiated between the two beings of fire.

Never once taking his eyes off Samayaza, Daniel raised his right hand and brought the pillars back to their original illumination in defiance and power.

Samayaza's eyes narrowed in anger. He knew the game Daniel was trying to play, and it took all his angelic will to hold back what his human form wanted to do.

Feeling Samayaza's struggle, Daniel tilted his head and grinned. This slight he dealt his lord was enough to subdue his rage at Samayaza's actions toward his guard.

He knew what Samayaza felt. Being in human form, he now knew how fragile yet supreme the senscs of mortals were. It was such an exciting formula—so delicately made but so receptive and open to the singularity that created them in His image. Nothing would have surprised Daniel anymore, as he was a creation of fire from long ago, but his clay form was a masterpiece. If only they knew how powerful they could become, his kind would be bowing down to them.

And with that thought, Daniel mockingly bowed his head to Samayaza and vanished.

Fuming at Daniel's disobedience, Samayaza's anger exuded out to the fire pits between the pillars and sent the flames shooting almost as high as the pillars themselves.

He closed his eyes and clenched his powerful jaw to regain his calm. Walking past the throne, he emerged onto a small balcony overlooking his new world. The fresh air did nothing to quench his rage; his human form stubbornly held onto his fury and commanded him to act.

"Control your anger," hissed the ancient dark voice within his thoughts.

Samayaza acknowledged the presence of the dark lord in reverence, even though he visited him only in thought. As he closed his eyes and bowed his head, he could not ignore the anger that roamed fiercely throughout his body. It was a nonstop assault on his senses, trying to push him to action. To crush Daniel and prove his supremacy over him once and for all.

"Control and discipline."

Yes, control and discipline. With an exhale, he opened his swirling, majestic blue eyes, and within seconds, the whirlpool of rage ended, the fires subdued, and the pillars' illumination of the throne room was once again returned to normal.

"Good," praised the dark lord.

It was good indeed. The control was good. Discipline was good. And looking out to the world Samayaza was to rule was good. Turian had listened well over the years. He had followed every instruction that was given to him. Whether it was how the dwellings of the humans should be to how his temple should look, inside and out, his magnificent temple towered over the large city. Yes, it had turned into something grand indeed. Smiling, Samayaza looked to every corner and felt the rush of power jolt through his veins.

Turian had done very well in controlling the masses to his will and creating his vision with such weak and pathetic mortals. But the best was yet to come, and now that he had Iris within his temple walls, there was no need to wait.

"Make your preparations and presence known throughout," instructed the dark being called Lucifer, the once bringer of light, now extinguished to be the bearer of darkness by his choosing.

It was time. Samayaza had to call a gathering of the fallen to direct and divide Earth. To create and teach according to each angelic craft and desire. Some were to learn everything, while others a specific skill to serve the purpose of the one they served. Covenants were to be made, some by oath and some by blood.

Samayaza's determined glare was so powerful that all the torches outside the dwellings grew brighter from his sheer will alone. He could sense the surprise of those who witnessed it.

Closing his eyes, he took in the praise and awe of the mortals. It was profoundly exhilarating. He now understood why praise and worship were necessary. It regenerated his will, determination, and celestial fire to burn brighter and become more powerful.

Slowly, he turned around, and with his back facing the city, he vanished into the night, toward the mountain where they had descended. Soon after, the winds blew and called all the fallen, summoning them to the mountain. He had instructions to give, including to the one he wished oblivion on.

# CHAPTER SIX

G rand was a word I fully did not understand until Boria led me through the many beautiful paths within the temple. From large pools of water with all sorts of floating flowers to a soft trickling of water from a fountain so beautiful, Boria had to nudge me to move. From the different stones used within the pools to the walls and pillars, this was something Grandfather Enok would describe as a place called heaven. Could this be what he was always speaking of?

"I noticed how you looked at him," Boria said with a sly grin.

"What look?" I replied with a frown.

"The look that makes your cheeks as red as the blazing sun!" she teased.

Shaking my head, I turned away and pointed to another large pool we were walking by. "Is this really the creation of our evil grandfather? It is so hard to believe the splendor within these walls. I can't stop admiring how beautiful everything is."

"It was at first. Like you, I spent much of the day walking through this temple, marveling at everything. Especially when Lord Samayaza would appear and speak with me."

This time I could see her cheeks burn.

"You have feelings for him?"

"I do, and know that you do, too."

"I do not, and you should be wary, Boria, not be infatuated with them," I chided. "Do you even know that they are not of this realm?"

Rolling her eyes, she ignored me.

"Boria, they can understand your thoughts like you speak to them aloud. If you have thought in your head, then they know."

"I know more about them than you do, Iris. I wished for them that night upon the rooftop! He heard and came down for me."

Scowling at her strange behavior, I was left speechless for a moment. Maybe she needed clarification, like how Grandfather Enok had explained to me. I was about to speak, but she turned towards me so hastily that I held back my words.

"He found me first, and I hope you do well to remember that the next time you look upon him," she warned with such fierce conviction that it was as though a different person stood before me.

My heart sank. I was used to her ignoring my observations, but this kind of admonition was new and hurtful; with no choice, I had to let it go.

I allowed her to believe she was right, especially since she had said she knew more about them than I did. Their magnificence and mystifying allure must beguile her. I felt it every time they were near, and the one called Samayaza had a pull that was stronger than Azazzel. How could she not see that or realize it? I needed to discuss this with Mother and Father later. Maybe they could make sense of what spell she was under.

For now, I just wanted to see my family again and feel safe in my strange new world. I simply agreed with what she said by nodding and blaming hunger and exhaustion for overspeaking. She took it as my submission and happily continued leading the way to our parents. She seemed so comfortable and familiar with the temple as we went through many hallways to finally reach my beloved parents.

The first person I saw as we entered a large room was the one who birthed me into this world. "Mother!" I exclaimed as I ran into her arms.

"Oh, Iris, my little babe." She tenderly said my name and enveloped me in her sweet loving arms.

The relief and joy I felt was immeasurable—finally, a moment of familiarity and warmth.

"Oh, my little Iris," she continued, looking me over to ensure it was me. Her soft, warm hands cupped my face as she kissed my forehead. My eyes closed instinctively; I missed her so much.

"Iris!" Father exclaimed as he came rushing toward us, encircling both of us in his arms.

I felt utter relief and felt safe in my parents' arms. My fear of never finding them alive vanished instantly—I felt at home.

I could not stop hugging my father. "I thought I would never find you alive."

"Oh, Iris," he tenderly said, allowing me to squeeze him tightly. "It's all right, child, you are here with us, and we are all safe for now."

"Why did you think you would not find us?" asked Boria from across the room, interrupting the peaceful embrace.

Frowning, I let go of Father and turned to look at her. "Did you forget how we were separated, and Grandfather came after us with his army!" I tried to remind her; I would have told her of my encounter with a deadly serpent, but how she behaved was very unfamiliar, making me hesitant to share anything from my travels. What was wrong with her? I knew her always to be a little vain, but this was more than I had ever expected, especially with all that was occurring around us.

"Oh, Iris, that was just to show our small and insignificant village his might. Do you not know how Grandfather is?" she said as she rolled her eyes, grabbed a platter of food, and set it down on a table nearby. "We were never in any danger, right, Mother?"

I looked at Mother, and she seemed slightly worried but answered, "No, I do not believe we ever were."

"Then why were we running from our home so early in the morning when we should have been sleeping instead?" I exclaimed.

"Iris, I know it has been a very long time since you have gotten some rest. Let us eat in peace and retire for the evening. We can discuss certain details once the morning sun arrives and our minds are anew." suggested Father.

Something felt strange. I could see it in both their eyes. I wanted to question them, but once I saw the pleading eyes of my father, I nodded and agreed to his suggestion. I closed my eyes for a second and took a deep breath. I needed to stop and be in this moment and only this moment. I could ask all the whys and how's tomorrow. Too much had happened, and I had seen too many strange things to try to understand it all in this short time.

"You're right, Father; I apologize." I was in no state to start something I knew I could not finish. "I'm just exhausted and hungry." I honestly was fatigued and needed nourishment.

Warm eyes looked upon me, and I knew my mother understood.

We supped quietly; the food was plenty and delicious. There were many new delicacies I had never eaten before. I was wary of having more, but Mother assured me they were not harmful and that I should eat as much as I pleased. There were these small brown dried fruits that had delicious meat within them. Mother called them *lochum* and said that they were her favorites when she was a young child.

The conversation was dull and minimal. When we finished supper, Mother ushered me into another room and kissed my forehead. "Tomorrow, we will have all the time we need to speak of each other's journeys."

Father had come in behind her and nodded in agreement as he kissed my forehead and thanked the heavens that I had arrived safely to them. Once he left, Mother started unwinding the braids within my hair and delicately removed all the flowers. Boria brought a warm wet cloth and handed it to me. She said it was for my eyes, to remove the colors so my skin would not become angry. I had no idea what that meant, but I followed her instructions.

Our room was large, and I sat on a vast, soft cot. It had many colorful blankets as smooth as a lamb's new wool. Some had symbols stitched with beautiful small stones, like what I had seen at the entrance of the temple. They were beautiful and very inviting. I just wanted to put my head down, cover myself with them, and finally rest. I was so delighted I had found my family; I was alive, they were alive, my belly was full of delicious food, and now, I could feel my eyelids grow heavy with sleep.

Mother noticed and smiled. "Until the morning, Iris," she said as she kissed my forehead and gently touched my cheek.

For a moment, I felt as if we were back home in our humble little village by the river. I was content even though I lay in a strange new cot within a grand temple I had feared for many years.

Moonlight shined through a large window on my left. Turning toward it, I could see the moon and stars. I thanked the heavens for uniting me with my family as I allowed the beauty of the night sky to lull me to sleep.

I awakened to someone softly calling my name. It was still dark, but the shadows in the room were longer, which meant daylight would be close at hand. Though I felt rested, it was a surprise to feel as refreshed as I did. I had thought I would sleep through the night and most of the morning, possibly having Boria or Mother come and wake me. Maybe I awoke from a dream?

"Iris."

There it was again. I knew I heard it this time, and it was not in my sleep. I knew that voice. I had heard it before in a dream. But I was awake now and not dreaming.

"Who is there?" I whispered. I was not scared, but I knew I was not alone.

Silence, I heard no answer or sound. I wondered if it were

Mother and Father speaking close by, and I overheard them, but that could not be it as the voice I heard was not my father's. It was gentle but deep and firm in tone. My father's voice was deep, but it did not have such timber or the tender note this voice did. Maybe I imagined it. I had seen a lot of unusual things recently, and this could be my mind just teasing me.

Ignoring what I thought I heard, I tossed over to my other side and tried to fall back asleep. I couldn't. It was strange to feel this rested in such a short time; maybe the excitement and exhaustion were overpowered by the peace I felt over being reunited with my family. Either way, I could not fall back asleep, and my mind raced in thoughts, so much so it began to throb a little. There was no use in sleeping. Taking a deep breath, I got up and wrapped myself in an outer garment left by the foot of my cot. The night air was warm, and a breeze came through occasionally. It reminded me of the nights we would have in our village. It was nice, which made me ponder if Boria would be awake. Maybe we could talk to one another like we used to on the rooftop of our home.

Stepping out of my room, I entered the main area where we'd all first met. I noticed the inner main room was almost in a circle, and three other doorways were on the edges. I knew the one across from me was how we came in with Boria. But which one of the other two would be Boria's room? As I was the first to sleep, I hadn't asked or waited to see her enter any room earlier. So now, I would have to guess and hope I didn't frighten any of them.

As quietly as I could, I began to walk toward the room next to mine. There she was, sound asleep in a cot similar to my room, with the same colorful blankets upon her. I am sure they were just as soft as mine were. Quietly, I walked toward her. I stared at her beautiful sleeping face for a moment; she had no colors on her eyelids or trinkets in her hair. She was beautiful; she looked like the sister I remembered and always confided in. I desperately wanted to awaken her, but she seemed so peaceful sleeping that I had no heart to wake her.

Letting out a breath, I decided to allow her some rest. Maybe in the morning, we could speak and understand each other like we always had. I wanted my sister from the rooftop back. There was so much I needed to tell her, but I would have to wait.

Walking out of her room, I was headed toward my cot again but remembered the beautiful fountain we had passed right before we entered the living area where my parents were. I was not tired, and a little walk and hearing the soft trickling of water would soothe me as the sound of the river in my village had. Just the mere thought of my river made me yearn for home again; how I missed the sound and scent of the river. With that memory in mind, I headed out of the living area in search of the trickling fountain.

As I walked through the halls, I was in awe again of the beautiful and intricate designs and images carved into the walls and doors. No temple had ever been described to me as serene and unearthly as this. I felt no fear though I should have been afraid walking in a temple built by an evil man for beings unfamiliar to us all. But my worry evaporated with every step I took in search of the fountain. At last, I could hear the sound of water. It was close. I listened to the trickle and smelled the crisp scent in the air. Turning a corner, I finally reached it; an expansive open courtyard surrounded by small pillars with green foliage between each post. It was dreamlike to see such serene beauty.

Just the scent in the air reminded me of our river. The closer I drew to the water, the more clearly I could see the colors that adorned the edges of the basin. Such vibrant hues encircled the inlet, and an image lay underneath the water.

How did I not notice this before? Could it be what I thought it was?

"Impossible," I whispered as I peered down further.

It was the same color and shape as the one I had found by the river! How could this be? There was no other like the single flower that floated down the river while I was gathering water. Somehow it had not flowed with the river but found its way to me. Boria and I had walked as far as we could alongside both river bends to find the plant that produced such a delicate and extraordinary flower. But sadly, we never saw such a plant.

I could not help but plunge my hand into the clear water and touch the stones that created my unique flower. Caressing the rocks, I swore I could smell its lovely fragrance. So many edges to each stone, but not one edge was sharp enough to cut into my fingers. They all met where the next one ended. It was fascinating, and I couldn't look away from its alluring beauty.

"Iris." The familiar voice echoed again.

Startled, I quickly pulled my hand out of the water and looked around.

There was no one I could see.

"Iris." Again, it called.

It came from behind the fountain.

I could not remember how or when I had heard that voice, but it was familiar. The way my name was whispered was unlike anyone that called upon me. It flowed effortlessly into the air and surrounded me with comfort and protection. It was piercing, yet polished, unyielding as it lingered in my mind. It called to me with every essence of my being.

Walking past the fountain, I saw a veil between two pillars. And past the cover, I could see a shadow that stood away from it. Cautiously, I walked past the veil and saw a man, a very tall and unearthly-looking man. The light of the moon shined upon him and glistened in his hair. I could see his body's broad outline against the night's dark blue sky. His hair reached the middle of his back, tied at the neck. He wore dark clothing that blended well with the color of the night. His legs were strong and clad in a strange dark cloth.

I stood for a moment looking, wondering who he was and if I should say something to let him know I was there. This was all unknown territory for me, and though I should have felt anxious to approach him further, I wanted nothing more than to see his face. The closer I walked toward him, the more I noticed that he was more prominent than Azazzel and Samayaza. I felt my body tense, knowing this was another unearthly being that stood before me. His height looked the same, but then again, they were all so tall it was hard to say. But his shoulders and upper body looked more considerable than the others. Could it be Samayaza? Biting my lip, I tossed that thought away; whoever this was did not have the same voice as him. No earthly man could be this grand and perfect in design. The magnificence of these beings was extraordinary, as was their ability to read thoughts.

A familiar scent was present in the air—home. I closed my eyes and shook my head to stop whatever hallucinations I was having. I missed my village, but I was not about to lose my senses in front of this being who stood so still against the night sky. Only wisps of his long dark hair swayed when a light breeze would come along. I took a deep breath and stepped past the veil toward him, and suddenly, night turned into day, and I was standing behind him by the river in what I recognized as our village.

I whispered under my breath, "How can this be?" Were my eyes deceiving me? I knew where I was standing a moment ago and what I felt in my hands as I pushed the veil aside. How did the hard stone floor under my feet with the night's breeze turn into daylight with my feet upon tall grass and my river in sight in front of me?

I felt slightly sick. What sort of beguilement was this? Was this indeed a dream? Yes, maybe it was. I must be sleeping and dreaming all this.

"If it were a dream, you would be in your old home. On the rooftop with your sister Boria," he answered knowingly.

He turned around as he said this, and I finally saw his face. He was magnificent, more so than I had ever imagined anyone being. I wondered again how beautiful he was for a man, as though a master artisan flawlessly drew him. Even from this distance, I could feel the intensity of his stare and the most tempting green eyes I had ever seen. His eyebrows were as dark as his hair, and he had thick lashes, similar to Samayaza. Every feature of his defined face was in perfect unison without a single blemish or scar. His lips were full and perfectly aligned with his straight nose. His jawline lacked any weakness, and the sun gently touched his skin.

This was a sweet vision, from the tall grass that swayed back and forth to how the wind caressed them into a dance. I could hear their song in the wind, an unusual yet sweet melody. I didn't know where it came from, but all I wanted to do was reach out my hands and touch it.

I felt so light and free. I was content with the sun shining upon my face, the smell of the river, and looking at this graceful being. I knew he was no mere man. He was one of them, like Azazzel and Samayaza. An angel not of this Earth, as Grandfather Enok had said.

Nothing about him was ordinary. Even the clothing he wore was something I had never seen before. Black cloth hugged him from the waist down and showed his powerful legs, which held his tall frame. His tunic was of the same material that covered his legs. It had no sleeves, showing off his muscular arms. Samayaza was close to his stature but was less significant than this being. He beguiled me. Maybe it was the color of his eyes or the sun shining upon his starlit skin that overwhelmed my senses.

He started to walk closer to me, holding that half smile that melted my worries away. I stopped moving as his eyes narrowed and kept me in place.

"I have long waited to see you in the flesh, Iris." My name flowed from his lips as freely as the river flowed behind him.

He stretched out his hand and took hold of mine, encasing my tiny fingers. He brought them to his soft, warm lips, gently touching them. I could feel my cheeks burn and could not help but look down in nervousness. His touch sent me a flurry of unfamiliar emotion, and I shivered uncontrollably in response. It was unlike what I had felt when Samayaza had looked at me.

A finger from his other hand tilted my chin to meet his gaze. Bewildered, I stared at the evergreen swirls in his eyes. It was as though lightning lived within them and churned the green color into a lush and vibrant field of grass. His eyes spoke of kindness, strength, and something similar to what I had noticed in Samayaza and Azazzel—*want*.

I felt utterly lost yet untroubled.

"Follow," he commanded tenderly.

I heard and obeyed.

Without much thought or resistance, I followed his lead. This was out of protocol for me, yet I did not care. His voice was the most enticing sound I had ever heard. Commanding in such a way that it made me obey like sheep to a shepherd and as desirable as rain after a long dry summer. Silently I wished he would continue speaking, and my heart desired he never let go of my hand.

He led me through the grass to where he was standing before. I felt the ground was no longer soft. Looking down, I saw we stood on an oddly shaped white stone. He pulled me closer to his large frame. I knew it was not appropriate, but the thought of resisting him cast a shadow upon my heart. His unique scent was enslaving. It reminded me of the sweet smell of juniper berries at their peak, sweet yet earthy.

"Close your eyes and place your other hand in mine."

Without moving my gaze from his, I did as he said. I was fascinated with the swirling gold of Honey Eyes and the churning blue waters of Samayaza, but these deep green swirls of lightning had me undone.

"Close your eyes, Iris." His voice continued to slip into the deep crevices of my mind with every word he spoke, bending my will to his instantly.

I felt a cool breeze caress my body.

A hand gently touched my face and slid through my hair. I shivered and felt heat rise to my cheeks again.

"You may open your eyes," he whispered.

I did and was astounded by what I was looking at and where

I was. We were back at the temple, standing by the balcony's edge where I first saw him. I was staring at the entire village, lit with beautiful lights. Looking down upon this large village was breathtaking. I had never seen so many homes that shone like the stars in the night sky. It was as though the stars had descended from the heavens to come and light up the ground below.

It was truly enchanting. Homes with windows revealed people were moving about with plenty of lights within them. How many candles were they burning to achieve such light, I wondered.

"None," answered the unearthly being beside me, quietly staring at me as I studied the city that belonged to my evil grandfather.

"It belongs to us," he corrected.

"How are you doing that?" I asked. How was he reading and answering my thoughts like I had voiced them aloud? "How can you hear my unspoken words?"

"You allow it," he replied. "Learn to guard your thoughts," he encouraged.

"How do I allow it?"

He reached his hand toward my neck and pulled out the stone Grandfather Enok had given me. His fingers' soft touch and caress sent a flutter to my being. I instantly felt my cheeks burn again in response.

"If ever you need a veil to cover your thoughts, touch this amulet."

But how did he know of the stone necklace?

"I am the one who gave it to your Grandfather Enok to give to you."

Again, he answered my question before I could voice it.

"Keep your mind solid like the stone. Let them be enchanted

by you and not you by them."

"Are you not one of them?" I asked.

"Yes."

"Should I be afraid of you or them?"

"Neither."

Slightly confused, I reached for the stone he had let go of. I wondered how he had given the stone to Grandfather and when he had given it. How long had these beings been here, and why couldn't I stop looking into his beautiful deep green eyes?

"Because I am not of this earth, your senses are overwhelmed with our light."

Scowling, I asked, "I thought no one could read my thoughts while my hand is upon this stone?"

"No one can." He paused momentarily, then answered, "Except for me." He winked and smiled, turning me into honey drips.

I wanted to ask him how he knew Grandfather Enok, but before I could say anything, he tensed, and a scowl appeared upon his striking face.

"Keep your hand on the stone," he instructed, grabbing my hand and placing it upon the smooth stone as his palm covered my eyes. He said some words in a foreign tongue. And just like that, he was standing no more but had vanished, and I was standing in front of the fountain with colorful stones. I felt slightly ill from the sudden shift, just like before, but another emotion was plaguing me more than the slight turning of my stomach—emptiness.

A dark shadow overtook my heart, and my mind descended into a sadness I had not felt before. Why did I feel so empty and alone suddenly? I had not even felt this sadness when separated from my family. And why did I feel his touch lingering on my hand?

I let out a deep sigh and stared down into the fountain with the colorful stones. A single tear rolled down my face and into the water. The stones shimmered as the light of the moon shined upon them. It was beautiful indeed to see such colors glisten in the moonlight. Sitting at the edge of the fountain, I gently caressed the water. I watched the ripples created by the small trickle of water coming into the pool; it made a beautiful interval of the moonlight hitting the stones.

I could smell my river again. Closing my eyes, I inhaled deeply and could see him again. His swirling green eyes were intently directed at me, and I felt nothing else mattered. I could hear my river again. I could see his face, so perfectly drawn in my mind. Feelings I never knew I had awakened the moment I saw him. Thoughts of him were not enough. I wanted to be in his presence again.

My hand went deeper into the pool to touch the stones again. I could feel the smooth and ridged edges. I felt a slight chill run up my back as the cold of the water touched my arm, and a cool breeze caressed me as it passed by, reminding me of those nights on my family's rooftop.

"Iris."

I heard him.

I opened my eyes and smiled. I knew it was him.

"*Keep your hand on the stone,*" he warned.

His voice spoke deep within my mind. He was speaking to me in my head! It was somewhat unsettling, but in some strange way, it felt reassuring to know how close he could be.

"You have always been easily amused, Iris," said another familiar and unearthly voice.

Startled, I stood and tightened my grip on my stone. It was the one called Samayaza. The one who rescued me from my evil Grandfather's wrath. The one who called himself lord. He stood between two pillars as the moon's light shone upon him. The blue of his eyes shimmered like the stones in the fountain, and his gaze was unwavering as he slowly walked toward me.

I slightly bowed, remembering Boria's warning as I held tightly to my stone. "Forgive me; I didn't mean to wander without permission."

"You are free to wander my temple whenever you wish." His allowance was gracious, yet I was weary as he continued to walk in my direction slowly. "Just be aware of those unbeknownst to you as you wander," he warned with a smile as his blue eyes began to swirl like I had seen in the throne room, a reminder of how he was not of this Earth. It was like staring at a collective of stars that began to spin and dance in a deep blue ocean.

"You are free to ask me what you wish as well," he smoothly offered as he drew closer.

My heart began to race from his mere presence; his intensity made me feel like a cornered animal, like prey, yet my curiosity wanted to stay within his sight and hear whatever temptations he could offer. I should be ashamed for thinking it, but I was so fascinated by his swirling blue eyes. They reminded me of the night sky when Boria and I would look up and speak of our future, hopes, and wishes. That feeling engulfed me now as he drew closer, inviting me, whispering to dive deep into his waters and stay.

He pushed a stray hair behind my ear. The slight touch of his hand sent shivers down my back. My skin tingled with excitement, but it all felt different. The calm I had felt with the one with green eyes wasn't present—instead, only excitement and intrigue. I should have felt fear as his tall frame quickly overtook mine. My shadow seemed lost within his massive one, as though only one being existed, and he had consumed me. Though I held his gaze in awe of his charm, I never once let go of my stone. I was aware of that and the slight burning sensation in my neck as I looked up at him in such proximity. He was so much taller than I, and at this distance, his scent was rich and potent as it stirred emotions I had just newly discovered.

He lifted me and placed me on the edge of the water. I gained some height and felt my neck ease as I looked upon him. But a frown was upon his face, a look of deep concern. He stood tall and stoic as the swirls in his eyes disappeared. Those beautiful dancing stars that moved so feverishly within the blue waters vanished suddenly and became unmoving lakes of ice.

"Go to your quarters, Iris," he commanded. He was stern, direct, and abrupt.

Feeling suddenly bereft, I stumbled as I stepped down.

He reached out and quickly supported me as I found my footing again, but the coldness in his eyes never left. What had I done to anger him so? Had I broken protocol or offended him? I somehow felt deprived of joy, of his presence, and for what reason, I had no clue.

He stared down at me now, and I knew not to stay any longer. I had seen first-hand the power these beings possessed. I slightly bowed and hurried to my quarters while holding tightly to my stone. I entered as quietly as possible and made my way to my room. Falling onto my cot, I finally let out a deep sigh of relief and released my hand from my stone. I felt calm again, and the uneasiness of what I experienced with Samayaza slowly drifted away.

How odd was the sudden shift in behavior, I wondered as I lay there in my cot. What had I done that brought forth such coldness from him? Though I was glad to leave when he commanded me to, I did not want to be accused of something that would infuriate Boria or bring shame to my family.

Honestly, all I wanted to do was recall everything with Green Eyes, what he had said, how he had made me feel. But I could not keep myself awake anymore. I felt drained of all my energy and decided I should rest. I knew the morning light would bring new troubles like Boria's enchantment with these beings; and mine. I understood the pull they had now and knew not to blame Boria to the degree I had intended. I pulled the blankets over me and rested my head on the soft wool bundle. Thoughts of green eyes and blue waters carried me to a restless slumber.

# AMONG ANGELS 2

Samayaza stared at the stones within the fountain incredulously. He knew the elements that lay hidden in each of them and what each one could influence within the hearts and minds of mortals. He knew of the healing properties and destructive energy that lay deep within. He knew how some could be used for their beauty while others could be used as currency.

He could see the depth of desire grow within each mortal that saw these stones. They coveted them shamelessly, and, already in their minds, they were willing to defy the fundamental laws of life to possess them. How easily they were lured to their destruction, he thought. So quickly, they ignored the truth etched within them at the sight of the glories they had once resided in.

He knew everything about the Earth and all the jewels that hid within it. Not one component was hidden from him as he had witnessed the creation of this world. Yes, he was in awe of the beauty of it all, at the complex and intricate design the Creator had formulated for the mortals. It, indeed, was the most fascinating realm he had ever witnessed the creation of.

How inextricably this world was built to function and heal itself with its own elements. Everything it needed to restore its waters, air, and life, including that of the mortals, all existed within itself. And it was all made for the honor of them to seek out and decide to use it according to the simple map the Creator had left for them. He knew of all of this, yet he neglected to see the simple reality that even with the knowledge and power of the stars, he was now part mortal.

Though he would not succumb to the toil of this world as they would, he could still become beguiled with its treasures. Elements that were hidden deep within the Earth and very difficult to reach. Ingredients no human could harvest. It would take generations of these mortals even to start scratching the surface of what the first layers of the Earth could provide them.

He huffed at the thought, cupped some water, and allowed it to fall between his fingers. Moonlight shined upon the water that dripped down his perfectly smooth mortal skin. It would never age or wrinkle like that of the mortals. Some secrets needed to remain hidden from them. He would make sure of that.

But never once did it cross his mind that these elements would hinder his powers here. At least not in the way he had just experienced; he was caught off guard and felt a hot rage wash over him. He felt a fool for not even crossing this scenario in his mind. What he had felt moments ago in her presence was only being held due to his angelic discipline. Had he not dismissed her when he did, he might have lost his patience at the continued lack of entry into her thoughts. He could not read her like he had earlier, which only meant one thing.

The amulet she held within her hand tied around her neck had given its secret away.

"Did you know?" he asked into the night air as he continued looking at his glistening wet hand.

Out of the shadows of the pillars, Azazzel walked toward the moonlight, revealing himself to his superior.

"No," he answered. He had suspected something but discarded the suspicion as he could read the female's mind while escorting her from her grandfather's home. But he was not about to tell Samayaza that. He knew better than to offer weak excuses.

Samayaza closed his eyes and inhaled deeply. He turned around, releasing his breath slowly as he looked upon Azazzel, the first one who had agreed to descend with him and help him recruit the others. He stood steadfast when those others had doubts about the repercussions of what they were about to take on, but because of Azazzel's allegiance, they drove forward into an agreement. And thus, paved the way to force Daniel into the pact.

"How do you suppose we handle this slight dilemma?" asked Samayaza.

Azazzel smiled slightly at the question. He already knew what he was being tasked with. "I will leave for the old fool's village upon the first rays of the sun." He bowed and turned to leave but sent a silent thought to Samayaza as he began to disappear into the darkness. *"Alive or dead?"*

"Alive for now," replied Samayaza.

Killing the old prophet now would bring unwanted wrath and attention from the realms above, something he needed to avoid for as long as tolerable. In this realm, time would be of the essence to him and his angelic brethren. Every minute that went by was used to its utmost potential. Though he had never been at the mercy of Earthly time when he was above, he now wanted as much of it as possible. Such a foreign emotion, likely due to his hybrid existence now. He would ensure his plans were laid out and executed promptly. Though there was much to accomplish, he had already established his rule upon Earth.

Walking out to the balcony, he stood by the railing and watched the large city below him illuminated like never before. The mortals were in awe of him and all that he had thus provided. A perfect smile crept across his lips. It was good and only the beginning of what he would create. So much had been given to these mortals, yet they had no idea how to wield any of their resources. They were not even aware of their status among the Earth and stars. And that was the way he wanted to keep it. The less they knew who and where they came from, the better and easier it would be to herd them into obedience.

A malicious chuckle echoed inside his mind. Lucifer was near and approved of his thoughts. Instantly, Samayaza's smile faded as he heard the command given. Bound by oath, he obeyed his dark lord and disappeared into the night.

# CHAPTER SEVEN

I awoke to the sound of arguing voices. It was Boria, and from her voice, she was very aggravated.

Rubbing my eyes, I sat up in my cot and yawned. Though I had woken up earlier in the night fully refreshed, I now felt the lack of energy one should have in the morning. It was all strange. Everything had changed in a blink of an eye, and though I was with my family, I still felt lost. The way of the people here was so different and obscure; nothing was like my humble and simple village.

The security I felt from reuniting with my family was a comfort beginning to fade as I noticed how quickly they were adjusting. It just seemed strange that no one questioned anything. I knew I had been terrified numerous times while getting there, but I still held on tight to whatever little amount of courage I had and spoke not only to my evil grandfather but to the one called Samayaza.

Just the thought of his name provoked memories of my encounter with him, how he had sent me away without even looking at me and had suddenly gone rigid and stoic. And how the once-charged air around me felt drained and bereft. I tried to think again of what I could have said or done, but nothing came to mind that would have upset him. Trying their patience or angering them was not something I would purposely do, as I had seen what they were capable of. But somehow, I managed to do it without even knowing. This unprovoked and unintentional slight worried me. I was in unknown territory without a guide.

I shifted my gaze down to the blankets that covered me. The rays of the sun revealed the intricate needlework. Never had I seen such imagery etched onto any cloth like this.

"What are you doing?" Boria asked from the doorway.

Startled, I bunched the blanket in my hand as I turned to her. "Admiring the threadwork on these blankets."

With one eyebrow raised, she looked down at my hand that fisted in the blanket.

She walked over and sat down next to me. "You need not worry about anything, Iris; no one will harm us." She slowly released my hand and straightened the blanket out.

"How do you know?"

"Because we are royalty here. Did you forget who our grandfather is?" She got up and walked toward the opening where the sun shined upon her, and the threadwork on her clothes glistened in the sun just as the blanket had.

It was amazing. "How do they make a thread that shines like the stars?"

"Oh, Iris! Why do you ask so many questions that do not

matter?" she snapped, mocking me as she walked around the room, pretending to be me. "How do you know? How do they do that?"

Though she saw the frown on my face, she continued as she came closer to where I sat. "Why ask why or how when we are here and seeing the amazing things happening to us with our eyes!"

"Why are you joyous about such mysterious beings we know so little of?" Now it was my turn to give her an earful of what I thought. "We are away from our village, forcefully brought to a temple made by an evil grandfather who would have had me killed had it not been for those beings...."

"Precisely, Iris! They are for us, not against us!" she quipped.

Sighing, I did not argue about that, as she was right. Yet I did not want her to be right on this.

"What if you are wrong, and—"

"Iris, enough." she snapped, "I know what I know, and I will not allow your infant mind to destroy our chance at a great new life here!"

Without another word, I moved away from her and sat with my back facing her on the edge of my cot. There was something wrong with her infant mind, not mine!

"Iris, you are behaving like a child."

And if I was, I had every right to be since she behaved like one herself.

I heard her sigh, then felt her slender arms wrap around me. "You know you want to embrace me, too."

She knew me too well. "I would if you could release my arms!"

She ignored me and began tickling my side. She knew my weakest point and went directly for it. I had no choice but to laugh and beg her to stop!

"Will you stop asking questions and just enjoy it?" she demanded as she continued the onslaught, bringing about an uncontrollable laughter within me. I could barely breathe, let alone answer her.

"Girls!" Mother had walked in.

Boria stopped and straightened as I took a moment to collect myself and catch my breath.

"Father is waiting on you two for morning supper." She smiled slightly and gave us a wink before turning around to leave, but not before she said, "Iris, embrace your sister."

We both looked at each other and burst into laughter as we embraced. Boria's lengthy arms engulfed me as always. I could only get my arms around her slender lower back. Burying my face in her beautiful hair, I inhaled deeply and remembered all the nights I would sleep in her arms.

I felt at home finally.

We both walked into the main area to find Father pouring Kas into his cup. Shaking my head, I smiled and joined my family for a morning feast. There was everything I could have imagined for morning supper, from sweet, braided bread to honey, dates, and fruits. This was a feast indeed! I was so famished that I began filling my plate without realizing that Father was holding the Kas pitcher and waiting for my cup.

He chuckled at my eagerness. "Always a rush for the sweet bread." He pointed to my cup with his eyes while Mother shook her head and continued filling her plate.

I had always loved anything sweetened with honey. Mother would warn me about eating too much and growing thick in the waist with no teeth, as it would rot them. At one point, the thought of losing my teeth and becoming thick made me stop eating bread and honey altogether. But this morning, all Mother did was shake her head and allow me to indulge in whatever I wanted without a single word of discouragement. Silently, I wished it could be like this all the time.

"Iris, can you pass me the dates?" Boria asked.

I nodded and grabbed a plate of the plumpest dates I had ever seen. I quickly threw one on my plate and leaned forward to hand her the rest. My stone came forth from my dress, and Boria promptly noticed. "What is that?' she asked as her gaze fixated on my stone.

I grabbed it and put it back underneath my tunic. "What?" I asked dumbly.

She squinted at me. "You know what I am asking about. Where did you get that stone?"

And just like that, my pleasant morning was ruined because Boria could not leave well enough alone. "By the river, a fortnight before we left," I lied.

"Let me see it," she demanded.

"No."

She knew I was hiding something. I had to think of something quickly, or she would persist until she received what she sought.

"What was amiss this morning? I awoke to hear trouble between you and Mother?"

Boria's face was no longer soft with sisterly affection but rather cold with calculated observation. I looked at Mother instead. She knew I had changed the subject on Boria, but she played along and allowed my question to linger as she looked toward Boria.

She looked at me with venomous eyes, and I knew she wanted to reach out and grab my stone. But one look toward Mother was all it took for her to retract momentary spite and answer, "We weren't arguing. We were discussing Lord Samayaza's kindness to us and how Mother should show more gratitude."

Mother stopped eating and looked down at her plate as she neatly put down the piece of bread in her hand. I knew her posture, back straight, head lifted high, but eyes looking down. Mother was irked by what Boria had just said, and I instantly regretted my question.

"If they require gratitude, then maybe we should be free to leave for our village." Mother's voice was stern and solid in rebuke.

Yes, I absolutely should not have mentioned anything. I noticed Father shift uneasily in his seat and stop eating. Anxiously, he looked upon Mother and gave Boria a look to stay quiet.

"I was just making sure we didn't offend these interesting beings and—"

Before Boria could finish, Mother abruptly answered, "And what, Boria? Throw ourselves at their feet because they saved us from one lion only to face another?"

The look on Boria's face was pure petulance, and I knew this would end badly. She opened her mouth to say something, but the sound of soldiers entering our quarters quenched the heated argument instantly.

Four soldiers and two unearthly beings I had not seen before entered and surrounded us. The feeling of almost being home fled instantly, and my hand instinctively went to my stone. One of the unearthly beings seemed to notice and came to stand directly behind me as the other one, who held a scroll in his hand, stepped in front of Boria and handed it to her.

The one that stood in front of Boria was similar in size to all the others, but the hair upon his head was ashen in color, making him seem older, yet his face was that of a younger man. His eyes looked dark, and his clothing was covered in armor.

Father grew nervous. He started to rise, but one of the soldiers pressed his hand on Father's shoulder, directing him to stay in his place. I saw Mother slowly try to get closer to Boria, but she had the same thing done to her by another soldier.

A deep timber of a voice came out of the unearthly being like thick, rich honey out of a honeybee's nest. "Do you accept willingly?" he asked.

"Yes," Boria quickly answered.

"NO!" Mother objected to whatever she had accepted. Again, Mother tried to stand, but the four soldiers had now encompassed Father and Mother, warning off any opposition.

Without looking at Mother, Boria opened the scroll and said, "I am summoned. I will obey."

"No child of mine will be summoned like she is chattel!" Mother cried to no avail.

Boria's stance was pure defiance. She calmly looked at Mother, knowing Mother had no rule over her. I sighed at my sister's stubbornness. She was purposely being wicked to Mother.

"Can I not go in my daughter's stead?" asked Father as he tried to intercede. But not once did the unearthly beings look his way.

"The summons calls for me, Father. It even has my name on it, look." She handed it to him, but Mother quickly snatched it from his hand and began reading it. Her face was worried, and I knew Mother saw something within that summons that frightened her.

She handed the summons to Father, looked at me, then Boria. "Whether summoned or not, if you choose to obey, you will be subject to this temple and his will." She finished with plead-ing eyes, "And I do not think you have the slightest idea of what that entails."

Boria scowled. "What do you mean *his will*? We are com-pletely safe here. Look at our clothing and our quarters! If we were to be harmed, it would have already happened."

Father sighed and looked toward me, but what could I say to deter her? I knew better than to convince her differently when she had already decided.

"Did you not even notice the symbol upon that summons?" asked Mother.

Boria shrugged her shoulders as though it meant nothing.

"It means that you will become a high priestess of some sort. That symbol represents the temple. The temple symbol can only be given to those of rank or those who will obtain rank. Did you forget who my father is and where I lived half my life? Were my stories not enough warning? You will never be able to leave!"

Boria looked as though she was trying to process what Moth-er was saying but disregarded it.

"Why would I want to leave?" Boria asked. "Look at me, Mother. I am clothed in garments of beauty, my heritage has earned me a place in this magnificent temple, and I am free to make my choices, unlike my previous life." Rebelliously, she continued, "I choose to make peace here and become someone great, unlike you."

"Boria! That's enough!" Father reprimanded.

Mother stood in disbelief, as did I. I was genuinely bewil-dered by the words my sister chose to speak. In an instant, she had changed into the worst parts of herself.

The unearthly being that stood behind walked forward and

stood next to the ashen-haired one. They now stood on either side of Boria. "It is done!" both exclaimed and began to walk with Boria in tow.

"Boria." I took a few steps forward in hopes of reaching her. "Do not leave," I begged. I could hear Mother sobbing.

Boria stopped, as did the unearthly beings beside her. She turned to look at me, her determined gaze colliding into my pleading eyes.

"I'm sure your summons will come soon, Iris." Her gaze went to where my stone was as she gently tapped her neck to confirm her knowledge of what I thought was hidden.

"Or you may choose to come with me now, and we can take on this journey together," she offered with a smile.

"NO!" Mother protested.

I stood where I was and did not move. I silently mouthed, *please stay* as my final attempt, but she shook her head subtly yet firmly, rejecting my plea.

"Hmm, I suppose it will be later then," she said as she turned away, continuing her path out of our quarters and into unknown terrain. Father tried calling for her, but whatever Boria had accepted was already done, and any objections were in vain.

I sighed in disappointment and dropped my hand from my stone now that they were gone. She was enamored. She was beguiled. She was blind to reality and unafraid when she should be treading lightly around this strange new place. I knew what she felt as I felt it every time I looked into their eyes.

I heard Mother's sobs and Father's quiet shushing in hopes of consoling her. Boria was determined. We all knew that, and now, with her blinding admiration toward these beings, we knew we had no chance of convincing her of anything. I had no idea what would become of her, but if anyone knew, it would be the woman crying in my father's arms.

I walked over and put my arms around them both. We had all been through so much in such a short time. We were brought back together, only to be ripped apart again. I was finally trying to grasp the reality of being reunited with my family, then Boria was summoned and left without any regard for herself or us and called for what and by whom exactly was still a mystery to me. I still did not understand it all, but it was not good from what Mother was saying. She was the one who had read the scroll.

"Mother, what will happen to her?" I asked, stepping back a little to give them space.

Her eyes closed, and she took a deep breath and collected herself. When she looked at me, it was with such defeat. "I do not know," she answered.

"Was not your father the high priest?" I hesitantly asked, hoping to inquire without upsetting her too much.

She looked at me and sadly nodded yes.

"My father's reign is no more. Even though he succeeded in taking my firstborn, I do not know what these beings are after."

"He no longer reigns over this temple?"

She turned and looked at me, ready to repeat herself, but I began telling her all I had witnessed. I knew this was my chance to tell them everything that had happened, so I recalled as much as possible. Father and she both stared intently at me as I told them all that had happened from the time Honey Eyes escorted me to this village, the bathhouse, the temple throne room where I met my evil grandfather, and finally, how the one called Samayaza rescued me from his wrath and froze him in place, then had him vanish before my eyes. One minute, he was standing, and the next, he was no more.

"I was in the throne room. Grandfather Turian was going to hit me, but the one called Samayaza froze him in place, and then he made him depart in a blink of an eye."

"What do you mean *depart*? How can one be no more when they stand before you?" asked Father.

"It was just as I said. He was there one moment, and the next, he was gone." I could see the confusion on his face, but I had no other way of explaining what I had witnessed. I still could not believe it, but it had occurred just as I spoke.

"Iris, are you certain of what you say, maybe—"

I interrupted him before he could blame my exhaustion from the journey for imagining things. "I know what I saw, Father! I am not delusional; it happened right before my eyes!" Why did they always question me and not Boria? "He stood there frozen in place, hand still lifted as though to hit me, and then he was gone with a command. Why do you not believe what I say, Father?" it hurt deeply to see the doubt in his eyes when I spoke the truth.

"I do not doubt you, child," Mother calmly interceded. "I know who you speak of."

Relieved, I sat down for a moment. Father looked upon Mother, trying to figure out if she truly believed me or was just too tired to argue. I felt the sting of betrayal, father was always on my side. Why now would he doubt me?

Mother spoke as she stared across the room. "After all this time, it's all true. I thought him mad; yet he was speaking the truth." She pinched her upper nose between her eyes and bowed her head. "This is far worse than I ever imagined."

Father took a step forward, his concern mirroring mother,

"What is far worse than you imagined?"

Looking at him, she grimly replied, "With my father as high priest, I may have known what Boria was summoned for. It would have been what we had feared regarding her future husband being chosen by him, but now, the protocol has changed. Everything I knew about how this temple worships is no longer familiar."

Oh my. I now understood why she was so worried. It had to be the unearthly beings. It had to be him that summoned her.

"Samayaza," I whispered.

"Yes," Mother answered as her eyes began to well with tears.

"Then we have not much to fear," Father replied. "Was he not the one, your father mentioned as *following his orders,* hence why we are alive? If he summoned Boria, then he would do her no harm. Or else what was the point of keeping us alive and in such lavish quarters as these?"

Mother looked at him in dismay. "Beguilement is a power, husband. My father spent years refining his speech and appearance to coerce an entire village to do as he says without question!" she spat angrily at him.

"Maybe your father did, but these beings are not like us. And if they could hold your father back, we may have a chance to go home unharmed."

She just stared at him as tears overwhelmed her. My heart ached for her, and I was about to go to her, but she turned and walked to her room. Father quickly followed.

I stood there motionless for a while, trying to process everything she had just said. I knew nothing of this new world other than that it was driving me to exhaustion every moment I was in it. There were too many new and unexplained things happening.

Things I could not even imagine, let alone see with my eyes and accept as real. I felt like I was in a story Grandfather Enok would tell us as children. Grandfather Enok! How I wish I could have just a few moments of counsel with him. He could bring sanity back to me and, most of all, to Boria! I wished I had paid more attention and memorized every word he spoke.

As hard as I tried to remember our last encounter, I could not recall everything he had told me. My visions of Honey Eyes, giant horses, cold night air, bathing pools, and swirls of blue and green eyes overlapped. They were all I could remember—beautiful, unearthly beings. Maybe I, too, was beguiled, much as I accused Boria of being.

At the thought, my hand instinctively reached for the stone around my neck.

I had neglected to tell my parents about the unearthly one with green eyes. Something within me did not want to share anything about my encounter with him with anyone. The need to keep it hidden nudged at me constantly in my thoughts. Yet, while I spoke of my journey, I wanted to tell them about the dreams where I saw these unearthly beings. I tried to tell them everything, hoping to figure out what was happening, but I knew they would not believe me. I could hardly believe what I had told them thus far.

Maybe I should tell Mother, but I should wait until she was calm. She might be able to explain any further knowledge she had of these beings. She must have seen many unpleasant things growing up with a horrible father. I wondered how often that evil man hit her as a little girl. How easy would it have been to beat his daughter if he were ready and willing to hit me without reason? He had sacrificed his wife from what my mother had told us. And that alone was enough for us never to want to be near that kind of evil. But here we all were, with Boria leaving and accepting her place within this temple.

How we'd ended up deep within a temple, I wished never to see was astonishing. How had fate woven this extraordinary moment into our lives and rendered me silent? Guarded by unearthly beings that had powers beyond anything I had ever seen—there was no escape.

With my fingers holding tightly to the stone around my neck, I wondered what mercy they would have upon us and, more importantly, what would become of Boria since it wasn't my evil grandfather who'd summoned her. Did this mean the old terms were null? What was their intention with her or Samayaza's for summoning her alone?

My mind raced through my encounter with him, his swirling green eyes, his imposing presence, and most importantly, his sudden dislike of *my* company. Could I have done something to have caused all that was happening now? The thought brought anguish deep within my heart.

Tears rolled down my face and onto my hand, as I felt my failure in rescuing my family. I had not made it back to them in time to prevent Boria from leaving us. I should have just been taken with them instead of fleeing as my father had urged me to do. Had I not left and escaped, I might have been able to steer Boria away from her stubborn thoughts and whatever beguilement was upon her. I could always find common ground with her and quell her need to sabotage herself, but it always took time and care.

I quietly walked back to my room and fell onto my cot. My whole body felt tired again for some reason I couldn't fathom.

My ankle ached a little. I felt defeated again and weak, physically and emotionally. I needed rest. I needed calm. I wanted to be home again, but I knew it would not be so.

Wet with tears and weariness, I closed my eyes and turned toward the window. A breeze made its way over me. I swore I could smell our village river again, but I knew it was just my mind doing its best to comfort me. Either way, it was calming and eased the ache in my ankle. Slumber came swiftly, and oh-so-sweetly, I surrendered.

# CHAPTER EIGHT

Slumber was sweet, indeed. I dreamt of my village. I dreamt of Boria and myself alongside our river, laughing and running with our hands brushing against the long grass. The sweet scent of the river and the smell of freshly cut tamarisk calmed our hearts. We spoke of our dreams as always, and I laughed at Boria's outrageous imagination. She combed and braided my hair, and all felt well again until she handed me the stone and sternly asked who gave it to me.

I was startled awake. I reached for my stone and felt its cool, smooth surface against my fingertips. It calmed my heart and brought a sense of stillness. I thought of *him* again—Green Eyes. I did not want to, yet I did.

I thought of him more times than I should have. His voice still echoed in my mind. How he looked at me with those swirling green eyes only made me yearn for his attention. I did not want us to part. I wanted to discover the mystery of who he was, where he came from, and what his thoughts of me were.

I felt my cheeks warm at the thought.

"*Iris.*"

I heard his soft melodic voice in my head. I welcomed it without fear this time. Hearing him that close made me feel safe, as though I was not alone in this strange new world. He felt oddly familiar, which confused me.

Maybe Boria was right—perhaps I was just as enamored with him as she had become with Samayaza. This led me to think of how I would have responded to a summons like the one she had received. Would I have gone? Would I defy my parents and leave at a whim's notice if he called? I knew the answer and shivered at the thought. Boria was right.

Shortly after I awakened, Mother came in and said we would go to the market to be fitted for new garments, per the summons that had just arrived. For what purpose, she did not know. The same four guards had arrived, along with the two same unearthly beings. The ashen-haired one instructed that we were free to choose anything we wished. Mother told him she wanted to go home and have her daughter back. He answered with a raise of his eyebrow and proceeded to escort us out of the temple into the busy streets.

It was busy with people of many trades. So many huts set up with various goods, and everything looked and smelled wonderful, from the fresh fruits, loaves of bread, and meats to the beautiful and richly decorated vessels. It was a stunning sight to see. People dressed in many colors and adornments covered their heads or ears, while their faces bore the same black color around their eyes. It was more prevalent with the women than men, but they looked so different from our village people.

One artisan drew on a beautiful golden vessel. I moved closer to see his work and observed an array of beautiful petals with a stick with some feathers at the end. The color was a rich blue with the colors of the sun within. It shined like the threads in my blanket; it was breathtaking. I wanted to get closer and see what material he was using.

I felt a slight breeze, and one of the two unearthly beings now stood beside me. His menacing frame cast a shadow so large that the young artisan stopped to see what had blocked the sun. When he looked up, I noticed his eyes. They were a deep blue like that of a clear night sky. He did not have color on his face like most men but wore the same garments. His hands looked strong, as though he worked in the fields, yet they were clean and delicately held the dainty stick. He had a handsome face and looked tall—his head was almost the height of mine while he sat on a stool.

"Do you wish for the vessel?" asked the handsome artisan as he cautiously viewed our escorts.

I shrugged regretfully for bringing about the unwanted attention. I knew at this point that the unearthly being had to be fiercely staring down upon him.

"I was just admiring your craft," I said kindly. "I have never seen such detail created by such colors. How do you produce them?"

He smiled at my compliment. "Your admiration is humbling." His eyes shined with genuine delight.

I smiled back and noticed the small pots filled with colored liquids beside him. They were so vibrant in color, and some had flowers or petals within. I saw one pot with a familiar flower. "Where did you get that flower?" I pointed directly at it.

He looked to where I was pointing, then reached for the jar. As he brought it close, I could see it was like my flower but not the same.

"They are picked by our apprentices and dried, then given to us to use. Would you like to see how I create and combine the colors?" he asked.

"I would love to—"

"Artisan, keep your eyes and thoughts to your craft, lest you lose them both," the ashen-haired being threatened as the air around me suddenly felt thick with pressure. The sole timbre of his voice was enough to warn the young man to bow his head in submission and return to his work without another word. Though I noticed he had a glare in his eyes when the being rebuked him, he dared not challenge as he would be no match against him. With all that I had seen them do with mere words and a simple glare, I also felt fear in the air and decided against even saying goodbye to the young man.

I turned toward Mother, who quickly pulled me close to her side, chiding me for straying and causing discourse with our escorts. I stayed silent and bewildered as to why the guards denied a simple, innocent request. I understood Mother; she always chided us when we gave any men attention. But why did the unearthly being interfere with such a mundane request? I was trying to see how those colors were created and where his apprentices found those beautiful flowers.

His offer to show me how he could create such beauty would have been a delight to witness. But it was not to be. Disheartened, I heeded my mother's warning and followed as they led.

But I knew I would somehow find a way to apologize to that young man one day. There was no reason to chastise him just because he chose to answer my questions.

As we continued walking through the vast, decorated streets, I noticed large stones with animals carved into them at almost every corner we turned. Some I recognized, but some were creatures I had never seen before. One, in particular, was that of a man on top, but his lower half belonged to a beast of some sort. Even Mother was staring at it, trying to figure out what it was. Of course, there were many other stone carvings throughout the streets. Some were of women carrying vessels with water coming forth from pools beneath their feet. I had to admit to myself how beautiful and wondrous this place was now that I could see everything without the panic or fear I had before. When Honey Eyes escorted me, all I could think of was who and what he was, and I wondered if I would live to see my family again.

I had somehow missed all the beautiful colors and drawings that adorned the walls and homes of these villagers. They, too, were decorated with colors and threadwork that were stunning. The women wore dresses of different colors, with adornments in their hair, their faces beautifully colored, especially their eyes. I was not eager to look like them, nor did I want to have my face painted like theirs, but the way the black line encased their eyes made them more appealing and alluring. I would have looked exactly like these women if I had given the girls at the bathhouse less grief.

The smells in the air were wonderful. We walked past many tables filled with bread and meats, making me feel hungry again. Our village never had this much food to trade or sell. At home, we already knew who was capable of what craft, and trades were made accordingly. But here, there was such an abundance of everything it made me wonder why my village was less fruitful. Trade between our villages would have been ideal, but I doubted there was anything my village could have offered as grand as the things found here. It looked as though they had everything one could ever desire.

Once we turned a corner, the street had colorful fabric hanging from one home across to the other. So many colors shined brightly as the sun glistened upon them. From where I stood, all the huts were selling garments—beautiful garments with more shiny thread than my blanket and even more appealing than the one Boria wore. I felt tempted to reach out and touch a beautiful green garment with threadwork, the color of the sun, throughout the fabric.

"Iris, don't touch anything!" Mother scolded. "Remember where your last curiosity led to." She pulled my hand away from the garment. "One lesson a day should suffice," she sternly chided.

"The maiden wishes for new garments," came a voice behind the hanging fabric. Pushing them aside, a beautiful woman came forth, wearing a garment reminiscent of fire and the sun's rays. Embellished with small, flat, shiny objects throughout the hem, it made an interesting noise as she walked toward us. She began sizing me for the garments, and my fear of causing trouble intensified. I looked at Mother with worry, but she shrugged, not knowing what to say as the woman approached us, unafraid.

Just then, the menacing unearthly being came and stood before the beautiful woman. He spoke no word, but the woman responded with a bow and assurance that meant they obeyed and served as he instructed. Mother and I looked at each other, baffled by what had transpired before us. I had not heard a single word come out of his mouth. And neither had Mother. The confusion on her face was as bad as mine.

With one foreign word, he ordered the guards to form a half circle that enclosed us to the table and kept us from anyone walking by. He stood in the middle with the other unearthly being, who was similar in stature but had brown hair rather than ash. His eyes matched the color of his hair, and though he looked wider in the shoulders, his face held a certain softness that the ashen one lacked. He wore all black with a belt from one shoulder to the opposite of his hip. The other one with the ashen hair wore the same belt, but his was green and black with stones on the edges. They turned as to give us privacy, I assumed, and the beautiful woman began to dress us, starting with me.

I could tell Mother did not like the order given. But we both knew there was no way around it. The woman proceeded to put the green garment on me. It was even more beautiful when worn. It wrapped around my body as though it was made just for me. The hem of the garment was the perfect length for my height, and the bodice held intricate stitchwork; I could have easily spent a whole day admiring it. I was glad the stone around my neck disappeared neatly beneath the garment. I had to push it to the side, but it hid perfectly. And even if it appeared, it would blend well with the tiny stones stitched into the neckline and waist of this dress.

"Sit and let us finish."

Us?

Upon her word, three other women came from behind the hanging garments. Two of them began fixing my hair while the other began to rub and cleanse my face with a wet cloth, then she proceeded to paint my face. I did not argue this time, nor did I make it difficult for them in any way. I had learned how quickly my harmless intentions could lead to harm to others. And if I were to be honest with myself, I truly wanted to see if I could be just as beautiful as Boria. Or at least as beautiful as these women.

They rubbed oil upon my feet, arms, and neck. It smelled similar to what I remembered my flower smelled of. It was delightful and calming. Inhaling the scent deeply, I wished I could return to that day when I had my sister next to me and my life was simple and plain. But I knew that would never happen. With my hair pulled and combed, it reminded of my new existence.

I looked over at Mother, and she, too, was being dressed, and by the look on her face, she was not pleased that it was against her will. She was cooperating like I was, but I could see it was only because she knew that rejecting the service was not going to work. They had her in another beautiful red garment with the same shiny threading as mine and Boria's. I could not stop thinking of her now, what she had said, and how she left us so quickly. What was it that made her leave without a single care about what we thought? So lightly was her decision made that I wondered if being more like her and appreciating all of this would make things normal and easier to live with.

"Such a rare gem, is she not?" said the woman who painted my face.

The others glanced my way and agreed with smiles and expressions of awe. I had no idea what they were admiring other than the beautiful green dress I had on. I did not know how I looked, but from their admiration, I assumed it was good.

The woman placed a large, very slender object before me. I

could not believe my eyes, nor Mother, as I found her standing beside me instantly. We could see our true selves as we looked upon this object.

"You are truly a beauty among us," said the same woman as the rest gave a slight bow.

"What is this?" I asked as I continued to stare and touch it. It was smooth and slightly cool to the touch.

"It is called a mirror. It reflects anything in front of it exactly as it is," she answered.

Mother quickly interjected, "Stop touching it. We don't know what it can do."

The woman chuckled. "It only shows your reflection and nothing more."

Mother looked at them sternly and whispered, *"Nothing here is harmless."*

I had to agree with Mother, but seeing myself in such a beautiful garment for the first time was appealing. I had never thought myself beautiful, but now, someone could easily see how Boria and I were sisters. My hair was combed straight with small braids on both sides, and my face was beautifully accented with colors. Thin black lined above my slightly golden eyelids; my lips were more vibrant than ever. It was all different but oddly lovely. Mother even stared at herself in her beautiful red dress and painted face. She looked just as beautiful, too. Whatever this *mirror* truly was, it made us admire ourselves quite a bit. Or maybe it was just Mother and I? Either way, I would take Mother's warning and tread lightly in this new wonder.

The sound of rustling feet alerted us to our escorts. They were back into the double line formation with the two unearthly beings on either side of us. Since our task was complete, they began to escort us back to the temple. Mother quickly grabbed our clothing from before but was told they would place it in our quarters along with some other new garments. She stood there, not knowing what to say. I would have chuckled if it had been any other moment. I had never known Mother to be speechless. She always had something to say, even if it was something about which she did not know. She gave them the clothing and turned away as the women went about their duties.

I stayed silent. I knew Mother had a lot going on in her head, as did I. The way of life here was so different from ours. Nothing was like our village, not even the way they made bread. Our bread was small, flat, and round; theirs was flat, long, and puffed up like lamb's wool. Though she would rarely speak of her life here, nothing she had ever mentioned came close to all we had seen. Unless she didn't intentionally tell of it to not pique our curiosity? It was so hard to understand her thoughts. I just knew that she was usually correct in her judgments.

"The princess is finally looking her part," came a familiar, haughty voice.

The guards halted, and I could see Azazzel standing between them. Though it seemed like they greeted each other with a simple nod, neither one of the two beings moved out of the way for him. He stood there as though waiting for them to part and make way for him to reach us.

Mother looked at me and raised her eyebrows in question. I nodded, letting her know it was the one I had spoken of while we were in our quarters. She turned back and stared him down as protectively as a mother could. But I do not think Azazzel noticed since the guards would not move, and Mother was off to my side while I remained in the direct center of his view. Azazzel was looking at them strangely, his eyes showing ire and contempt. Could it be that they were speaking to each other through their minds? Like how my unearthly being did?

"*Yes.*" His voice came as a whisper in my mind.

I touched the stone immediately and kept my thoughts as straightforward as possible. Azazzel and the other two would have had no trouble reading me if not for the stone. In fact, they had to have been able to read my thoughts this entire time! I had gotten too distracted with all the new sights, smells, and people that I had never once reached for my stone. Until green eyes just whispered to me and reminded me of my misstep. I wanted to tell Mother, but there was no way I could talk to her without them hearing.

"What is happening?" asked Mother.

I looked at her and shrugged. I hated that I was blatantly lying to her, but it had to be this way for now.

No one moved, not even the human guards. Looking around, I noticed people in the street cautiously maneuvering into whatever corners they could find, hiding within shadows. The air around us began to change and thicken. A chill swept through me. Mother pulled me close, as she must have felt the shift and chill in the air.

Then all at once, it was gone, and so was Azazzel. I looked at Mother and saw the disbelief on her face. Her eyes wide and mouth slightly open, she looked around, trying to figure out how he had just disappeared. I knew that feeling. I had felt it in the throne room and during my encounters with these beings. I hope she now knew that I was not exaggerating what I had experienced on my journey to them. What just happened might make her remember more of what Grandfather Enok had spoken of and taught for so many years, how his lessons and stories were not for amusement as most thought.

"You believe me now, Mother?" I whispered as I kept my hand on my stone.

Wide-eyed, she looked at me and said, "I always believed you, Iris; I just never believed my father."

"Your father?" I questioned.

"My father always spoke of a craft that was of the gods," she responded solemnly.

The guards began walking, and we followed suit.

Leaning close as we walked, I asked, "What craft of the gods? You mean of God, as Grandfather Enok would speak of?"

At the mention of my Grandfather Enok, the unearthly beings both tilted their heads to stare at us.

Mother pinched my hand and pretended not to hear my question. The mere mention of my grandfather always irks these beings. I kept quiet and followed Mother's lead, speaking only of the beautiful garments and village adornments. I knew what she was doing and played along. I kept my hand on my stone most of the time. I needed to get a better hold of my thoughts. I could not keep holding on to a stone and expect no one to notice. I knew Mother would soon notice, and I did not want that attention on me.

We were nearing the temple again; I could see the enormous stones between the homes becoming more prominent as we drew near. It was so grand and magnificent; each stone looked the size of an ordinary house. How they got them to sit upon one another like this was amazing. As much as I did not want to admit it, this place was magnificently enchanting. So many colors existed from within and outside these homes—the people and their faces, clothing, artistry, and of course, the food and scents that surrounded us everywhere we went. Everyone seemed to be happy and smiling.

Our village was the complete opposite. Though we were sufficient in providing for ourselves, no one had such colors on their garments or faces. No one had baked anything like the loaves of bread or food we saw and tasted here. None of our homes were this large or decorated with colors and plants. And sadly, most of the people in our village were so burdened with their harvests and herds that they looked worn and tired. How were these people so prosperous and happy? Where were their flocks, and where did their crops come from?

We came around another corner, and I noticed a table with many flowers placed on it. And a large area beside it with what looked like a wall of dried flowers. More were being hung to dry while others were placed together to form a beautiful array of colors and petals on the table. I looked at Mother, and she already knew what I was going to ask.

With a shake of her head at my request, she asked, "May we pick through some of these flowers, my lords?"

The two beings stopped, and the one with the ashen hair nodded and gave the order to allow us to pass through the guards surrounding us.

I was puzzled over why Mother called them lords, but I would not question her choice of words in their presence.

We walked over to the table while the women continually placed flowers as Mother began gathering them. They all looked so beautiful and smelled so lovely. Some were familiar flowers that we had in our village, while others were very different from anything I had ever seen. Since Mother was picking through the fresh stems, I headed toward the wall of delicately dried flowers.

The smell was just as excellent from the dried flowers as from the fresh. I gently touched the dried petals, and some fell to the ground. One of the women came forward, handed me a small bowl, grabbed a small bundle from the stems, and placed them within. She smiled and walked away before I could even thank her. I knew how to handle dry flowers as I had one of my own, but seeing a wall of such colors was too tempting not to touch.

I picked enough bundles to where my bowl was full, and I was happy with the vast selection of colorful and fragrant flowers. I wished I could have known how to make colors like that young man had done with them. Another time, when I could walk freely without any escorts, I would be able to see him again and ask.

We continued to the temple. Before we got close to the entrance, we noticed many people were going in and out with hands full of garments, food, and flowers. Once inside, preparations were made and were carried out by many people. Some were cleaning, and others placed long black curtains directly between the white ones that hung between the pillars throughout the temple. A black substance was put into every fire pit we walked by—even our quarters had a black door with a strange symbol. How had they added a door so quickly?

The guards had left us already, and only the two beings stayed. They stood on either side of the new doors, both about the same height as the door. None of them spoke a word, but each time they looked at me, it felt like they were looking into my innermost thoughts. No spoken words were needed, just communication placed directly into my head on what they wanted, needed, liked, or disliked. No matter if I had the stone in my hand or not, I could receive their intent. Both stared at me with an emotion I was not familiar with and made me nervous to be in their presence. They made sure I knew they were there and kept nudging me in my mind.

With all I had seen and felt thus far, this type of communication was becoming less alarming. I wondered if Mother experienced the same or was quietly nervous about it.

I knew Boria did not, as she denied such a feat when I confronted her the night we were reunited. But she could have easily lied just as I had when it came to my stone.

Once we were inside and realized these new doors and our unearthly escorts were staying, Mother went inside her room in search of Father, and I went into mine to collect my thoughts without interruption. I needed to set my bowl of dried flowers down somewhere away from their view, as I could not enjoy them with the constant stare of two beings that made me feel like prey.

I placed the bowl on the foot of my bed as I sat beside it. Gently, so as to not ruin my new garment or hair, I allowed myself to lay down on my cot. I sighed in relief and closed my eyes as I recounted all that had transpired that morning. From our new appearances, the flowers, the young man, and Azazzel. What did he mean by saying *the princess was beginning to look her part?* I guessed my mother is considered the princess since her father ruled this village, but I did not recall Mother ever mentioning anything about her father being a king.

But I wouldn't be surprised by her withholding that information. She had many secrets about her youth, and when we tried to ask about anything other than what she was willing to share, we would be confronted with an icy stare and silence. We learned not to ask questions early on, as she would assign us more chores anytime we became too curious.

Yawning, I stretched my arms above my head and lay still for a moment. It was quiet even though I had a small opening within the wall to see the outside. I could smell the dried flowers next to me and allowed the peace of this moment to wash over me like fresh rain upon a dried, parched land. It was soothing to have familiar scents around me.

I looked through the flowers and discovered I had picked some that we had in our village! Though they were utterly fragile and dried, I could still recognize them and seek them out from the wall of flowers. All that was missing now was my hand being caressed by the river in our village as I lay beside it, letting the day's worries flow away.

I wished to go back home; closing my eyes, I stretched my arms as far as they could go and envisioned it.

I felt a soft caress from my elbows down to my hands. Startled, I quickly rose in surprise and looked around my room. No one was there.

I walked towards the window and stood there for a while, hoping to feel the wind coming through, thinking it was just the breeze I had felt. But there was no wind, just the beautiful sun and many busy people below.

Turning back around, I felt the wind, but it wasn't coming from behind me as it should have been. Instead, it was in front of me, gently blowing at my hair. I could smell the river, the flowers, and *him*.

I felt every worry and thought melt away. He was near.

My heart impatiently awaited his presence.

I felt the wind pass by my one side, then the other. I smiled.

"Iris," the wind whispered as it lifted my hair.

My eyes instinctively closed to the sound of his voice. He

brought calm to my thoughts. As though he had always been there, but I only now realized it.

I opened my eyes, anticipating his presence, but he was nowhere in my room. My heart fell in disappointment but was quickly revived by a small blue flower in the middle of my cot. It was my flower, the one I had found by the river. It was just as beautiful as I remembered.

"Iris, we are summoned to the throne room before twilight for your sister's confirmation into the temple priesthood."

Mother's heartbroken voice jolted me out of my serene moment, and I dropped the flower.

She noticed. Even with how heartbroken she sounded and looked, she managed to enter the room and grab the flower that had fallen from my hands upon her announcement. "It's beautiful," she said, bringing it to her nose. A small smile appeared on her face at the scent. "It smells heavenly."

I smiled in agreement.

"Is this why we were taken to be dressed and prepared?" I asked as she gently placed the flower back down on the cot. She must have assumed I picked it up from the hut.

"I believe so."

"Is there any way to stop her?" I asked.

"No. She has willingly chosen to submit. The fate I thought I had escaped has now fallen on my eldest child."

"You were given a choice?"

She chuckled lightly. "Yes, of course, I was. Nothing can be forced. Everything must be given willingly through consent." She walked around the bed toward the window and looked at the village.

"Boria is enamored as I once was, and I can understand that

allure. This village has blossomed in ways I never could have envisioned. It was already grand when I left, but I never imagined it becoming as beautiful and evolved as now." She turned toward me.

She looked lovely in her new garment, with the sun's rays shining behind her. Her long hair was braided to one side with flower adornments intertwined within the braid. Her river-blue eyes were captivating with the thin black line drawn around them. I could now see so many beautiful similarities between my mother and Boria. They were both strikingly radiant.

"Is there nothing we can do, Mother?" I asked.

She walked over to me and tenderly grabbed my hands. "All we can do is pray that she will be safe, and maybe by some grand power, she will wake up from this beguilement." She kissed my forehead and reminded me to prepare myself emotionally to see her again. She warned me what would be required of me once she was bestowed the title of priestess. I would not be allowed to call her sister as she would no longer be a part of the family but would belong to the temple.

With her words, I felt a rush of despair. I would lose my only sister.

She saw my anguish and said, "Iris, you cannot change what will occur." She cradled my face in hopes of comforting me.

"If Grandfather Enok was here—"

"Shh," she quickly whispered as she looked around. "Do not mention his name while they are close. They become very agitated by the mention of his name."

I was glad they did not like to hear his name. If I remembered correctly, they had been defensive when they came for me at my grandfather's home. And I vaguely remember an argument between my Grandfather Enok and one of these beings. If Grandfather could survive a discussion with one of them, he knew something we did not.

"Where is Father?" I asked.

"He is in our room, praying to his god for guidance," she answered as she sighed.

Of course. Father believed, as Grandfather Enok did, that only one god existed. Mother believed in many, as her father taught her.

"What if he is right?"

"Right about what?" she questioned.

"Right about there being only one god."

She gave me an incredulous look. "Iris, have you not seen what is happening around you?" She rose and waved her hands around. "You are witnessing the many gods around you and live within their temple."

No, how could it be, as she said?

"Iris, I made a mistake a long time ago." She walked over and sat next to me. "I should have told you and Boria everything I knew from my time in this village with my father." She looked down as she continued to speak, as though in shame. "I should have told you every word he taught me about what was coming. The sad truth in all of this is that I did such a good job forgetting everything that I am having difficulty recalling everything he taught me."

I had never seen her this distraught. "If you could remember, would you be able to save Boria?"

She shook her head.

"Then what is the point of remembering anything if we cannot save her?" I said impatiently.

"Because if I can remember, then maybe we might have a chance to live a life out of their sight. I know it is late for Boria—"

"What do you mean it is late for Boria?" I was not leaving her behind. How could I? How could she leave her daughter behind?

"She has already consented to their will. There is nothing you or I can do to change that. It is done."

So, she had given up all hope for her eldest child this easily? Without a single fight, she was willing to let them have her!

"I am not leaving this place until Boria leaves with us." I left no room for compromise on the matter. I could be as stubborn as Boria, and she knew it.

She looked away in thought and sighed again. Probably thinking how unreasonable I was being, but I did not care. My sister was not going to be some sacrifice for us to flee.

"All right then." She walked towards the door but stopped short of leaving as she turned back and said, "After the ritual, let me know if you believe Boria would ever leave this place willingly."

Then she walked out, leaving me to my thoughts again. It seemed like a torrent of emotions was all I had ever encountered since we had had to flee our village. One moment, I feared for my life; the next, I feared for my family. Not to mention the overwhelming new, unfamiliar emotions I felt around these beings—mostly Samayaza, Azazzel, and the one with swirling green eyes that only I could hear and considered mine. That thought alone was disturbing enough for me.

Why did I believe him to be mine? And why did I feel this energy, or pull, whenever around them? It appeared all of them had it, just some with less intensity than others. Even the two standing guard at our door gave me that feeling. Azazzel was the strangest, as it felt like the excitement and fear measured the same whenever I saw him. I remembered how he had felt with my back leaning against him on that horse. His arms engulfed my entire being in a protective manner that gave no quarter for escape, yet I knew he smelled my hair and had to have been the one who brushed it.

I felt exhausted again with all these thoughts. Every emotion led to another, and none made sense.

I walked over to the window and looked out toward the clear sky. It looked so calm and peaceful. Though the sun was shining, it was beginning to descend for the day. We would soon be escorted to this ritual that would take my sister from me.

I reached for my stone and felt the smooth coolness of it slowly calm my soul. I closed my eyes and thought of nothing. Any thought that tried to make its way, I denied it entry and just kept touching the smooth round edges of the stone. I needed to absorb whatever peace I could get at this moment.

I remembered Father saying how praying to God was peaceful and calming. He was doing it, which meant he sought help and peace from a higher power. It was more than what Mother was doing, as she had given up. At least Father was trying to fight in his own way.

Yes, he was right on this. Mother always seemed to know and lead, but not this time. If Father would pray and Grandfather Enok quarreled and prayed, then I could do the same.

I kneeled.

I prayed.

And I was ready to contend for Boria.

# CHAPTER NINE

Adorned with the garments from earlier that day, the guards escorted us out of our quarters shortly before supper. Father was given a black robe with black stones on the outer edges that went down along both sides and stopped before hitting the bottom hem. The material was soft to the touch and seemed thick. This material was new to me and interesting, but Father paid no attention to it and just proceeded to put it on as instructed.

I tried to remember our path, but the temple was so vast that I lost track once we went past the fountain where Boria and I had first conversed. Everything within the temple was grand. The large white flowing fabrics between the pillars all had black ones in the middle of them now, with just a tiny bit of the white material showing on either side. And others had the fabric pulled back to reveal the night sky. Stars were beginning to awaken, and it reminded me of my sister.

We continued to walk through the outer terraces, where the fires contained in small pits had been replaced by much larger ones that allowed the fire to be twice as intense. Incense burned as it effused into the crisp night air. It smelled like Grandfather Enok's home but stronger. Flower petals were upon the stone ground. In fact, women dressed in similar black robes continually spread flower petals as we passed them, replenishing what we walked over.

As we came around the outer corner of the temple, we saw the many villagers below by the base of the steps. They were chanting something I could not understand. All held red flowers, and some light shined within some of their hands. It looked like the entire village was there, waiting at the foot of the steps that led up to the temple. I looked toward the doors and noticed more unearthly beings standing guard. They showed no emotion upon seeing us or the crowd. They all seemed to have black garments that fit tightly around their legs and upper bodies. Some wore armor embedded within their garments, and others wore long cloaks.

We stood there, waiting on the side of the upper steps with guards on either side. Straight ahead, toward the other end of the stairs, unearthly beings stood tall and loomed over everyone below. Looking down, I saw flowers covering the entirety of every single step. Long stems with lush green leaves, prickles, and a beautiful head of red petals that were thick and bountiful; the air carried their lovely scent. It was like a river of red and green, with no sight of the colorful stones that were embedded in every step. The flowers continued toward the entrance and stopped a mere hand away from the unearthly beings standing in front of each door, facing the crowd.

All at once, the chant stopped. The crowd divided in the middle, and a slender, beautiful woman came out from the group, escorted by two unearthly beings on either side as she walked toward the temple.

Mother tried to step forward, but Father stopped her before she could. I knew where she wanted to go; it was Boria that had emerged from the crowds, and Mother knew instantly.

The doors to the temple opened with a sound that demanded attention. Out walked Samayaza, every bit domineering and engulfing the awareness of everyone present. If I were to think of a ruler, it would be someone like him; dressed in dark robes with red stones stitched within the edges that shined in the moonlight. He walked forward without glancing at us; instead, he stared straight toward Boria and his brethren. I could see his eyes homing in on Boria, and the edges of his lips turned slightly upward.

Boria continued to walk steadily forward with garments that glistened in the moonlight. The bodice revealed more of her breasts than any other garment I had seen on her. I knew Mother and Father would not be happy with what they were witnessing. Her hair was in a beautiful braid upon both sides of her head and pulled back into her long straight hair that hung behind her. Her face held color like ours, but there was particular coloring I had never seen on anyone here. It was like the sun dusted itself upon her. Or it was the moonlight that made it seem so. Either way, she looked very unearthly herself.

A wind came through, gently moving the leaves of all the flowers thrown on the steps. An unusual hum was in the air, a soft thunder from the heavens, yet no clouds were in the sky. The smell of the flowers intensified the closer Boria got to the temple. There was something familiar in how one of the beings walked beside her. I could only see their mouths; both wore robes with hoods covering half their faces.

Samayaza's presence was intense, and his gaze unwavering from Boria. Even she bowed the second she reached the foot of the steps. I grasped my stone and looked toward my Mother and Father, and they had their heads bowed. I knew it was not in reverence to Samayaza but instead in despair at witnessing the loss of their firstborn daughter.

Seeing them in such despair brought about a wave of anger deep within me, steadily overcoming my fears. My fist clenched the stone so hard I knew I was bruising myself, but I did not care. Something was happening or was going to happen, and I needed to stop it.

I looked down at Boria; she was still bowing as though waiting for permission to stand. I knew what I had to do. Whether I feared the consequences or not, I could not contain myself. I lifted my foot to take a step forward when the being standing to her right suddenly raised his head slightly, grabbing my attention. I saw the green eyes.

I stood motionless as my gaze held his. Why was he here, standing next to Boria, of all places? Seeing him blurred everything around me; it was just him. The green swirls of his eyes reminded me of our encounter by the village river. I released a breath I didn't know I was holding. My anger melted away, and I could hear him whisper softly, "*Not here, not now.*"

His voice brought the calm of the river, the sweet scent of the grass in the morning, and the sun's rays that soothed my soul. Without hesitation, I abandoned my protests and took caution as he directed.

His gaze released me, and I instantly looked away, hoping not to be noticed. Samayaza, was still admiring Boria then looked at the two beings beside her. Upon following his gaze, I saw the angel on the other side of Boria lowering his hood to reveal himself; it was Azazzel. I took a sharp breath at the sight of him standing next to my sister.

His honey eyes sensed my surprise, and he focused directly on me with a mischievous smile.

"*Look at me,*" Green Eyes summoned.

I obeyed. And I saw he had lowered his hood, revealing himself to all. He stood so much grander than the rest. His entire being radiated strength, virtue, and magnificence. The distress I felt began to melt away with every churn and ripple his green eyes seemed to make. His unwavering gaze held me steady, protecting me from a foolish move I was about to make. I held tight to my stone, hoping no one noticed or picked up on my intentions.

"Daughter of the Realm of Earth, rise and concede to my will with each step you ascend to me." Samayaza's voice echoed loudly.

The night went silent; the hum was gone, the thunder stopped, and so did the breeze. No one moved; all the people from this village remained kneeling. The unearthly beings stood motionless like carved stone. Mother and Father held on to each other as they looked down upon Boria, as did I.

She raised her beautiful head to Samayaza, rose from her kneeling position, and began her climb one step at a time. I wanted to scream at each step she took, for her to wake up from whatever disillusion she was in.

Then I heard *him*. A constant whisper of calming words

within my mind, as serene as a river, his words tried to soothe me. Reminding me it was her free will. I could not understand the complexity of free will, as all I wanted to do was warn her to step back a little. But Boria had proven to reject anything we had said. She was stubborn and wouldn't listen to anyone when she set her mind to something. Her eyes fixed upon Samayaza; not once breaking away to see her whimpering Mother, father, or sister helplessly and hopelessly watching her.

With each step she climbed, the fires in the pits roared as though cheering her on. The hum returned, and the heavens began to thunder. The fragrant scent of the flowers returned and became stronger as she approached him. I noticed her feet were bare with adornments upon her ankles. As she stood on the final step in front of him, she looked small and delicate compared to the large, menacing stature of Samayaza.

He looked down at her with a pleased smile and spoke in words I could not understand. Boria bowed her head in response.

He then raised his right arm to his waist and opened his palm, revealing a circular light. I heard gasps from the villagers and Mother and Father. The small light, like the sun, merely radiated within his hand.

Looking at Boria, he asked, "Are you willing to concede your will and partake in what I offer?"

"I willingly take all you offer, my lord," she answered and bowed her head in submission.

"Azazzel. Daniel." He called upon their names, and both raised their right arms as he had, and those same orbs appeared within their hands. I wanted to revel in finally knowing my unearthly being's name, but the sudden burst of light that shot up from Azazzel and Daniel to Samayaza was blinding.

Everyone gasped and squinted to see what was happening. Mother tried to sprint forward again, but Father held her tight as we watched the light hit Boria and illuminate her entire being.

My heart felt like it jumped out of my chest! Where was Boria? All I could see was intense light, so blinding I could barely see my hand in front of me.

"Boria!" I cried out.

I heard Mother scream.

And all at once, the rays of light were gone; Boria stood precisely where she had before, completely unharmed. Her clothes shimmered, and her face had a glow about it the likes of which I had never seen.

I reached for Mother's hand in hopes of comforting her. Her tears were rolling down, creating a faint black line on her cheeks as they fell to the ground. The colors of her face were fading as she kept wiping away her tears. I felt so torn and useless as I could not do anything to help her. Father looked at me with such sorrow that my eyes filled with tears.

Samayaza extended his hand to Boria, and she placed hers in his and finally took the last step to stand next to him.

Samayaza looked toward the people. "Behold your oracle." As he lifted her hand, the crowd below began to cheer and applaud. It soon became the strange chanting from earlier, a tongue with which I was not familiar.

It was done. Whatever this ritual was to be and whatever it meant to be an oracle, Boria had become it, and I couldn't have felt more defeated. I knew Mother and Father must be feeling so much worse than I. Boria was my sister, but to them, she was their firstborn.

Samayaza spoke again. "Daniel, Azazzel." He gestured toward the unearthly beings around us. "Guardians of the great temple, let us celebrate." As he turned with Boria's hand still in his, he led the way through the grand doors as the rest of us followed closely behind. Right before turning toward the doors, I caught a glimpse of him. I now knew his name, *Daniel*. I wanted to be excited about this discovery, but my heart was heavy over what I had just witnessed. And what I had noticed as we walked into the temple. Boria's bloody footprints were more apparent at the entrance, and I did my best to keep Mother's gaze away from the ground. I noticed it when I saw her climbing each step barefoot. The flowers had prickles, and though she showed no distress, her feet were bloodied well.

I knew Daniel was behind us. I could feel his gaze upon me. It was strange yet comforting at the same time, especially now when I thought about what was happening to Boria and what it meant for her to be called an oracle. I could see Samayaza and Boria ahead of us. He still held her hand within his as he led the way. We made a few turns through halls I needed to familiarize myself with. The temple was vast, and I was sure I had only seen a small portion.

We passed by large rooms with pillars within them, like the throne room, but these were different. They had no fire pits, no large fabric hanging from the ceilings to the ground. Instead, there were sitting pillows everywhere and food with drink placed every few feet. Servants ran back and forth, preparing a feast, but not before bowing to Samayaza and the rest of us as we passed.

We strode through that final large room and arrived at an outdoor area with a grand fountain I had not seen before. It was simple in its design and only the depth of one hand, if that. The night sky was still clear, and the stars shined brightly next to the full moon.

"You have desecrated your purpose and that of my grand-daughter!" came a booming voice that echoed throughout the area we stood.

I knew that voice. It was Grandfather Enok.

"Spare me your rebuke, old man," hissed Samayaza.

He swiftly pushed Boria behind him, and four unearthly be-ings surrounded her, enclosing her completely.

"If you believe I am here to rebuke you, you are gravely mis-taken," said Grandfather Enok, mockingly.

As swiftly as the wind would move, Daniel and Azazzel were no longer behind us but now on either side of Samayaza. The three unearthly beings stood like massive mountains against my humble grandfather.

Father quietly switched places with Mother so that he was in the middle. He reached for my hand and Mother's. He then soft-ly nudged us to follow his lead as we edged closer to the guards on our sides.

"Time belongs to us now." Samayaza stepped forward. "Leave before yours runs out, Enok." Samayaza spat his name out with such disgust that I cringed.

"I do not fear you, nor do I obey your brief dominion upon Earth," Grandfather Enok calmly responded as I saw him come closer to where we stood.

I could now make out what he was wearing, and of course, it was the same garments as always. It warmed my heart as it reminded me of our village and how simple and great our lives were before these beings appeared. I felt a strange sadness in my heart at that thought. I nudged it away as I could see my grandfather moving closer to an unearthly being that was guarding us.

He looked at me and gave a quick wink before he began his verbal assault again at the beings. "Release my son, daughter-in-law, and granddaughters now, and I will leave without further trouble."

With a deep throaty laugh, Samyaza taunted my Grandfather Enok. "You, old man? Are to cause trouble...for me?" he sarcastically questioned as he walked around to face my grandfather, and that is when I noticed Daniel flanked him and spoke in words I could not understand.

They went back and forth in a tongue I had never heard. Samayaza spat out words while Daniel sternly replied. All the while, Grandfather listened. To my surprise, he responded to them in the same tongue. Whatever he said sounded very much like a demand as all went still. No words were spoken aloud, just Grandfather and Samayaza staring at each other with such contempt that I could feel the hatred and loathing in the air.

Daniel had positioned himself where he could directly see me. His face was solemn, and his eyes held no swirls of green as he reminded me what I failed to retain. *"Remember your stone,"* he whispered impatiently.

With the shock of seeing Grandfather Enok, I dropped my hand from the stone; I tried to remind myself to not let go, especially now.

"Take them," Samayaza ordered. "If they are willing to leave."

The guards moved away, allowing us a clear view and path to Grandfather Enok. Father did not hesitate and led the way, rushing us over to Grandfather. I could not believe he was letting us go! We could go home and never venture into these lands again.

"Allow Boria to pass," demanded Father.

Again, laughter burst forth from Samayaza. "And you are the son of this prophet?" Samayaza *tsked*. "How have you not taught your son the laws of free will?"

I looked at Grandfather, whose face had lost a bit of strength and determination I had seen just a moment ago. Mother frantically looked at him, waiting for a response but realized, as I did, we would not all be going home.

"Boria, come home with us," cried Mother as she stretched out her hand towards Boria.

"Son, take hold of your wife," Grandfather quietly whispered to Father as he placed a comforting hand on his shoulder. "Boria has declared her will. Her decision has been made."

"No!" Mother screamed. "I am not leaving without her!"

I tried to look at Boria, but the guards were so big that they blocked most of her. I could only see her lower half.

Samayaza looked amused. "Then stay if you wish."

Daniel was staring at Mother, as was Azazzel. But the way Azazzel looked at her was reminiscent of the bathhouse incident with that older woman. I felt the need to protect her from him. I tried to walk in front of his vision, but just as I did, Mother broke free from Father's embrace and ran toward the unearthly beings guarding Boria.

Azazzel's threatening smile was all I saw before he raised his hand, and all around the guards surrounding Boria, a translucent wall was erected. The air had ripples like a rock thrown into a pond would disturb the water. My heart racing, I looked toward Daniel, knowing this was not good. Whatever was erected was meant to harm my Mother.

The unearthly beings guarding Boria took a slightly wider stance but did not look bothered by my Mother's charge. She was like a fly running toward a group of beasts. Nothing she could ever do would harm them. She was only going to hurt herself. Looking at Daniel with pleading eyes. I hoped to stop what was to come, but he was looking at Samayaza.

A burst of light came forth, blocking the air ripple and stopping Mother from colliding with it. The light was so intense that she hit the floor in surprise. We had to use our hands to shield us from the blinding light.

An authoritative masculine voice spoke, and all of a sudden, the light disappeared along with the translucent wall Azazael had erected. Looking toward Mother, I saw her slowly get up as Father rushed to help her. Boria was still behind the guards without even trying to peek through to see if Mother was all right.

Samayaza, Azazzel, and Daniel stood right where they were before the light appeared but looked somewhat reserved and tense.

Grandfather Enok approached my parents and whispered something into Father's ear. Father immediately nodded and started taking my dismayed Mother back toward the path we came from.

"Nothing is unseen, whether it be above or below," Grandfather definitively said as he turned from them and walked toward me. Mother and Father were out of sight now, and I knew why.

Grandfather came close and embraced me, quietly whispering, "I know your love for your sister and how stubborn you both are." He released me and smiled lightly as I could see his eyes tear up. "Are you sure you wish to stay?" he asked.

I did not want to stay, but I was not going to leave and go home without her.

"Yes," I answered nervously.

He sighed as he saw the fear and uncertainty within my eyes.

"You alone might be the only one that can reach into your sister's heart." He embraced me again. "You are stronger than you believe, child," he whispered.

I nodded and held him tight as tears fell down my cheeks. I did not know how he knew or what was happening, but I had to stay. And knowing that he was giving his blessing, in a way, was the comfort I needed to stay.

Worried, I asked, "What will you tell Mother and Father?"

He thought for a short while before he answered, "That their daughters must fulfill their destinies."

With that, he turned and spoke directly to the beings in that strange tongue. Whatever he said, all but Samayaza slightly bowed their heads as he turned and walked toward the direction I'd last seen Mother and Father.

I stood there unmoving as he walked away, and I could no longer see him. I felt abandoned for some reason and unsettled more than ever. I wanted to curl into a ball and cry in front of all the unearthly beings. My loss was now more significant than the fear I had of them. I wanted to run after Grandfather and go home, but home would not be the same without my sister.

Tired and frightened, I turned to see all the unearthly beings staring at me. My hand still held the stone, so I was not worried about my thoughts being revealed. Yet I knew my face could not hide what I felt.

Then slowly, Boria stepped out from behind the guards and started to walk toward me. I let out a sigh of relief as she was smiling warmly. Her voice held kindness I had not heard in a long time as she said, "Come, sister, I will show you our new world."

Wearily, I smiled back and took her hand as she led me past

the beings staring at us. Even Daniel seemed concerned as he looked at me. But he whispered no words in my mind. Samayaza was not smiling but looked pleased, nonetheless. I did not even want to look at Azazzel, as his cruelty to my Mother wouldn't be overlooked by me. I would remember.

I held Boria's hand as she led us away from the beings and through an area of the temple decorated with the same colors she wore. Flowers were thrown upon the ground, and servants rushed about. I noticed similarities to the throne room, except this was less grand, with no pillars, large stones, and no large throne to sit upon. A less great throne was set in the center above a few stairs. Though small, it shone like the sun, and many red stones were encrusted upon it. The crown had a symbol of an eye right in the middle. Very unusual to see a single eye set in the middle, yet stunningly beautiful.

We stopped, and she let go of my hand. "This is my throne, sister," she said. She smiled and made her way up the few steps to eloquently sit on the throne perfectly made for her size. It made sense now why it was so much smaller than the large one I had seen. This one was for her, my sister.

"Rise," she said and lifted her hand in gesture.

I looked at her, confused by what she meant, but heard the shuffling of fabric and looked around to see all the servants that had been running to and fro a moment ago now rising from a bowed position. Whatever title she had been given, they all bowed to her as she sat upon her throne.

She had a content smile as she watched them all rise and return to their duties. She was beautiful as always, but something in her eyes seemed different. Maybe it was all the colors or the way the black line above her eyes was drawn, but something was missing when she looked upon them and me. The light within seemed dim, like the twinkling of innocence I once knew was gone.

"Will you not bow to your newly appointed seer, sister?" she said thoughtfully.

With worry and confusion, I was about to answer her with a slight bow, but her soft laughter filled the air before I could bend a knee. "Oh, Iris, I will allow you time to learn protocol. After all, you are a princess as well," she revealed.

"I do not understand?" Throwing out specific titles without explanation was not helping my confusion or concern.

She rolled her eyes at me. "Iris, you are the granddaughter of a king. A king who ruled these lands."

She was referring to our evil grandfather, and it made me sick listening to how she reveled in his title. "That grandfather would have killed us if he had the chance, Boria."

"No, he would not! Look, he has given us the throne!" She pointed all around her. "This is our inheritance!"

The excitement in her voice and face was too real for me to even hint at how blind she was to everything around her. She had somehow believed this was all for us. Had she not seen the larger throne room? Did she not meet our evil grandfather or hear of his horrible deeds?

Maybe he hadn't raised his hand against her, which was why she thought this way? But if so, why had he wanted to strike me, and why did he vanish? The last time I saw or heard of him was then. Samayaza had not mentioned him once, not even during the ritual. If our grandfather was the ruler of these lands, then where was he now?

"Where is our grandfather, Boria?" I asked.

Without much thought, she quickly answered, "Why does it matter? We are heirs to his throne." She stretched out her arms. "Our destinies can be whatever we make of them now," she said, barely containing her excitement.

Sighing, I knew now why she was so blind to everything around her. How had I missed it or forgotten her despair when she was faced with a destiny that was not of her choosing? I had forgotten her pain from that night on the rooftop, her tears, and her fears of a life that had been picked for her without her consent. But she needed to put that behind her and try to see everything as it was, or at least what we could make sense of.

"How have you embraced this without concern for yourself or us?" I persisted. I knew she just wanted to forget her pain, but this was not the right way. To turn a blind eye to everything that had happened thus far.

"Acceptance is essential to survival, little sister,"

She stared at me sadly. I knew she just wanted me to accept everything as she had. But I could not. Something was hidden here, dark yet cloaked in light with all these rocks and colors.

"Have you even cared to ask? Or did you not see what happened to Mother before you?"

She rolled her eyes again and vehemently denied the incident. "Mother was never in harm's way." She turned around and sat back on her throne.

"What about you, then? Look at the bottom of your feet! You were walking upon prickles and bleeding as you walked into the temple, yet you did not even flinch," I exclaimed. "How is that possible?"

"Pain is nothing more than an emotion, like happiness, sadness, or fear. You can shut the door on it with your will at any time," she said imperiously.

I stood baffled at her words and behavior. She had shifted so quickly from who she once was to whatever she believed herself to be now that I was bereft of words.

"You are heir, as I am. Accept it. Become it," she said fiercely as her eyes pleaded for my agreement.

Her voice almost had a tone I remembered our evil grandfather having. Something was happening to her that was so foreign to me that it frightened me a little. I had stayed for her, patiently waited for her return to us; to who she was. Yet at this moment, I doubted my ability to help her. She refused to even acknowledge the danger Mother was in, in order to continue believing the throne she sat upon belonged to her.

"It is a lovely throne, fit for a seer. Is it not, Iris?" came a deep cunning voice behind me.

"Lord Samayaza," Boria quickly announced and jumped out of her throne to give a bow, as did all the servants. They all bowed low and slowly backed out of the room.

His smile at their obedience was as dangerous as the serpent that bit me. Strange as it was, he somehow reminded me of that serpent.

His eyes quickly met mine, and the blue swirls began to storm. I felt held in place, beyond my control. Shivers of emotions bombarded me, waves of emotions so strong and unfamiliar I could barely hold myself up. What was he doing to me?

"Samayaza!" bellowed a firm, angry voice.

Suddenly, it stopped, and I barely caught myself from collapsing to the floor. I looked toward Boria; she was still bowing with her head down. Could she not see what was happening to me?

Daniel walked in and now stood in between Samayaza and

me. No words were spoken, but I knew they were communicating with each other within their minds. What did he want from me?

"Heir or not, respect and fear must be shown," Samayaza said in a chiding tone.

He had just answered my question. I closed my eyes in disappointment. How could I have forgotten my stone? I felt somewhat at ease in the presence of Boria and neglected to protect myself. He must have read all my thoughts. I quickly grasped the stone and hoped it was enough to hide my fear.

"Lord Samayaza, she is young and unversed in protocol. Please accept my regret on behalf of my sister," Boria sweetly said. She added, "A gift after the feast tonight, I hope, will atone for this lapse of thought."

Samayaza sternly walked toward Boria with no smile but eyes that held fury. Scared for Boria, I tried to walk past Daniel, but he extended his arm.

"*Leave it alone,*" he whispered, ordering me to not intervene.

My hands clenched into fists, my nails digging into my palm. If he so much as pulled a hair on her head, I swear I would find a way to hurt him.

I could see Boria was nervous as he neared, but she kept her ground and did not flinch.

He stood towering over her as she stared up at him with a tinge of fear in her eyes I had not seen since that night in our village.

"I am no mortal to be bribed so easily." He placed his hand upon her throat and brought up his thumb to gently caress her chin. "But you have found favor in my sight, so I shall grant you your request." His hand dropped, and Boria bowed again as he returned to where Daniel and I stood.

His unwavering gaze was like a knife slicing through any and all barriers I thought I had. I felt my cheeks flame up and heard my heart's loud and fast beating. Daniel moved slightly to the left, halfway blocking his view.

But it did not deter him; his eyes were homed in directly upon me as he said ever so calmly, "Stones are useless without knowledge."

He finally released his gaze as he walked past us, back into the hallway where we had entered; a shiver shook my entire being. The feeling of being exposed was great within my soul. I looked down, embarrassed over knowing Daniel knew what I was feeling. I had let go of the stone again and realized too late.

Without a word or whisper in my head, he turned slightly to look at me with the corner of his beautiful green eyes, and I knew he had read my thoughts. I felt flustered and startled that I reacted the way I did to Samyaza. It just happened when he looked at me.

As Daniel was turning around to leave, Boria bowed slightly per protocol, and though I was not bowing in the same manner as her, I bent in shame as he walked away.

# AMONG ANGELS 3

T he wind rushed into the throne room as Samayaza sat on his royal chair. He knew who was coming by the charged ripples in the air. Though he
despised his brother for his devotion to their first
purpose, he had to admit his powers were astonishing. If only
he would stop fighting against him in everything he tried to do
within this realm, they would accomplish greatness that could
never be matched.

The doors burst open, hitting the walls behind them in a loud
thunder that would have woken the dead. Samayaza grinned at
Daniel's display of power; he had always wondered how strong
and deep his powers ran. The Creator had made him with special care, and now, Samayaza was getting a glimpse of what
they were.

The wind whipped stronger, the veils in between the pillars moved violently, and Samayaza's grin was no longer there. Azazzel materialized, along with three other unearthly beings. Two stood on either side of the throne where Samayaza sat, on guard and ready to protect the one they pledged allegiance to.

Eyes upon the doors, they waited, but it was in vain as Daniel began to descend directly behind Samayaza's throne with all his angelic glory. Samayaza was growing impatient. He needed to know where Daniel was but could only see him through his mind's eye. He could see Daniel's grand and enormous wings but could not locate him. Lightning crackled all around the throne room, creating an atmosphere of chaos. He knew it would not take much effort for Daniel to fold them all into his wingspan and suffocate the life out of each of them. But something kept him calm, which irked Samayaza. He could sense Daniel's clear state of mind and controlled temper.

Anger had made them both stumble once, and that was more than enough for either one of them to never allow that to occur again. There was something far more at risk than petty human emotions.

Samayaza still could not locate him. He was near or even within the room, but he couldn't attest to it. He looked at Azazzel for validation, and he also confirmed the same. Daniel was here somewhere.

Samayaza's demeanor shifted drastically. He knew Daniel was quick to learn, which meant he would gain control faster than any of them. Where only a mere moment ago he had sat confidently waiting for Daniel's predictable behavior, he now sat on the edge of his throne, legs at a wide stance, elbow resting on one leg and ready to rise and defend if the powerful guardian appeared. This feeling of anxiousness was new to Samayaza;

how his mind made his human body react was most unpleasant. The mortal shell he had taken on was not what he'd expected, nor was he prepared for how his will was so easily swayed by such emotions. He needed discipline and control, so he homed in on the angelic fire that was his true self. There was no red blood in him but only glorious fire that would consume all.

"Show yourself, Daniel!" he belted out in rage.

Now it was Daniel's turn to grin, and he did. As he brought his wings in, he made sure they heard the rustle it would make, but right before they turned around, he dissolved into thin air.

Samayaza, Azazzel, and the other angelic beings turned in a battle-ready manner that would have frightened the soul out of any mortal. But Daniel was not there, Samayaza realized one second too late, and as he turned back around, Daniel was already dangerously standing before the throne, showcasing his superior strength and how easily he gained the upper hand.

Samayaza fumed inside like the fires of hell. He wanted to crush him now and get rid of the nuisance that had plagued him since existence. They stared at each other with such venom that the air became thick with smoke that lingered low and flowed in and out of every corner. The elements of the Earth molded and became anything their mind wanted them to be. Manipulating matter was as easy as breathing the air. They used this knowledge for their purpose on Earth and were starting to use it against each other in an ultimate show of power.

Azazzel and the other angelic beings waited for orders from Samayaza. They were anxious, as they knew Daniel was the most powerful angelic being created within the Gregori. Azazzel looked to Samayaza from the corner of his eye but received only a quiet response to wait within his mind. Samayaza would not start anything he knew he might lose, so he would wait for Daniel to make his move first.

"Boundaries are created and kept as a bond," Daniel said, factually. "Yet you continue to push them, Samayaza." He enunciated his name to make it known that he was defying the oath of calling him lord.

Samayaza seethed in anger but held back all the rage as he answered, "You break your oath, brother."

With a slight tilt of his head, Daniel fired back calmly, "As did you." He paused, then added, "Brother."

Samayaza wanted to destroy every part of Daniel's being and throw him into the depths of purgatory. But he knew that power was not yet his and now was not the time to war with Daniel. That time would come soon enough, and he needed as much knowledge from him as possible. But right now, he needed to collect himself if that dream were ever to come to fruition.

"Name your request, and I shall grant it," Samayaza said, knowing it was the only way to look as though the power was still in his hands. It was the only way to show that he was still alpha within them among the rest of the beings.

Daniel raised an eyebrow at his question but decided to play along. He knew now that Samayaza understood who he was and what he could do. "Do not impose your will in any way, shape, or form upon my guarded," he demanded.

Samayaza thought for a moment and then solemnly answered, "You have my word." he promised.

Both stared restlessly at each other, knowing that neither trusted the other nor was this far from over. But for the time being, it would suffice. Daniel left without another word, and immediately the air began to clear. The charge within it dissipated, and the smoke turned into white clouds that drifted out through the windows between the pillars and into the night sky. His powers were magnificent and far more superior than Samayaza had predicted. This was cause for concern and would require patience, practice, and discipline to reach the heights of power Daniel had just demonstrated. But until that time, there was no way Samayaza was going to allow Daniel to believe he ruled in this realm.

He ruled this realm, and soon, Daniel would bow down to him willingly.

He rose from his throne and walked down the steps as he boldly stated, "Her will is mine to do as I wish."

The three angels looked at one another in hesitation, for they had just witnessed Samayaza giving his word to Daniel. To disregard this would be against protocol whether in this realm or the one they came from.

Bakru, the one that had stood next to Azazzel, asked, "Is it not against protocol, my liege?"

Samayaza knew what Bakru meant, but if he did not show defiance and rebellion to them now, he would seem too weak to lead. He could not allow the surprise of Daniel's powers to put doubt in their minds. "It is, Bakru." He nodded at him in appreciation for his attention. Then without warning, Samayaza was right in front of him, hand around his neck as he lifted him above the ground effortlessly.

Bakru grasped Samayaza's hand to release the hold, but the fury that burst forth from Samayaza was great, and Bakru was no match to stop him.

"Do you think I don't know what is and is not protocol!?" exclaimed Samayaza in rage that echoed throughout the throne room.

The other two angels squinted in anticipation while Azazzel smirked at what he saw. No angel was going to cover another's inequities in this realm. Each would be after everything and anything they could gain. If one were to throw themselves into the depths of hell, then the others would simply watch and divide what was left behind. The only oath they had taken was allegiance to Samayaza, and that was all that they would honor.

Silently choking but looking straight at Samayaza, Bakru spoke into his mind. Asking for forgiveness for his false assumption while within this human form.

Samayaza knew what a nuisance it was to control such mortal emotions and released him. "I suggest you send a replacement for your position here at court until you master your bodily form."

Bakru bowed and disappeared into the air as commanded.

"Azazzel." Samayaza called the angel to attention.

He knew Azazzel would be concerned about what he had just witnessed with Daniel and Bakru, but Azazzel showed no such emotion as he bowed and waited for his master's orders.

"Do you remember what the sweet scent of her hair smelled like?"

Azazzel's eyes met his master's as his eyes swirled of honey gold at the memory. "I do, my liege," he answered as they both grinned from ear to ear.

The other two angels just watched and listened.

"Good. Then let that be your reward for the task at hand."

With a simple nod and bow, he accepted the mission that was spoken silently and directly to his mind. As he began to walk out of the throne room, Samayaza called out, "Hair only, Azazzel."

he warned, knowing Azazzel enjoyed stretching his commands.

With his back turned, Azazzel listened to his order. In response, he gave a small grunt of laughter and left to begin his task.

The other two angels were dismissed; they bowed and dissolved into the air as Bakru had.

Samayaza now stood alone at the foot of his throne, feeling the fire within his body calling for action, for a penalty that should be paid for Daniel's insolence.

*"Such desires are sated through sacrifice."*

He heard the dark one's voice within his mind and welcomed the solution. Nodding in acknowledgment, he waited for his orders.

*"Blood is the only way to pay for such a penalty,"* demanded the excited yet diabolical voice of Lucifer.

Samayaza mused it over in his mind. As much as he wanted to relinquish the rage that Daniel had brought forth, he just could not let the rage distinguish itself. He needed to pour it out on something to the point it no longer existed. The fury within needed to be released; needed to destroy and cause pain to the point of death.

An image of a large animal with horns entered his mind. *"Kill and be at ease,"* coerced the voice.

Samayaza closed his eyes and searched for the beast. He found its location, and in a blink of an eye, he disappeared into the night. The blood would sate his anger and pay the price for Daniel's transgressions.

The fires within the throne room went out, and all became dark. The cool night air blew in from the openings of the walls, and in came a dark mass that slithered and swirled around the throne. As it circled, it grew and raised itself above the throne and then slowly descended upon the chair in the form of an impressive male figure. The dark mass rested its arms and leaned back into the throne. Darkness surrounded him, yet his soul was darker than night itself. With an unearthly voice, laughter bellowed as it sat upon one of the many thrones he would be sitting upon. His reign on Earth had just begun.

# CHAPTER TEN

I felt a loss I had never experienced before and did not know how to proceed. I walked away from Boria the moment Daniel left. She had neither tried to comfort me nor acknowledged what had happened. Instead, I heard her speak with her servants in preparation for the celebration feast.

I had not eaten all day, nor did I feel hungry even though people were swiftly carrying large trays of food into the room. Her servants set large, colorful, pillow-like blankets on either side of the room. Some had threads that shined like the sun when the fire light flickered. Others had beautiful symbols and birds that were so detailed that, had it been any other time than this, I would have enjoyed running my fingers across each stitch. The entire throne room floor looked like the wall of flowers I had seen at the market. So many deep, rich colors were so inviting to the soul. Whoever owned this skill of artistry was genuinely gifted by the heavens.

But standing here now made me feel so alone and ashamed. I had willingly stayed behind with the hopes that my beloved sister would awaken from whatever dream she believed herself to be in, and we would escape back to our village together. But I realized that she was not the one living in a dream. Rather, it was me. I had deceived myself that I would be strong enough, brave, and wise and somehow convince my sister that treading lightly in this new world would be prudent. Thus, doing so, she would return home with me.

They started bringing in large trays of meat now, and though it looked and smelled enticing, I wanted to be alone. I headed toward the balcony hoping to have a moment of quiet and solitude. My thoughts and everything around me felt restrictive, suffocating, as though someone had their arms around me and was squeezing tight. I needed air, and with each step I took, I could smell the fresh air, leading me to the coolness of the night that was comforting and familiar.

I walked past the translucent veil and closed my eyes upon seeing the night sky. The air was warm, with a pleasant cool breeze every so often. I took a big breath of air and released it ever so slowly. I felt every part of my body ease, and my mind finally calmed to where I had no more thoughts in my head. I was clean and just an empty vessel with no artistry upon it. Simple and plain but solid and stable was how it felt to breathe in the cool air.

I placed my hands on the railing and looked over to what was one of many courtyards within the Temple. There was no water fountain; a small river came through a pair of doors far across where I stood. It intertwined throughout the relatively large area and disappeared below my balcony. Flowers of many colors were throughout; strangely enough, there were some small trees. Large stems with large green leaves, yet the trunk was short. I had never seen such greenery.

"Does it remind you of your village?'

Startled, I turned with a gasp. A young man stood in the back corner of the balcony with colorful pillows on the floor around him.

"Do not be afraid. I am not here to harm you," his voice sounded tender and sincere.

He looked familiar, as though I had met him before.

"I was just startled," I assured. "I thought there was no one here but me."

He smiled.

I knew now where I had met him! He was the young man from the market! The empyreal artist who used such colors and drawings I had never seen before!

"You are the artist from the market, yes?" I asked.

"I am."

"I'm sorry, I don't know your name?"

"My name is Gabril," he kindly answered.

I said the name in my mind a few times to avoid forgetting. It was an interesting name and must be familiar to those in this village. He was kind, like most people I had encountered here. Abruptly, I remembered the horrible way the unearthly being had treated him, and my smile faded as I tried to apologize. "I—I'm sorry for how…they…" I stuttered, not knowing how to describe these beings.

"You do not need to explain. I know who they are," he claimed, as though everyone here knew these beings and how they behaved.

A moment of silence fell over us; I still felt guilty and responsible for how he was treated and wanted to apologize. But he seemed not to want it. So, I let it be as he wished.

I noticed he had a thread in his hand. "Are you the one who threads the pillows?" I asked excitedly.

"I am," he said humbly.

I was amazed. "Your artistry is heavenly. I have never seen such lovely threadwork on a pillow before." The excitement and awe in my voice must have been noticeable as he chuckled lightly.

"Do you wish to create one of your own designs?" he asked.

Earnestly, I replied, "Yes!"

He laughed and motioned for me to come close. I stepped forward, excited at his invitation, but to my surprise, Boria burst forth from behind the veil. "Hurry! It is almost time!" she announced as she grabbed my hand and pulled me back toward her throne room while giving Gabril a look of disdain. She rushed us past him so quickly that I did not get a chance to mouth an apology. And yet again, my encounter with him was cut short.

Once in the throne room, Boria seated me next to her. There was another throne next to hers now; it was more substantive and had black stones upon the head of the chair. It was not hard to figure out who would sit there now, but why would he sit next to her? Was he to be her betrothed, or was this protocol within the Temple? She was Seer, or Oracle is what Samyaza called her, but what did that mean? I still needed to learn what Boria's part within this Temple was. I assumed I would find out soon enough as many villagers were present now—women and men dressed in garments as beautiful as the one Boria wore. Some women had fabric on their heads that were of the same material as their garments.

It was foreign to see yet pleasing to the eyes as it brought more attention to their adorned faces. Interesting how their eyes were always what caught my attention. Some had a black line that curved so precisely it made their eyes alluring. It was intriguing to see such artistry upon a woman's face. The men were no less worthy of attention as they wore the same garments I had seen in the market, but there were two colors only, black and a warm color reminiscent of the sun. They all sat on either side of the room, allowing for a large walkway in the middle.

Boria instructed me where to sit and to leave only when granted permission to do so. That irked me a bit, treating me like a child. She then left her throne and exited the room with some women. I watched as she gracefully walked away, she was never heavy or clumsy in her steps, but there was something softer and more graceful about how she carried herself now.

I wanted to stay displeased with her, but she had mentioned how Samayaza was on his way right before she had left, which brought to mind why she would go if he were about to enter her throne room. I felt panicked at the thought of Boria leaving me alone. But I had no choice and could only follow the simple instructions she had left for me.

Just then, the room fell silent. Women and men rose and bowed their heads as the two large doors to the room swung widely open. In came the four unearthly beings that had held Boria within the center of them shortly after the ritual. All wore the black garments as before, as did Samayaza, who walked in right behind them. All of them stood taller than any man in the room. They radiated power with every stride they took and demanded reverence with their presence. Daniel and Azazzel were the last to enter, walking side by side. They all had black robes on, except for Daniel. Though dark, his color looked like the color of burnt ash.

Each step they took was like two of ours. The feeling of being crushed under their feet was the first thing that came to mind as they walked past every villager, as though signaling the threat without any words. The four prodigious beings walked past the throne chairs and stood behind them, spaced out evenly to protect and cover their lord. Samayaza took his seat on the throne and looked magnificently terrifying. He glanced and smirked at me as though sensing my anxiousness. I had the stone in my hand, so I knew he could not read my thoughts, but I knew my face was another issue I did not control very well. I scolded myself for being distracted by the sight of him. This was going to be a challenge with him and his kind; I seemed to have this reaction to them whenever they were near.

Daniel and Azazzel stood on either side, in front of the thrones, with Daniel slightly adjacent to me. He was so close that I could reach out and touch him if I wanted to. As strange as it was, I felt comforted and protected knowing he stood close to me and blocked me from Azazzel's view.

I watched them closely, anxious about what may happen since they were here and Boria was not. I waited for Samayaza's fury, but no such burst of anger appeared from him or any of the beings. In fact, they all paid attention to the doors they had just walked in from. I looked toward Samayaza. There was no anger upon his face but rather anticipation as he sat slightly forward upon the throne. For what were they waiting?

Suddenly the sound of hands thumping on an object began, just like during the ritual, and the women and Boria came through the large opened doors. They swayed and moved their hands in a dance of sorts. They were moving accordingly to the sound of the thumping. Their hips moved from one side to another, revealing the skin underneath garments made to betray modesty. Two women in front of Boria moved to either side, allowing Boria to come forth freely on her own in a very uninhibited and captivating dance.

I could not believe what I was witnessing. Mother and Father would have scolded her to no end had they seen the way she was moving her body. Her hair was loose as it fell down her back; her garment revealed her stomach and arms. Her legs would peep through as she moved and swayed closer to the throne in a dance that had everyone mesmerized, including the unearthly beings.

Samayaza stared, devouring every movement she made. He moved his hand toward his chin and rested his elbow upon the arm of the throne. His body leaned to one side as he enjoyed the entertainment. I wanted to slap him and take Boria away from here, but the look on her face was far from entrapment. Her sly grin and how she looked at him only made me assume that it was precisely the reaction she wanted from him. She was utterly enthralled with him as much as he was with her. I wanted to see Daniel's response, but the way he stood did not reveal his face. He had been quiet and had not spoken to me or within my mind since that moment earlier with Samayaza. A small part of me felt disappointed over not hearing him in my mind.

I moved forward in my seat a little to see if Azazzel was staring at Boria, but instead, I came eye to eye with him and his mischievous smile. I quickly sat back in my seat, tightening my hold on my stone. I noticed Daniel take a wider stance; whether he noticed or not, it shielded me from his gaze. Azazzel's eyes and how he looked at me made me want to seek shelter and hide. It was an all-consuming stare that tried to find my soul from deep within and muddle it as he wished.

Boria continued to dance her way closer to the throne with the women flanking her. The thumping grew louder and faster as they all moved in closer. Boria began to swish her hips slowly from side to side, her arms swaying gracefully, then up in a twirl as she brought her wrists together and down to her chest. All the while, she was inviting the stares of all who looked upon her body, watching how it could bend and turn more alluringly than a serpent. As she reached closer to Samyaza, just mere steps from his throne, she began to twirl as the thumping gained speed, and her arms went for the loose garments on either side of her, grabbing them and lifting them above her head as she continued to twirl. She looked like a flower in the wind, with delicate petals that fluttered.

Then suddenly, the thumping stopped. She purposely collapsed upon the throne's steps with her arms stretched out and her palms openly laid down as though in worship. The other women behind her did the same and fell to the ground. It became so quiet I could hear the labored breathing from Boria and the other women. Heads still bowed, they waited for Samayaza's response. I leaned back to see his face but only got a glimpse as he rose from his throne and walked down to where his feet almost touched Boria's fingertips.

Boria looked up upon seeing he had approached. He extended his hand for her to take, and she did. Samayaza spoke so softly that I could not make out what was said, but I knew it must be praise as Boria smiled, then the entire room erupted in applause. He led her back to her throne and allowed her to be seated before he sat upon his.

"Your Seer has gifted you all with her grace. Now bestow the same favor unto her," he ordered as he motioned his hand toward the people and sat beside Boria.

Everyone looked nervously at one another; I sensed they were not expecting such a request. I sat motionless, wondering how these people were supposed to entertain such beings and Boria. She had danced in a manner I had never seen nor heard of. No such dance I knew could compare to the one she had accomplished. What more enjoyment could these people provide other than the magnificent feast that was waiting? Was it not enough that the colorful pillows etched with such threadwork surrounded them? That alone should be enjoyment for an entire day, let alone a night.

A woman dressed in garments of green and gold approached the throne and bowed as she spoke. "My Lord, and graceful Seer, we have prepared a feast and celebration of song for this evening, if you will allow." She raised her head slightly to see their answer.

I moved to the edge of my seat, not caring that Azazzel was staring. I wanted to get a closer look as to who this lady was, as her voice was very familiar. Ah, yes, it was the woman from the bathhouse! She remained bowed, waiting for Samayaza or Boria to approve or dismiss her.

I noticed Azazzel looking at her with bitter disdain. I knew he would have harmed her the first chance he got, but she must be protected, as he mentioned, or else she would have already met her demise.

At Samayaza's curt nod, she clapped her hands, and the people roared in anticipation as the drums began to play and dancers came out from every corner to entertain. Samayaza nodded in pleasure as his companions feasted on cheese, fruits, nuts, and delectable meats placed in front of them. They laughed and praised Samayaza and the gods at every sip of their wine, constantly bowing their heads.

I sat there staring at the complete obedience and worship they mindlessly gave these beings. I could understand the fear that would push such compliance, but they looked as though they were happy to honor them. From their lips came such things as *gods with us and masters of our destinies.* I wondered how long my evil grandfather had prepared them for this moment and how he knew of these beings.

I guessed I would not know since he had disappeared from that moment in the throne room. When I believed Samayaza was protecting me and my family. I was wrong in that belief and knew now that the only protection I had came from Daniel, who still stood with his back toward me, continuing to block Azazzel's view. I knew he was one of them, but he always protected me when in distress.

A tray of fruit, bread, and meat was suddenly in front of me. A young girl held it towards me, waiting for me to pick and eat what I wanted. She looked very young; I felt horrible allowing her to stand beside me while holding a large tray of food. She had a solemn look and would force a grin anytime we made eye contact. She looked too slender to carry such weight of the food tray. She wore clean and beautiful clothing like all the villagers, but my heart broke seeing bruises on her arm.

Without much thought, I grabbed the tray from her; though she looked at me with dismay and fear, I kindly asked her to sit beside me. I scooted to one side of the chair and then continued to hold the tray and offer it to her. She looked worrisome, always looking around as though she would be caught and punished. I knew that fear in her eyes, and though I could not protect her, I knew who could. "Do not worry, little one, no one will harm you," I said, smiling at her and pointing to Daniel.

She smiled tentatively and, upon my insistence, grabbed some bread and cheese.

She relaxed a bit and took bigger bites of her bread and cheese. A strong urge came upon me to protect this young girl. Maybe I was trying to put forth the effort of saving someone to one who looked like they required protection. Or it was my way of consoling myself since I knew I had failed Boria. Either way, I felt useful and instantly needed. Everything I had seen and done so far had been fruitless in my eyes except for this.

"What is your name, little one?" I asked.

With her big beautiful brown eyes looking at me, she said, "Selah."

"That's a lovely name," I genuinely replied.

She gave me a broad smile and nodded as she continued to pick at the tray. At that exact moment, I decided I was going to take her back with me to my quarters. If I were to stay here, I would be helpful to someone. Obviously, whoever was caring for her needed to do a better job. Those bruises on her arms did not look harmless. Someone had caused them by grabbing her too harshly.

"When the feast is over, you will come with me to my quarters. There are many rooms, and you can have one for yourself!"

Her faint smile disappeared, and panic filled her eyes as she said, "I must go back to my master's house once my service here is no longer needed,"

Her master's house. "Do you have no mother or father?" I

asked, surprised.

A look of utter sadness came over her face at the mention of her mother and father. "They owed a debt they could not pay."

I wondered what she meant by debt. "Are they imprisoned?"

"No, they are home with my sisters. I was just taken as payment when they could not pay what was owed."

In disbelief over what I heard, I thought of how horrible a village this was! What amount was owed that this child was equal to it? I felt utter rage and disgust upon this discovery.

"*Keep her with you. I will take care of the rest,*" Daniel whispered in my mind, bringing a wave of relief to hear his voice again.

"*She looks so frightened at the mention of my request. I do not know if she will willingly come with me,*" I waited for his response.

"*She will go if you order her to,*" he insisted.

I frowned at his suggestion; how could I order her to come with me? Wouldn't she see me as the brute who took her as a form of payment?

"*No,*" was the simple answer Daniel gave. He was reading my mind.

It irked me a bit that he could not wait for me to ask him and instead was intruding upon my private thoughts, but I knew he was right. And at this point, I was willing to take his judgment on this matter.

Looking at Selah, I said, "You will no longer be a debt that was paid. You will be with me as I order it." I tried to sound as confident as possible, but I failed.

"No, no. They will only go back and take one of my sisters," she said fearfully. Tears were starting to well in her eyes, making me tear up. The fear and pain she had known was breaking my soul.

*"I will take care of the rest. She has nothing to fear for herself or her family,"* Daniel reassuringly repeated.

Without question, I knew he would do as he said. And upon that promise, I calmed little Selah down and told her nothing would harm her or her family and that tonight she would stay with me until morning when we would rise and search for her family. She struggled to believe what I was saying, but all it took was a quick glance from Daniel to reassure her. He had turned and smiled so warmly at her that she felt comforted, and her tears were no more. I knew what she sensed as I, too, experienced the warmth wash over me. These beings were astonishing; how they could send such waves of energy to one another or any of us was astounding and unnerving.

She nodded and continued to eat from the tray. On the other hand, I wished I had not eaten anything, as the sight of Boria and the villagers worshipping Samayaza as a god made me want to heave. Villagers were bowing at every chance, while some presented their daughters and sons as homage to the Temple. For what reason did they do such a thing? What would the Temple or these beings do with children?

I looked down at my side, at Selah, who was happily eating the last remaining bread, and realized that the answer to my question was sitting right next to me. They enslaved them and cared not how young and innocent these little children were as long as it was for the service of the Temple.

I felt numb at the horrible thought and to this village, this Temple, and all I had seen my sister do this night. Only a tiny part of me felt relieved to have this little girl by my side.

Boria soon dismissed me for reasons unknown. I asked no

questions and didn't look at her or anyone else as I grabbed Selah and left the hall with Daniel leading the way out. I felt anger toward my sister. Her selfishness and disregard for our family were abhorrent to me. Seer or not, I was going to confront her and try to remind her of who she was.

As angry as I was with Boria, Selah was slowly melting that anger away. She stood close to me as we walked behind Daniel as he escorted us to my quarters. I felt a little healing in providing Selah a way back home. At least she would have a chance to return and grow up with her family as she should.

As hard as I tried to sleep, I could not. I felt the cool night air blow in as my mind raced with thoughts. At least Selah fell sound asleep the moment she placed her head down upon the cot. I knew her little body was tired from all the labor she must have endured today. Her poor little hands were calloused and hardened. My heart ached with the knowledge that she had to have been enslaved for some time for her hands and body to look like this. Even when we worked in our village, weaving baskets, washing clothing, or bringing in the harvest, our hands still did not look as worn as her little ones did. This village was not at all what it seemed. Though they had such pretty homes, clothing, flowers, and faces, they lacked something that made them distant from mercy.

Now that I thought of it, the only mercy I had seen in this cruel village was in the eyes of Gabril. I thought of him freely now as I lay in bed, remembering his humble eyes and low voice that held kindness and strength. His hands were beautiful, like the images he created on pillows and pottery. I felt silly calling his hands beautiful, but they were. I saw no callouses on his palms or dirt underneath his nails. Nor did he have anything to enhance his face as the others in the village did. How I had overlooked that baffled me, as that was one of the first things I had noticed about everyone here. He did wear the same clothing, though, which might have allowed me to overlook that part about him. I wondered when I would see him again, not out of some intense allure like the unearthly beings but out of admiration for his humbleness and kindness.

As I turned and covered myself with a blanket, I realized I had let go of the stone in my hand. A part of me felt unsure and troubled, knowing Samayaza would know all I thought of and what he would say, but I was too tired to think about it anymore. I had not the will to keep my eyes open any longer. Maybe it was my tired imagination, but the continued sound of the drums was still pounding in my head, along with an unusual hum in the air. I needed to sleep and put all of this away for the night. Come tomorrow morning, I would awake anew.

# AMONG ANGELS 4

Daniel heard every thought that went through her mind that night. Like always, her observation of everything was vast, but her understanding of them overwhelmed her. He knew he had to put her mind at ease and allow her to rest. She had experienced more than he had ever wanted her to. He sent a sound repetition into the air in her quarters to calm her soul and put her to sleep without dreaming. She needed rest without the interference of her mind or that of anyone around her. With hopes of a restful slumber, she might forget her questions and stop reassessing her emotions toward Gabril. He could not help but cringe at the notion that she found solace in Gabril rather than himself.

He had not expected her to find that comfort in another being, let alone his heavenly kin. Gabril was not fallen as he was. In fact, he was upon Earth at the request of Daniel and of another whom Daniel knew nothing about. Since Gabril was not fallen and created for a higher realm than Daniel, his descent and ascension between the heavenly realms and Earth was free. This was a significant advantage that Daniel longed for again. As the leader of the Gregori, only he had had this privilege of travel. He was favored for his allegiance, leadership, and strong dedication to his purpose. No one within the Grigori knew of this allowance that had been given to him by the Seventh Realm. As the first Gregori to be created, he was made to lead, and for that reason alone, he was given authority over all the Watchers and was welcomed to report freely to all heavenly realms. But most of all, his love for his Creator allowed him access and freedom throughout all domains, including Earth.

"You requested my presence, brother," said a tall, radiant being whose eyes rimmed bright with light as he appeared.

Daniel bowed in reverence to the light and in appreciation that Gabril answered his call.

"My guarded has found solace in your presence," he said painfully. He knew not to feel the way he did, but deep within him was a raging beast that was being muffled only by his celestial fire.

Gabril nodded and waited as he knew what lay heavy upon his brother's heart. He felt his troubles controlling his mortal emotions and pitied him, as Daniel was once the most disciplined and devoted of all angelic beings until his descent with the rest of the Gregori.

"Her affection should not burden your heart; it is true and clean in intention." He reassured him, though he knew mortal emotions were quick to change.

Daniel nodded in acknowledgment. He knew his brother

would not ever be afflicted by the same curse as he and the rest of the fallen Gregori.

"There will be times I will not be able to be near her to protect as I once was able to." He looked straight at Gabril, now in a plea. "I need you to be close at those times to protect her."

Gabril knew what he meant since part of his mission was exactly what Daniel just requested. Without saying a word, he nodded and allowed the silent oath to take root between them.

"He knows of your intent and struggles, Daniel," Gabril kindly reminded him. "Though I know not of your fate, I know of his mercy and understanding. Take comfort in your struggles as they set you apart from the rest for the time being."

Daniel instantly caught his warning of what was to come. If he allowed his mortal temperament to take hold, it would only lead to utter oblivion for him. All chance of atonement would be lost. At the thought, Daniel felt an ache in his heart that he had never experienced in his mortal form. It was a crushing sensation, a feeling of losing something he could not be without. It was the drive, the light, and the will within him that felt vulnerable, and he knew it was only going to become more difficult the longer he stayed within this realm. But he had no choice, as he had to protect his guarded and the future of humanity.

"Your words are taken to heart, brother." Daniel nodded and bowed in gratitude.

Gabril nodded in return and was about to take his leave when he received a message from the higher realm that needed to be relayed to Daniel.

"Samayaza has put Azazzel on the path to your guarded. Be wise in this knowledge and allow her to see the truth herself. Do not take it upon yourself to choose for her, as all mortals must decide upon their own free will."

Daniel furrowed his eyebrows in concern at what Gabril had just announced. He knew of Azazzel's wicked intent upon her but believed Samayaza to be true to his word. This was the beginning of many betrayals he sensed would come from Samayaza, and he needed to take heed and be on alert, as Gabril advised.

With a final nod and bow from Daniel, Gabril ascended back to the realm of light and purity. He looked at him until the last elements of light disappeared and felt the bitter tinge of regret slice at his heart. Atonement would be his only defense, and in order to seek that, he needed to protect the sacred line of mortals that would bring about indemnification for all of them now and until the end of the age.

He must continue his mission and not allow mortal emotions to interfere. As Gabril advised, he must maneuver wisely amongst his fallen brethren, not be tempted to anger, greed, or lust as it would doom him for all eternity.

# CHAPTER ELEVEN

U pon hearing little Selah calling me to wake, I opened my eyes to her lovely smile. Though the morning had arrived sooner than I wanted, I knew she was excited to be reunited with her family as promised. Weary-eyed, I slowly got up and readied myself to go on our little journey.

"You must have slept well. I'm glad to see you refreshed, little one." I said as joy entered my heart upon her keenness.

She bounced around the room in anticipation. "I am, I am! Shall I help you dress or braid your hair? I know the prettiest braid, and I can put flowers in it if you wish." Her excitement was infectious, and I could not deny her.

I nodded as I said, "You may braid my hair if you wish, but no need for flowers. The sooner we ready ourselves, the earlier you see your family."

Her eyes sparkled like stars upon the mention of her family. So, I quickly dressed and sat down so she could braid my hair. She spoke of how she would tell them about everything, like the Seer's ritual and how she slept on a cot with such beautiful veil covers. She continued about how much she missed them and could not wait to embrace them. I knew her feeling, as I missed my sister, too. Even though she was within my reach to see and hold, she had somehow changed into someone I could barely recognize.

A slight knock at the already open door alerted us of someone; Daniel stood unmoved by our chatter. He only acknowledged me with a curt nod and returned to stand guard like he had the night before. I smiled back at him and remembered the questions I had but thought it best to leave it until after Selah was home. We ate without wasting too much of the morning, and I packed whatever food and clothing I could find for little Selah. She was not going to go back empty-handed after all she'd been through. I even put in the beautiful veil covers without her noticing. She would be thrilled when she found them when unpacking. Hopefully, they would add to the joy of her return to her family.

With Daniel as our guide, we made our way out of the Temple without any trouble or interaction with anyone. Once outside, I welcomed the warmth of the sun upon my skin. Though it was never so cold within the Temple that I would shiver, I always enjoyed and preferred the golden rays of the sun warming me in the early morning. There was something about how the sun shined upon awakening; it was never too harsh and nourished the body.

Horses waited for us, but I did not want to ride one.

"May we walk if the distance is manageable for Selah?" I

asked Daniel. Selah was about nine summers old. She should not have had too much trouble, but I did not want to push her to exhaustion right before seeing her family due to the hardships she'd had to endure.

Daniel looked upon Selah and assessed it would be all right. "If she tires, there are other ways to reach our destination," he offered as he began to lead us out of the village.

He took us through the market; everyone bowed as we passed but otherwise went about their daily tasks. I noticed so much more of the market than before. The smell of spices, both sweet and spicy, filled the air. Smoke rose at every other merchant stand, and the chatter of people haggling with each other overwhelmed the senses. It was comforting not to be stared at like we were the last time we had walked through this place.

As Daniel escorted us farther away, I could see how vast and enormous the Temple was. It was built so prominently high for all to see near or far. I knew there had to be more hidden passages and paths within it or behind fountains and pillars that I had yet to see. I would pay closer attention when we returned. I needed to know as much as possible about this new world I found myself in.

Daniel walked slightly before us but made sure only to be a step ahead. He stood tall and looked so strong that no one dared to offer us any of their goods. His hair was pulled back and tied at the nape of his neck, but small strands fell on either side of his strong jaw. His arms were bare, and he wore smooth cloth covering only his torso and back. You could see his muscles move in perfect uniform with every step he took. It was mesmerizing. I knew I was resting my gaze on him longer than I should have, and I forced myself to look away, but it was no use. He noticed and turned his head in my direction. I quickly looked away, hoping to look less like a fool.

Thank goodness Selah was with us and started speaking about everything she would teach her little sisters once she got home. Her excitement burst through her as she began to skip more than she was walking. Her joy warmed my heart repeatedly, reigniting the hope of maybe one day soon, Boria holding my hand as we walked away from all this and returned home to our parents, village, and river.

As we made our way past the market, we ended up going past many of the beautiful large homes. Many were the color of the sun-kissed sand and had enchanting plants covering the walls' sides. Some even had trees that looked like they had burst through the roof and rooted from within the home. It created great shade and brought about a cooling effect for the home and those inside it.

As much as I did not want to give the people of this village any of my admiration because of what had been done to Selah and to who knows how many more children, I continued to look upon the magnificence of what they had created. It was too appealing to look away, just like the beings themselves. My weakness to them and this village was bringing about constant guilt. A part of me wanted to enjoy and revel in it like Boria, yet the other part knew that what I saw and felt was shallow.

"It is a matter of view and belief," Daniel smoothly injected as he interrupted my thoughts.

He wanted to converse, and I was only happy to oblige. "How would it be a matter of view and belief when everything in this village seems to be built only to make you feel powerful."

He raised an eyebrow at my question as he looked at me curiously. "If you only knew the capacity of which you were created, you would not think so."

He was starting to sound like Grandfather Enok, which was not helping.

"A bit farther, and we will soon be home!" exclaimed Selah as she pulled on my hand to walk faster.

Our conversation would have to continue another time as I could not deny her request to hasten my steps. Daniel looked at us with amusement but did not say a word as we continued on and came upon a less densely populated area of the village. I realized Selah's home must be in the harvest lands, away from the Temple. I had wondered where these lands would be as I didn't see it when I first arrived upon the horse with Azazzel. Just saying his name made me anxious.

"*Then do not say his name,*" Daniel teased with a wide smirk as he looked at me from the corner of his eye.

As much as I wanted to roll my eyes at his taunting remark, I could not help but smile. His attempt to relieve my fear by being playful was endearing and duly noted.

The homes we walked by were humble in appearance, so much so that they reminded me of my house by the river. And, of course, the land they tended to was very grand. I noticed a large smoke plume in the distance, and Daniel extended his arm in front of Selah and me, signaling us to stop.

He took a position in front of us, completely covering us both behind him. Selah could not help but try to peek from his side, but with one gentle push, he placed her back between him and me. Something had to be wrong for him to stand so protectively.

"Should we turn back?" I quietly asked.

"No! We are right here, right by that plume!" Selah exclaimed as she popped right back out, pointing to it.

I reached out to grab her hand, but Daniel nodded. "We may proceed." He gestured to move forward. He did make sure we were a step behind him, in any case. Which I was fine with. Even though he allowed us to move forward, I could sense he was very alert as he scanned the area.

"*Yes, you are correct. Tread lightly and do not stray far from my side,*" he warned softly in my mind. For once, I liked our connection and appreciated the link.

I nodded and pulled Selah closer to me as we continued to walk. She was so excited she could not feel the slight shift in the air and how the clouds seemed to flatten like a veil over the once-blue sky, the silence of animals, from the birds to the sheep in the fields. All were huddled and not grazing as they should at this time of day. And the unusual hum in the air rang in my ears as a signal, as a warning that something was not as it should be.

I braced for the worst as we neared the trees covering Selah's family home.

Upon passing through the tall thin line of trees, I sighed in relief as I noticed the house was intact and two men were burning a pile of old harvest waste. I relaxed my hold on her, and she took that as a cue to let go and start running toward them.

"Selah!" I reprimanded, but Daniel reassured me to let her go as we continued to walk toward them.

One of the men lowered his rake and squinted in disbelief. He cried out in joy as Selah ran into his open arms. He hugged her tight and swung her around as he cradled her head in his hands.

"Selah! Oh, Selah!" Tears fell from his eyes as he continued to hold her. I assumed this was her father as I saw similar facial features. The round cheeks and full lips were a family trait.

The other man looked on in joy as he watched the sweet reunion of father and daughter. Putting down his tool, he came closer to them and welcomed Selah home with a gentle pat on the head and a smile.

"What is all the fuss out here?" said a woman coming out of the home with two little girls that peered through the door as she walked toward us.

Upon seeing us and noticing Daniel, she abruptly stopped and froze in fear. Until she heard her daughter Selah call out to her from her father's arms, her face warmed, and her eyes filled with tears as though she could not believe what she was seeing.

She cried aloud as she rushed to Selah, and they reunited in a clash of emotions and a joyful embrace.

"Oh, my Selah!" she cried out. "My precious Selah!" She kissed and embraced her as she grasped her face to look at her.

Tears began to fall down my cheeks over witnessing such an intense homecoming. One I hoped would be mirrored one day when I returned home with Boria.

Once the reunion had calmed down, they approached Daniel and me. They bowed to him and me alike. I wondered why they would bow to me; I was not expecting or wanting such homage. I was neither a king nor a being of another realm.

"*You wear the seal of the temple upon your garments,*" answered Daniel within my mind.

Seal of the Temple? What was the seal of the Temple? I quickly looked over the garments I was wearing.

"*The serpent thread that shines without the sun is the seal,*" he replied.

Could that be true? I looked around us and noticed that he was correct. The trees had blocked out the sun, and yet, the golden thread upon my garments glimmered like the sun was shining.

"Our deepest gratitude for the return of our daughter," said the father as he humbled himself by bowing deeply.

It touched my heart as I reached out and pulled him up. "I am a mere daughter who loves her father as well. I am humbled to bring Selah home and request forgiveness for her forced service."

He looked at me in confusion as he tried to understand what I had just said. Daniel stepped forward, and I could see fear enter their eyes momentarily. But not Selah; her eyes twinkled with joy as she knew she had a strong protector. She continued to smile and enjoy the bliss of reunion.

Daniel lifted his hand slightly, and calm entered our hearts. I was astonished at his power and wondered if they knew it was coming from him. Either way, he relieved their fears, and he was able to speak to them.

"I know I am not the first one here," he stated. "Did you pledge yourself or your family?"

I looked around me, suddenly in fear of what he said. Which one of them was here and why? This was a humble home with an ordinary family and a poor farm. What use would they be to any one of these beings?

"No, we have not pledged to anyone." replied the father, a bit confused.

"Selah, go inside and see your sisters. They have missed you terribly," said her mother. I could tell she did not want Selah to hear more of what was just said.

Selah was about to run inside, but she quickly approached me and embraced me. "Thank you for bringing me home."

I squeezed her back and placed a kiss on her head. She was

home now, and my fight to stay for Boria was not in vain. At least one innocent child was reunited, which strengthened my heart.

I looked toward Daniel once Selah went inside, and he looked toward the other man as though waiting for his answer. But the man stayed silent and looked away.

"For returning our daughter, we pledge our family to you, my liege," said Selah's father as he bowed again. His wife and the other man followed, but he just lowered his head and did not bend the knee like the other two.

Daniel nodded. "So let it be." He waved his hand over them and the area. I saw a ripple in the air the moment he raised his hand. It was just like the one Azazzel had created, but this had more giant waves of rippled air than the tight-knit one I witnessed Azazzel do. Daniel looked at the other man with trepidation in his eyes. I knew something irked him about the man, but whatever it was, he let it be and began our walk back to the Temple.

"Why did they pledge themselves to you?" I asked, curious to know.

"Each mortal will have to choose who they serve among us. We are lord over them, and they will receive protection in return for their allegiance. No other will lay claim on them as it is against protocol," he explained.

"Would that mean no one of your kind would harm them or Selah ever again?"

He turned to look at me as he answered, "Yes."

I smiled in gratitude and took a deep breath, relieved knowing Selah and her family would be safe.

After that, our journey back was quiet. Though I wanted to question him about my stone and what they were here for, I felt a sadness I was not expecting. I missed little Selah. She had been with me for such a short time, yet her presence was soothing and distracting from what my reality had become. I had to remind myself that she was home now; the farther from that Temple she was, the safer she would be.

"I concur," said Daniel aloud.

I looked at him curiously and asked, "I know the stone doesn't matter to you. How and why is that?"

He again glanced at me from the corner of his eye, "You are my guarded, Iris."

His guarded?

"What does that mean?"

Looking straight ahead to the village near the distance, he sighed and answered, "It means that I can read your thoughts with or without the stone."

I scowled at his response. Then what was the point of the stone to begin with?

"To teach you how to guard your thoughts from the others." He sounded as though this should have been obvious to me.

I pondered that for a while. I knew he would be able to read my thoughts, but I kept thinking of Grandfather Enok and how he had been the one to give me the stone, not Daniel. Did my thoughts betray me to Daniel before I even knew of him? How had he come to know of the stone's ability?

"Do you wish to know?" Without looking at me, he asked the simple question.

I paused, unsurprised that he knew everything I was thinking, "Yes."

He stopped and turned toward me. Blocking the sun with his massive frame, he extended one hand to me in a request to take it.

I did.

He pulled me in close, and the world around us began to swirl and turn. He cradled my head gently against his chest, and I closed my eyes instinctively. I knew not how it happened nor where we would be upon opening my eyes, but I knew he would not purposely cause me any distress. Though his slightest touch was exhilarating to my senses, his scent this close untroubled my heart. I felt the wind whipping around us franticly, but I felt safe and knew no harm would come to me while in his embrace. Though no ground was beneath us, I knew his power grounded me.

With no words spoken, I could hear his thoughts as clearly as if he had said them aloud. He was praising me for being so brave and strong. I always felt it was an intrusion when he read my thoughts, but this felt different. He was allowing me to read his.

*"I'm not allowing. You found the link to me,"* he revealed.

*"Link?"* I asked.

*"A road,"* he corrected.

*"There are roads that lead to another's thoughts?"* This was interesting yet confusing.

*"There are many roads. This is just one."*

I did not fully grasp what he said, but before I could ask more questions, the winds subsided, and I sensed the ground beneath my feet. I felt the sun again as he slowly released me from his hold. The moment of heaven I found myself in gradually diminished as I stepped back from him. Realizing he would have read that thought, I felt heat rush to my face. I shook my head slightly at my lack of control when this close to him.

"Iris?" said a familiar voice I longed to hear.

I turned around to see Grandfather Enok standing in front of his hut, so engulfed in how close I was to Daniel that I had not realized where he had brought me.

"Grandfather!" I exclaimed and ran straight toward him.

He embraced me tightly. "Heaven's blessings, child."

I clung to him firmly. It was not the reunion I had envisioned, but I was grateful, nonetheless. I quickly asked him about Mother and Father, and he reassured me they were safe in their home. I wanted to ask how they were doing with Boria and me being absent, but he ignored me and settled me against his side as he looked at Daniel. He looked irritated, and I thought nothing but rebuke would come out of his mouth. Instead, he slightly bowed his head as his demeanor went soft—a small gesture of thanks, I believed, for bringing his granddaughter to him.

Daniel nodded back in acknowledgment.

Grandfather wasted no time. "Come, we have much to discuss." He motioned to Daniel as he turned around and escorted us into his hut.

I was so elated to be back in the familiar lands that I took no time to step in front of Grandfather Enok and lead the way to what I considered my second home. And upon entering the old hut, it was just as it always had been. Everything might look old compared to the things I had seen in the Temple, but I knew that these things that belonged to my grandfather were made, collected, and used for good things by his own hands. Nothing was made forcefully by the free labor of another.

Seeing what I had thought I never would visit again felt so refreshing to my soul. The dingy shelves that held uneven pottery, the small wooden table with crooked legs that always worried me if I placed anything heavy on it. And, of course, Grandfather's collection of oils, dried flowers, and dried fruit, how I cherished the things I had overlooked before.

I touched small pottery that Boria had made when she was less than five summers of age. It was meant to carry water, but it was so small and lopsided that it would barely hold any water. Yet Grandfather kept it throughout the years. My life was simple and humble before, yet I was happy with what little we had. I had thought Boria was also pleased, but I knew now she was not.

I turned around to the sound of Grandfather closing the door. Daniel was standing close by, watching me as I caressed the uneven water jug made by my sister. It did not bother me that he knew what I was feeling. I was sure that even if I knew how to hide my thoughts, the sadness on my face would have given away what I felt.

"I was expecting you towards dusk, but I will not complain about being able to see my brave granddaughter sooner rather than later." Grandfather said as he walked over and embraced me again.

"There are some new revelations that brought me here sooner than we had discussed," replied Daniel.

Grandfather frowned and gestured to take a seat on the old stumps he had as chairs.

"And what are these new revelations that have emerged?" he asked, with concern in his voice.

Daniel, who still stood, replied, "He knows of the stone and has devised a plan with Azazzel against my guarded."

His guarded? Wait, that was me!

Before I could say anything, Grandfather motioned for my silence with a single raise of his finger. He knew me too well and was ready to silence me before I could speak. I noticed a slight smile on Daniel's lips begin to form, but it disappeared when Grandfather asked a question.

"In what way has he devised a plan with Azazzel?" he leaned forward now with worry.

"I do not know, but I was told to move wisely in this knowledge as Samayaza does not know of my discovery."

Grandfather listened intently. He asked, "By whom was this knowledge made known to you?"

"Gabril," answered Samayaza.

That name sounded familiar.

"Ah, I see." Grandfather shook his head in thought as he looked off into the distance.

I sensed that I was not supposed to know whatever it was that they knew, hence such short responses to one another.

"His presence lingered earlier today on the outskirts of the temple, but he hid himself from my sight," revealed Daniel.

Grandfather rose from his seat. "So, he chose to hide rather than appear to you?"

"Yes."

Grandfather sighed and looked at me. "Then, indeed, he has set Azazzel on a dark task."

My patience was running dry, and I was getting frustrated with all this discussion that seemed to be about me!

"What does this all mean?" I asked impatiently. "Is Boria in danger?" Was Samayaza planning on hurting Boria through Azazzel?

They looked at me, somewhat surprised at my outburst, but Grandfather answered, "Not Boria, my child, but you."

"Me?" Why me, I wondered.

Grandfather approached and sat next to me. "Iris, some

things must remain hidden to restore order."

Again, he spoke in riddles that made no sense.

"She is confused," Daniel interjected. Though he was correct in that observation, I could not help but feel daft in front of them. And a little embarrassed. I was confused and had no idea what had happened to my once peaceful existence. My home, family, and life were calm and full of love. Whenever I felt like I stood on solid ground, the Earth beneath me moved and shook until I lost my footing and fell.

"Why would Samayaza consider me a threat?" I asked, looking at Daniel.

"Not a threat, but a conquest."

A conquest?

*"Yes. You are more than you think."* This time, he whispered it in my head.

Grandfather got up and stood in front of me, blocking Daniel. "You must now learn what I should have taught you and Boria long ago."

He brought his sitting stump and sat down, facing me. "Where is the stone I gave you?"

I revealed the stone from under my garment.

He nodded. "Pull it off your neck and hold it within your palm," he instructed as he waited.

Upon seeing the stone within my palm, he continued, "Now close your eyes."

Again, I did as he said without question. Anything Grandfather instructed always had a purpose, and I knew this command was no different.

"Now, describe how the stone feels within your hand."

I scowled at his question but answered when he looked at me

sternly. "Hard, yet smooth and cool to the touch."

"Precisely. Now imagine within your mind a wall made of this stone. Build a solid, impenetrable barrier," he answered after a moment of my silence.

I tried to do as he said, but I had no idea how to build a wall. Was the stone not supposed to supply that protection for me? I looked at Daniel, hoping he would be of some help.

"No," said Grandfather as he gestured his hand toward Daniel. "I believe it would be best if you waited outside. She must strengthen her will on her own."

It was amusing how Grandfather had no fear of these beings and ordered them as he saw fit.

Daniel straightened from slightly leaning against the wall, and though a look of concern grazed his face at Grandfather's request, he nodded and walked out the door.

Once he was gone, I asked my grandfather about their purpose here. "Who are they, and where do they come from? Are they from the heavens you spoke of to Boria and me as children?"

With a sigh, he said, "In the proper time, all things will reveal themselves, but for now, you must learn to protect your thoughts." He grabbed my hand and advised, "I understand your fascination, child, but you must be wise in your thoughts. Discipline your will, and your mind, body, and soul will follow."

Although I wanted to adhere to those words, I knew that whenever I was near Daniel, I felt a pull unlike any other. Sometimes that pull of emotion for him was strong like a river, and other times, it was just a steady pour of trickling water into a fountain. But it was always there, so how was I supposed to stop that?

"How do I discipline what I feel?" I asked earnestly.

He ran his fingers through his white beard in thought. He sighed as he said, "By knowing that the truth in all matters is more important than what we feel. Our feelings can be tempted or compelled to become something that is not for the greater good." he warned.

"And what if what I feel is true but not for the greater good?" How can one tell the difference is what I wanted to know.

"Then that is where discernment is key," he said kindly, comforting my hand.

I was unsure if I understood him and did not want to seem daft, so I just nodded and accepted what he said. I would ponder his words later, hoping to figure out what I needed to discern. For now, he wanted to continue strengthening my mind.

He had me close my eyes again with the stone in my palm. "Now envision a home deep within your mind where no one else exists except you and that home."

Letting out a sigh, I began to find a space within my mind that no one else existed in except for me. It was not easy. So many people were in my thoughts, along with many things that I had seen that were all new. I continued pushing them all behind me as I walked through my memories. I needed to find an empty patch to create a home and wall.

"Do you envision it?" he asked impatiently.

I was not quite there but nodded.

"Now, I want you to think of a great wall. One the size and thickness that you have never seen before. One that is impenetrable and strong."

I did. My home was small but solid. Beautiful flowers with lush leaves grew and rose from the ground to climb the walls. I even envisioned a small creek alongside it, with pleasant birds and small animals along its edge.

"Do you have your wall, child?"

"No." I was too busy imagining my beautiful little home.

"What are you doing then?" he retorted, annoyed.

"Building my home," I answered calmly.

He let out a deep sigh. "Iris, envision your wall, then you may continue to create your home," he said, exasperated by my lack of haste.

My eyes closed; I shrugged in remorse as I began to think of a wall, one that was as thick as a row of wild bulls and as high as any tree I had seen.

"I have my wall now, Grandfather," I said confidently. "What shall I do?"

I heard him scoot closer. "Now, all of your thoughts and emotions are to stay behind the wall and within your home," he instructed.

Hmm. That was going to take much more work than anticipated. How was I going to imagine all this at every thought?

"You must learn to cloak your thoughts and not allow the—"

The door suddenly opened, and Daniel stepped in. "We must return now."

Grandfather stood. "We are almost at an end to her lesson; a few more moments and—"

"We do not have moments. I must leave now, or they will be in danger due to my absence," Daniel insisted.

I had a horrible feeling that began to form in my belly. Though I did not want to leave, I knew Daniel knew something we did not.

Grandfather realized the same thing and turned to embrace me. He whispered, "Practice what I taught you with everyone, and soon, you will no longer require the stone for protection."

I nodded, reassuring him I would remember. I held him tight for one more moment, looking around again, trying to keep the memory of all familiar to me locked away in my home within the walls of my mind.

Daniel held the door open as I passed and took a final look at Grandfather as he watched us leave. With a look of concern, he did his best to give a final farewell with a faint smile and nod.

I felt Daniel's arm pull me close as he shut the door with the other. The wind howled around us, the ground beneath disappeared, and I closed my eyes intuitively as I rested my head against his chest. I breathed in the smoky smell that emanated from the strange yet soft material that covered his being. The gentle touch of his strong hand cradled my head again, and all the worry I had felt just a few moments ago melted away. Though a part of me wanted to open my eyes and see what was happening all around me during these journeys, I decided to opt for the peaceful embrace of my guardian.

*"That I am and will be forever,"* he promised.

His words enveloped my soul, consoling it whenever I felt uncertain. And all too soon, I felt the ground beneath my feet and the familiar room within the Temple. We were back in my quarters, and I felt a slight sinking of my heart as he released me.

Gently lifting my chin with one finger, he said, "Stay within your quarters. I will return shortly." He then turned and walked away.

I stood in the middle of the large room within a Temple filled with many people, yet I felt alone. Not even the comfort of knowing my kin was somewhere within these walls brought me any solace. I laughed at myself as I stood alone again in the room and Temple I wished to have never seen. Though every finery was within these walls, it did not give me the comfort and love my humble home in my beloved village by the Euphrates would provide. I yearned for the dirt floors, chipped pottery, and baskets worn from use. At least in that home, there was family and happiness.

I wished I could be near my river again, even if it were for a little while. Just long enough to clear my thoughts and allow the rush of the water to run through my fingers.

I needed to leave this room; I was feeling trapped. But where could I go? Where could I find a peaceful moment to search and regain my strength? The solitude of my mind was no longer a refuge. I needed to feel and turn off my thoughts. But where could I go in this strange place?

The fountain!

I remembered there was a fountain nearby. And if only I could recall the path, I could possibly find that beautiful garden I saw upon Boria's balcony. I knew the fountain was close by. I could start with finding that first.

I knew I was not following Daniel's request, but if I did not go now, he would likely find me in the corner of this large room, curled up like an infant and crying for home.

"I'm sorry," I whispered into the air as I rushed out of my quarters and hit an unseen barrier that sent me back down to the floor.

# AMONG ANGELS 5

D aniel took the path of the angels and was at Selah's family home within a blink of an eye. Standing on the outer edge by a cluster of trees, Daniel observed the area. Though his mind raced with images of Iris, he leaned on his angelic discipline and focused on the task at hand. He could see the family within the home going about their duties. Selah and her sisters played while their mother was kneading bread and watching her children. There was peace in her heart as she watched over them. Her heart still ached at the thought of Selah being taken and enduring the pain she had. Daniel waved his hand in her direction and subdued the emotion of guilt. The mother had no say in Selah being taken; she did not need to feel such deep guilt, which brought Daniel to locate the father and Uncle. He did not need to look far for the father, as he was on the east side of the home fixing the plow that kept breaking due to poor design. He would have to fix that later, he thought to himself.

Now, where was the Uncle? He further screened the surrounding area.

He found him quite a way out from the home, waiting on a rock. What was he doing out there alone and with anticipation within his heart? Daniel could see his heart beating fast, sweat building upon his brow as he fidgeted his hands. He realized this was going to lead to unpleasant findings about this fickle man.

Daniel shifted closer and stood motionless and undetectable near a giant boulder. His ability to cloak himself was his most valuable and powerful tool in this realm. He could easily manipulate the energy of anything upon the Earth and use it to cover himself as though he was part of the object.

He watched intently as the Uncle's heart raced wildly. Who was he waiting for in such anxiousness?

He did not have to wait long as Azazzel burst through a gateway and stood menacingly before the man.

Nostrils flaring, he looked at the mortal before him. Azazzel's eyes did not hold back his disgust. "Where is the girl?" he asked with pure disdain etched in every word.

With fear resonating throughout his entire being, the Uncle fell upon Azazzel's feet. "Forgive me, lord, I…I could not separate her from her mother and sisters," he admitted cowardly.

Daniel saw the rage travel through Azazzel as he flexed his hands, trying to hold back obliterating the mortal kneeling before him. Daniels's anger flared at the Uncle's admission, but resisted as he sensed a tinge of regret in his mortal mind.

"Take me instead, my lord; I will serve. I am stronger and can work harder than any child," pleaded the Uncle.

Azazzel lifted the man with a simple motion of his hand, and held him captive in the air. Like an invisible noose around his neck, the Uncle squirmed and reached for his neck as though trying to free himself from an invisible force cutting off his air.

"It is not your strength, nor you, that we seek. You are nothing but a feeble being of clay," spat out Azazzel as he tightened his hold around his neck. The man was fighting for breath by hitting all around his neck, but no physical form, neither suffocation nor suspension in the air, existed for him to assault. His attempts were futile as the outcome favored the being created of fire.

Daniel counted the seconds the man had before he would have passed out. He would intervene, but that would reveal his power and advantage. He would have to allow this punishment and death to the Uncle.

Suddenly, the man dropped to the ground and gasped for air as Azazzel towered over him once more.

"You have one last chance. If you fail, I will have to get her myself." He bent down low to peer into the eyes of the mortal.

The man fearfully stared into the swirling eyes of Azazzel.

"And the rest of you will not survive," he threatened.

Daniel knew Azazzel would be true to his word. He was the one who had begun teaching the mortals how to formulate better and more significant weaponry. Teaching them what each mineral upon the Earth was for, how to harvest it, and the art of working each metal for power and adornments upon themselves. He had already prepared them well by adorning their faces with earth minerals.

"You have two sunsets to deliver her." Azazzel stood. "Or else I will make good on my promise." The cool cunning glint in Azazzels eyes only solidified his promise of punishment if the man did not comply. He soon disappeared, leaving the man shaking in a heap of dirt.

Daniel realized the situation was not over as he had hoped. He was correct in feeling the disturbance around the man. The touch of Azazzel was not hard to miss; he left a strong residual of power that the angels were known for.

The man slowly stood, still rubbing his neck from the force that was mere seconds away from silencing him forever. Daniel was not fond of mortals like the one he was observing. They were the ones that carried the blood of a serpent, cold and un-feeling. They allowed fear to rule them so easily that they failed to realize how quickly they snuffed out the light within them-selves and infected others with doubt. They were fools to ignore the greatest gift in creation over something as temporary as fear.

But Daniel waited to hear his thoughts and what his decision would be. The man pondered his assignment repeatedly in his head yet could not push himself to surrender the girl. Though fear was rampant throughout his being, he had a fondness for Selah. He admired her strength and sacrifice. He was conflict-ed and figured he had two suns to think before he had to do something.

Daniel pushed guilt upon the man to stir up his morality. It seemed to work as he sat down upon the rock again and closed his eyes in grief. He had never been in such a dilemma that would cause him to choose between the only family he had left and his eldest niece. Either way, he knew he would live in shame and guilt. If he gave up Selah, the family, including himself, would be saved. But if he disobeyed Azazzel, then they would all perish.

Daniel heard the faint voice of Iris call out to him, "I'm *sorry.*"

Iris. What was she doing? He needed to get back to the Temple quickly. He had only left her alone in hopes that she would rest, but instead, she seemed to have made other plans. He alerted Gabril and received confirmation that he was watching her. Daniel furrowed his brows at the thought of Gabril with her. Again, that emotion that plagued him was trying to make its way into his mind—jealousy. He pushed it back down and chose not to partake in it.

Quickly, Daniel waved his hand and sent a wave of strength to the mortal to help him make an honorable decision. He hoped he would find courage instead of a fearful heart. It was better to face whatever punishment he would by disobeying Azazzel with his kin than to live with the guilt of causing one of them to fall.

He waited a moment more until the man had made up his mind and would not surrender Selah to Azazzel. But Daniel knew this might not be the end, as these mortals were very indecisive. He would have to return and continue nudging him on the right path. It might yet be possible to help him regain his courage and valor as a mortal man. And make the choice that led to light, not darkness.

So, he left and headed straight to the Temple. Taking the path of the angels, he was instantly there, right outside her quarters. Purposely hiding behind the pillar, he stood quietly and watched as he knew Gabril was already with her. His curiosity over how they would interact with one another convinced Daniel to stay behind the pillar and quietly observe. He wondered why he felt this way toward Gabril. He was not fallen and would not cross that line as he would never defile his purpose. The light of the Creator dwelled within him.

Upon that thought, longing and grief for that connection

rolled over Daniel. He quickly herded it away as there wasn't anything he could do about it now. He continued to watch them, knowing that Gabril would have already sensed his presence, with or without the cloak.

# CHAPTER TWELVE

A re you all right, princess?" asked a familiar voice.

I looked up and saw Gabril looking down at me with concern. Flushed with embarrassment, I apologized for my lack of attention as he helped me get back up.

I wondered how much he had seen. Had I hit the side of the doorway in my haste to leave? I wanted to ask, but still feeling abashed, I apologized to him again.

He did not seem bothered and reassured me that all was well.

"Was there somewhere you wished to go, princess?" he inquired.

Being called a princess always made me uneasy, but hearing it from him was tolerable. Maybe it was the sound of his comforting voice, his compassionate eyes, or his affable presence. Either way, I felt no guilt about being the granddaughter of an evil man who had built the Temple I stood in.

"I was...I just wanted to go by the fountain to clear my thoughts."

A look of concern came over his graceful face. "If you allow, I would gladly escort you to this fountain you seek?"

I wanted to accept his offer, but a part of me wanted to be alone with my thoughts.

He saw the conflict in my eyes, "We do not have to speak if you do not wish it," he said gently.

Though a part of me still wanted to reject his offer, I knew it might not bode well for me to be alone roaming around the Temple, as I did not know whom I might encounter. And it was hard to say no to him when his presence was always so comforting.

I nodded, and we began to walk in silence. As we walked further away from my quarters, I felt silly not speaking to him. Here he was finally, without any escorts near to threaten him or anyone to interrupt, yet I was wallowing in self-pity instead of all the questions I had wanted to ask him.

I turned to look at him once, twice, and ask, but words would fail to form.

"Do you miss your family?" he softly asked, breaking the awkward silence.

I felt relieved when he spoke, but he asked a question that brought a flood of heavy emotions.

"I do," I said sadly.

I wanted to go home. I wanted things to return to how they were before everything was torn from me.

"What do you miss the most?" he probed.

"My home. My village. And the river."

"It must be a wonderful place if you miss it so greatly. Can you describe your village?" he kindly asked.

That question made me smile, and I began to tell him everything I could remember, from the details of my home to the flowers by the river. Oh, how I missed the sound of that river and the smell. Oh, the smell would bring relief to all my troubles. I left out all the farming, herding, kneading, sowing, weaving, and preparations we did, but we welcomed all those chores, as we knew it led to many days and nights of calm, peace, and plenty amongst the people.

"It sounds lovely, simple, and peaceful," he concluded.

With an ache in my heart, I answered, "It was."

I realized we were near the fountain; I had spoken so much that I did not get to ask him all the questions I wanted. About his drawings and sewing and how he had come to this village. Was he born here, or had he or his family traveled from another village?

I turned toward him to ask when suddenly, he stopped. It was so abrupt that I was a step ahead of him already.

"Is there something amiss?" His face looked so concerned it worried me.

He considered me and said, "I cannot go beyond this point. If you would like, we can walk toward another area of the Temple?"

I looked at him, confused by his admission. "We are almost there. Why would we go to another?" I wondered.

"Iris!" yelled a female voice.

It was Boria calling out to me. I turned toward the fountain and could almost see her. I took a few steps and noticed other women were accompanying her, cloaked in white robes.

"Iris!" Again, she called out loudly.

I turned to tell Gabril it was my sister, but he was no longer there.

I looked from one side to the other of the long hall and found no trace of him. He had just vanished. How had he walked down the path without me catching a glimpse of him leaving? I stood bewildered, not even hearing Boria's footsteps running toward me. She grabbed my hand.

"Iris, did you not hear me calling?" she spoke, slightly cross.

Startled, I turned to her. "I did. I was looking for something I dropped." I had to lie as I did not know how she would react to Gabril escorting me; I remembered the cold glare she had given him on her balcony.

Boria looked at me and then down the hall and shook her head as she led me to the fountain without another word.

"Come, meet my priestesses." She gleefully smiled. "They are mine to command and teach. I will show them the ways of our lords, and if they learn quickly, then maybe they, too, shall be chosen to become a Seer of another temple."

Another temple, I wondered in surprise.

The girls lightly chuckled at the notion of being chosen Seer. They were young like I was, maybe a couple the same age as Boria. But it was hard to tell with all the coloring on their faces. They were all lovely, with sun-kissed skin, eyes of blue and green, and long hair flowing freely about their shoulders.

But another temple? There was more than the one we stood in right now?

I had to know. "What other temples do you speak of? Is this not the only one?"

With one eyebrow raised, she smiled at me. "No." She shook her head. "There are others already built and being built for our lords. They will each reign according to what Lord Samayaza allows them." She looked at the girls as she mentioned Samayaza.

The girls slightly bowed their heads at her mention of him. They were already obeying mindlessly, whether they knew it or not. I felt pity for them and myself as I understood these beings' pull. They were magnificent in stature and beguiling to the mind. They walked with such authority that young or old women would seek to have just one of them defend and stand beside her. I knew how it felt, how they felt, as I, too, wanted to covet one for myself.

"They look so young." Though I knew I was the same age.

"As they should be. They need to be pure for their lords," she said as she walked past them toward the fountain. "As I was for my lord."

I gasped at her words!

I neared her side and asked, "What do you speak of, Boria? Have you lain him?" This would be the most devastating revelation if what she said was true.

With a coy smile, she answered, "I am his Seer."

"What does that mean?"

"It means I am his chosen, Iris," she stated. "I am the one he has appointed to rule beside him," she said boastfully, and my heart sank.

This was not what I wanted to hear. I hoped she would have calmed from all the festivities, and I could have convinced her this was not the way. I remembered Grandfather Enok! I should tell her I saw him today, and that might turn her from her beguilement.

"*NO.*" Daniel's deep voice boomed in my mind, instructing me otherwise.

I frowned. What was I supposed to do now?

"Oh, Iris, do not worry. I know of a powerful one that has his glorious eyes upon you." She winked as though what she had just revealed was to make me happy.

And why would she say not to worry? Did she genuinely believe I would be jealous of her?

I was not.

I was just dismayed at Daniel's tone forbidding me to mention grandfather. I had never heard him raise his voice to me like that. All I wanted to do was help my sister remember who she was and where she came from.

I could not let go of her new revelation. Again, I neared her side and whispered, "Did you lay with him as a wife to a husband?"

With a smile, she repeated, "I am his Seer."

I took what she said as confirmation of what I feared, what I knew Mother and Father would have worried about. This was such a horrible outcome. How would she ever return to our village without bringing shame to our family and herself?

"Come, I will show you how a daily offering must be carried out to satisfy our lord and receive his praise."

Upon her command, the girls moved about in different directions, grabbing things that were on the ground. Once they had what it was they wanted, they gathered around Boria. Some had baskets of flowers, others jars of what seemed like oil, and another a basket with the top covered.

Boria's voice was controlled and unwavering, as though she had done this numerous times. She specified where they were to stand, what to prepare first, and who would hold the oil. They all looked at her eagerly, yet all I could see when I looked upon her was my sister drifting further and further away. Even her voice seemed to have changed, and her movement was different. The kind, inspired, and courageous sister was gone. Replaced by a bold, unsubtle, blind woman who had too easily and too quickly forgotten who she was.

"Iris, stand next to Amala." She pointed to a young girl who stood on the other end of a line they had formed. She had some flowers in her hand, as did four of the six girls there. One held the jar of oil, another the small basket with the cover, and the rest divided the flowers within the baskets.

Boria stood at the fountain's base, the rays of sunlight still beaming down upon the open area. This was the fountain I liked as I could see the sky. She began to speak foreign words as she lifted her hands. And as she brought them down, the girls started to sing. It was soft, like whispers. All were in unison with each word as it flowed out of their mouths and into the air around us. Had this been anywhere but here, in this situation, I would have said they sounded lovely, but I could not describe the uneasy feeling my entire being felt over what I was witnessing.

"Lord Samayaza, your people, your worshipers, your Seer offer you a small token of gratitude and love." She knelt and bowed her head. The girls moved forward and slowly released the flowers they held into the fountain while continuing to sing a lovely melody.

Then the girl that held the jar approached Boria and poured a little of whatever was in it on her. It dripped down her head and her back. Boria stood motionless and unmoved by it.

A slight shudder of noise came from the covered basket as the girl holding it placed her hand upon the cover as though to lift it, but she stood waiting for what I assumed would be Boria's command.

The girl with the oil began to pour the rest on the flowers in the fountain, and Boria stood and stepped into the water. Her face was solemn, as though she was in deep thought; after a few steps into the fountain, the girl with the covered basket followed and handed it to Boria. She took it in the same manner it was given to her, one hand upon the top and the other on the bottom.

Standing in the middle of the fountain with the flowers all around her, she looked up, said a few more strange words, then opened the basket to reveal birds that rapidly fluttered their wings and flew up and away from the Temple. The girls stopped singing. Boria watched as the birds flew away, and all became quiet again with just the sound of the water trickling into the fountain.

What the purpose of this was, I did not know. What would an unearthly being as powerful as Samayaza want with flowers, oil, and birds? How did Boria even know this and how to speak a language I knew she did not understand?

Once Boria emerged from the fountain, the girls dried her feet and gathered the baskets and jars. She instructed them with new tasks about another ritual for the morning, and then they left, leaving us alone by the fountain.

I had not moved from where she told me to stand. I was not seeing the sister I once knew and loved. The grief of that revelation brought a trail of tears that rolled down my cheeks.

She saw and tilted her head to one side as she squinted her eyes, trying to understand my reaction. "Why do you cry, Iris?" she asked.

I could not hold back anymore and cried as I spoke. "Because the sister I once knew is no longer standing before me."

Emotions crossed her face. She did not answer me right away.

She stared at me as my tears fell. I could see her thoughts were conflicted as she did not dismiss what I said.

She finally sighed and said, "I am she, Iris." She neared me now and wiped away my tears with her hand. "I am just not a girl who fears the future anymore."

For that brief time, I honestly thought I saw my sister again. Her eyes softened, and her smile was kind. Overwhelmed with emotion, I threw my hands around her in a firm embrace. She held tight for a moment but began to pull free hastily.

"Iris, your embrace is strong enough to kill an ox!" she laughed as she straightened her garments and hair.

Letting out a sigh, I gave her a halfhearted smile. I wanted the moment back. It felt like a little piece of home was here when we embraced, yet she ended it quickly. She must have felt the same, hence my disappointment at her quick dismissal. I knew her, or at least I knew the Boria I grew up with. She was not cold; she wasn't as boastful or arrogant as the Boria standing before me now. I had almost lost all hope for her, but that moment gave me hope. I could get through the cold demeanor I just had. It would just take time and patience. Both of which I had.

"Walk me to my garden, Iris; you may enjoy it." she offered.

My eyes lit up as I knew it was the garden I had seen while on the balcony in her throne room.

I felt our sisterly bond slowly returning. "I knew that was to be your garden!" Eagerly, I followed.

She smiled as we walked through the Temple. All the while, she spoke of the many gods that were now here on Earth. They all had great things to teach us and how most would require priestesses and Seers. She continued to speak of rituals and things I could not understand, but I didn't want to question her since we had finally broken the shell that was so thick between us.

"Once you take on your robe, you will have to obey my commands and follow the temple law in which you abide." she eagerly informed.

"What robe and commands do you speak of?" I asked, confused.

"The robe for becoming a priestess, Iris," she said crossly as if I should have known. "You are the granddaughter of the King, who was also a high priest; thus, you will take your place." She added, "Since I am the Seer, that would leave you with becoming a priestess under my rule."

Her rule? I thought Samayaza was the ruler of this Temple. "So, as Seer, you are to rule this Temple and not Samayaza?"

"Lord Samayaza," she sternly corrected. "I am to rule by his command as I am his favored. And you are to become a priestess or a Seer of another temple if you wish," she said pompously.

This new revelation was troubling. I did not want to be priestess or Seer, nor to abide under her rule or anyone else's. I would not blindly accept what was offered to me as she had. But if I voiced my rejection, she would slip further away from coming home.

"I need time to understand all that you have said." If she believed I was seriously considering all she said, it might gain some trust in our new bond.

"The Temple is gracious, and so are the gods we serve, as long as we do not stray from their teachings." She gently grabbed my hand in comfort but let go all too soon.

She continued speaking about the Temple and the unearthly beings she called gods. I could not help but remember Grandfather Enok's teachings. I kept nodding to her words, but all the while, I started to think back on his stories. It was a distraction I needed to continue gaining her trust, or else whatever little progress I had just made with her would be severed instantly.

He once said there was only one god, for the power that abided in One made no room for others. I tried to remember the other part of that story. Still, with Boria constantly speaking and me trying to pretend I was listening, it made it hard to remember the great history of creation.

Soon enough, we came about her throne room, and she walked behind where she and Samayaza had sat. There was a door I had not noticed; it had a narrow stone passageway leading down to the garden. I could hear the faint sound of the small stream and birds chirping as we neared the opening.

"All you will see is a gift from Lord Samayaza to me," she boasted as she smiled and walked into her garden.

It was enchanting from the moment I set foot upon the soft ground of this majestic area. It was breathtaking. When I was standing above the balcony, I had not seen the details of every plant and creature that lived within this charming garden. Nor had I seen it when the sun was still in the sky. Every ray that came through the opening in the ceiling only elevated the serenity this place breathed. The smell of fertile nature, the sounds of birds singing, the ever-soothing sound of water slowly gently flowing over pebbles, and the smell of exquisite fragrances that the flowers released, were heavenly. My heart felt light and happy. The weight of my burdens lifted away with every step I took further into the garden and toward the stream. This enclosure was the most otherworldly place I had seen since entering this village.

"It is of another realm, is it not?" asked Samayaza, confirming my thoughts.

Abruptly, I turned and watched as he walked in from the entrance we had.

"I favor it as well," he added as he passed by Boria without so much a glance.

She just stood there with her head bowed in greeting as I stood motionless, feeling the weight of all that had lifted quickly return.

I nodded but could not force myself to bow. Boria finally lifted her head and glared at me for not following her lead. I was not bothered by her disapproval but somewhat concerned about why he had appeared. I swiftly grabbed hold of the stone that I had tied around my wrist, hoping to hold it without drawing too much attention. I tried picturing my home and the wall surrounding it, but I could not concentrate. His presence was engulfing, and all I could envision was a faint outline of a home.

"Forgive me—" Boria's started to speak but was silenced as Samayaza lifted his hand.

"She is free to be as she wills." Not once did he look at Boria but was intently looking at me.

Boria's reaction was troubling. She looked dismayed and hurt but obeyed as she stood where she was and said not another word.

"I created all this for one such as yourself. Knowing the elements of this Earth calls to you and those of your kind," he revealed as his voice took on a note of sincerity I had not heard since I first saw him in the throne room.

Scowling, I questioned what he had just said. Boria had mentioned that this was her garden and belonged to her. And by how her face looked vexed, I knew she was not pleased with what Samayaza had just revealed.

"Boria and you are kin, are you not?" he asked amusedly.

Of course, we were. He knew this; I assumed everyone knew we were sisters.

He raised an eyebrow as he took a step in my direction. "If you are kin, you are of the same blood, little Iris."

How was he answering me without hearing my response spoken aloud? I never let go of the stone. Was he reading my thoughts?

Like a vessel of cold water dumped upon my back, I stiffened at this new revelation. He was reading my thoughts like Daniel; my stone was not working.

He winked and teasingly smiled, confirming my suspicion upon my discovery; he was toying with me.

He walked to the stream, all the while holding our gaze. I wanted to look away, but it was like he moved in unison with the flow of this garden, as though he was one with it, like another living creature that dwelled within its flourishing beauty.

"My Lord, the priestesses are waiting by the throne..."

She went silent as he turned toward her. Though I did not hear him speak, I could see the emotions that crossed Boria's face. She reluctantly bowed and left the garden with a final glance toward me as she turned the corner. She was angry, and I knew any progress made with her would be lost now.

With Boria dismissed, I was utterly alone with him. And if my stone did not protect my thoughts, how was I supposed to get out of this place and away from him? I tried to concentrate on my home within my mind, but it was to no avail as the tension and anticipation I felt from his presence overshadowed my will.

I had but one hope; to call upon Daniel, which I did, but I could not hear or sense him. My hands began to tremble as I looked around, hoping to see him appear like he had many times before.

"You look for him—why?" Samayaza's eyes churned blue intensely for a moment. His manner tensed, and I felt the energy in the air thicken. There was no doubt that he controlled the elements in this garden.

"*Daniel!*" I urgently yelled his name in my mind but heard no word from him.

"Am I that frightening to you that you would seek his comfort rather than explore what I offer?" Ignoring my alarmed state, he walked closer; he raised his hand slightly before him, and a majestic colorful bird landed upon it.

The bird, just like everything within this garden, was vibrant in color, perfect in its design, and breathtakingly beautiful as it opened its wings, revealing stunning colors upon its feathers. I was in awe of the bird, but it did not subdue my fears of being alone with him. I knew he held great power, and that alone was frightening enough.

"You are correct; you should not forget my power and strength."

He let the bird fly from his hand as he walked toward me again. Instinctively, I took a step back.

"You are wise to fear me but foolish to think I would harm you in such a way." He stood a mere arm's length away now, and I could see the swirls of blue beginning to churn as they tried to pull me into his will.

I continued walking back, wondering where I would end up other than another step away from him. He did not seem to care; he never lifted his gaze but continued to follow. Rubbing against flowers and bushes, I knew not where I was going. Too afraid to lose sight of this beast of a being, I dared not turn and run. He could outrun me; he could read my thoughts; there was no place I could go that would be safe.

He stopped and grinned at me as he tilted his head in amusement.

I kept walking back until I hit something solid. I reached my hands behind me and felt the bark of the only tree I had seen in this garden. I cringed. In my rush to be as distant as possible from him, I misjudged where I was going. I had strayed as far as possible from what I knew as the only doorway out. Nothing was safe in my mind, so I just continued to call out to Daniel. It did not work the way I had hoped it would.

"You have nowhere to go, Iris." He took two steps and stopped. "Why not embrace what I offer; I can enlighten your mind and show you wonders never witnessed by mortal eyes before." His voice was smooth with temptation, inviting me into unknown territory.

"You are created for so much more than this, Iris." His words became softer, warmer than I had ever heard before. They carried a caress I did not want from him, a comfort I didn't seek.

I looked around in need of escape. Where was Daniel when I needed him most? I called out again and again but heard only silence.

Samayaza eyes narrowed, as it looked as though his patience was running thin. "I can give you what no one else can. I can give you knowledge of all things and make you more powerful than any mortal upon this Earth."

He spoke, but all I could hear were unfamiliar words and the constant reminder that he had lain with my sister and defiled her.

He lifted an eyebrow and smirked at me. He heard what I had just thought.

"Now, why would I make that choice so soon?" he questioned.
What did he mean? "Boria is your chosen, is she not?"

"She has chosen," he corrected. "Yet whether she is *my* chosen is still to be determined."

What he meant by that, I could not understand. He had lain with her, according to Boria. That made her his by his honor. Nothing was making sense—his words, my stone failing, Daniel abandoning me, Boria as well, even if against her will.

"Your fear is of no purpose to you. Calm your heart, Iris. I give you my word; I will not harm you." A look of sincerity crossed his face as he promised, but all I could remember was how he had impaired me in Boria's throne room.

Had Daniel not intervened, I did not know how long I would have endured his onslaught. I opened my mouth to remind him of that but noticed an expression of concern cross his face as he looked down toward my feet. Instinctively, I followed and understood why. A giant serpent had slithered its way around and between my feet!

Terrified, I gasped for breath and screamed for Daniel. I heard nothing in return; he had truly abandoned me.

The serpent was so immense in size that I could hear the rest of its body slither from behind the tree. I felt its cold, scaly skin move against mine and stiffen at the unpleasant feeling. It was indeed the most enormous serpent I had ever seen. It had scales of many colors and shined as though oil were upon it. With no choice, I looked at Samayaza, I pleaded for rescue, but he was still staring at the serpent with furrowed brows.

Its long tongue flicked against my ankle, and it began to throb. The memory of the bite and pain returned to me as I stood frozen. I whimpered in desperation as sweat began to form on my brow. A whimper escaped my mouth, and Samayaza's attention shifted. He finally noticed my distress. He strode along the path over to me, and without even touching the serpent, he lifted me into his arms and began to walk away from the tree.

The pain I felt was not as intense as when first bitten, but it was strong enough that I whimpered in his arms. My head was against his chest, my cheek against the soft yet thick tunic he wore. It smelled of rich spices and smoke. I could hear his heartbeat. It was loud and steady, just like every step he took. He gently put me down by the stream and reached over with his large hands to cup some water. He poured it over the ankle, and suddenly, the pain disappeared.

Relief washed over my face as the pain was no more. I was thankful for it, but how did he know which ankle it was that pained me? There was barely a scar, and I was not holding my ankle at any time. Looking straight into his eyes, I spoke to him like I would to Daniel, "*How did you know?*"

He did not fail me and answered, "*I know everything about you, Iris,*" he whispered as softly as Daniel had. His blue eyes swirled as waves danced within them. He held out his hand and helped me up. I was completely free of pain.

"Who are you?" I needed to know in order to make sense of things.

"I am the one who will make this life bearable for you and your kind." His deep voice was as soothing as the water poured over my aching ankle. But did he speak truthfully?

"You doubt my intentions, little one. Many would perish if they were even to think what you have thought of me." He took a step closer as I again instinctively took a step back. "But I am going to allow you a concession."

He proceeded to explain. "You may ask whatever you wish without any repercussions or punishments. Ask anything at all. I will answer truthfully and allow you to obtain secret knowledge unknown to man. However..." He paused as he walked, circling me. Letting me know he was still in control as he stood right behind me.

"You must be willing to seek me in my garden of your own free will." His voice held an ominous tone that made me weary of what he just offered.

I heard him approach from behind me; then, suddenly, I could feel his breath on my ear. "And willingly open your mind to me, always," he whispered. His words fell like raindrops upon my neck and back, sending a shudder throughout my being. I had no understanding of what he asked for other than the sudden urge just to agree and allow it.

"Where did you come from?" I asked, trying to pull myself out of whatever beguilement I sensed.

"Do you seek me now, Iris?" he whispered in my other ear. "Do you give yourself to my will?"

I could think of no defense, no wall, and no home to protect my thoughts: only his voice and the urge to give him all he requested. Yet I could feel my essence trying to fight this impulse to allow him in. Why did I feel a reluctance and the upper tip of sorrow slicing its way into my soul?

He slowly, almost cautiously, walked around to stand before me. All I could do was stare up at him, bewildered by his presence and captivated by his voice. He silently observed my thoughts, doubts and waiting for my response. He had just saved me from death and pain, had he not? If he wanted my demise, he could have already accomplished that the first time I had approached him. He could have even allowed my evil grandfather to do that in his place.

I thought of offering him my gratitude, followed by more questions: how did he know everything? Was Daniel the same as he was, or would his answering any of these questions now consist of agreeing to his accord?

"Ask anything, Iris," his soothing voice coerced. "Just submit your will to me."

As though in a dream, I thought of no severe consequence to what he asked. I did have many questions that no one would answer truthfully. I could first start with what happened here to test him; why was there an enormous serpent within his garden? Then ask why did Grandfather Enock not warn me of him or Daniel and Azazzel? Why would no one speak the truth of what was happening around me?

"Do you seek me, Iris?"

"Yes," I answered without thought and hesitation.

"I will give you all you seek and more; just will yourself to me?"

Will? Again, he asked for my will. What did it matter if I willed or not? I wanted answers, and I wanted the truth.

"My Lord." Boria's loud voice echoed in the garden and broke whatever enchantment I was in, like out of a dream. I felt heat rise as I stepped away, as his gaze lingered on me.

She hastily continued, "Forgive my disobedience, but Lord Daniel instructed me to summon you immediately." She threw herself to the ground in submission but not before I caught a glimpse of the anger I had seen in her eyes before she was dismissed. I knew our progress had soured. Each time Boria looked upon me with hesitant eyes, I felt a wound within my heart open. We were sisters, bound by blood and family, yet she saw me as a threat to what she coveted. I kept failing her trust and losing any solid ground I had made with her. I bowed in defeat as I did not know how to regain her confidence.

Samayaza's hand lifted my chin as he heard all my thoughts. I felt a tear roll down my cheek as I looked up at him. *"Feel no shame or remorse when in my presence."* The whisper was as light as a bird's feather, yet an order, nonetheless. But those deep blue swirls churned, and I noticed something I had not before; warmth.

I looked away, conflicted.

Without a word, he unexpectedly placed a flower above my left ear and turned around to address Boria.

"Azazzel, take our Seer to her throne room. I will be there shortly." His tone was terse as he ordered Boria away by an escort, none other than him!

Just hearing his name, I turned wildly in Boria's direction. He was standing behind the still-bowing Boria. Compared to the grand, tall, unearthly being that stood menacingly over her, you could barely see her. Though Boria saw me as a threat, I did not see it that way and felt an immediate need to protect her from Azazzel. I took a step forward, only to hear Samayaza in my mind.

*"She is under my watch. No one will touch a hair upon her head,"* he reassured.

His words were not as comforting as he assumed they would be. Daniel had said the same thing, yet he abandoned me when I needed him the most.

Sudden silence ensued. Birds no longer flew about or made a sound. Even the stream seemed to have quieted.

And once again, the air took on a thick cloud of tension, and

I saw Boria slowly lift her head as she looked my way. Though she looked upset, she sensed the shift around us. I could feel the weight of his anger at the mention of comparing him to Daniel; I had fanned a flame that burned bright.

Boria looked as though she was to speak but bowed her head back in submission. He had to be speaking directly to her mind, and whatever he had said silenced her completely.

"My Liege," said Azazzel, bowing his head slightly with a smirk. He waited as Boria got up and escorted her out of the garden as commanded.

Samayaza walked past me, no longer looking at me, as his nonchalant voice entered my head. *"Stay if you wish. The serpent will not harm you. You have my word."*

I stood there motionless yet somewhat relieved to be alone. Somehow, he punished me without lifting a hand or saying a word. I felt chided like a child, punished for something I did not understand. My head pounded with the weight of all that had just transpired. The continued onslaught of my questions became my cane and hindered my cause. How had he done that? How had he made me punish myself with none other than my thoughts and fears? I felt confused and shaken by all that had happened. He had allowed me to stay if I wished. But did I want to stay here? No, I did not.

I ran out of the garden quickly and headed toward my quarters. I could see past the pillars that night was close upon us. The sun was beginning to set, giving off beautiful colors blending and overshadowing the approaching night sky. Temple servants or worshipers looked like they were taking their leave as they gathered baskets and turned incense. Every pit and torch upon the walls were lit with a fire within the Temple, illuminating every hallway. Every fountain I passed had many flowers, except for the fountain near my quarters; there were none. How strange. There had been plenty not too long ago.

I neared the water and did not even see a petal of any flower below or floating above it. No trickle of water was coming in; the water was serenely still and completely clean.

I leaned closer and saw my reflection and something I had forgotten behind my ear. The flower Samayaza had placed. It was the same one I had found by our river and given to me by Daniel. I began believing my unique flower was no longer such a rarity until I smelled it. It was different in its scent. Strange. How could a flower of the same kind hold a different smell?

Of course, his offer of compromise was this flower. I had never imagined him in a moment where he would gently place a flower in my hair as he did. The entire encounter had left me in much doubt. The being I once thought of as cold and as sinuous as a serpent became the one that saved me from such a creature.

Moreover, the one that had promised to protect me was nowhere in sight. Where was Daniel, and how had he not heard me cry out to him? He had always sworn to protect me, and like a fool, I believed in him. I thought that whatever he was and wherever he had come from, he would stay true to his word. Maybe I was as beguiled by him as Boria was of Samayaza. Either way, he had lied and denied my calls to him when I needed him the most.

"I did not deny you," came Daniel's powerful voice from behind me.

# AMONG ANGELS 6

Azazzel stood motionless behind a pillar as he watched the two sisters walk by and enter the crystal garden. A crooked smile appeared on his perfectly chiseled face. "They have entered, My Liege," he said, and Samayaza appeared.

He stood by the entrance, looking to where Azazzel hid in the shadows. "Be on guard. He is aware," Samayaza warned.

Azazzel acknowledged with a nod and stood as ordered. He knew Daniel would have felt the disconnect from his guarded the moment she entered the garden of her own free will. Undoubtedly, he would soon appear at the one place he could not enter. Excitement ran up and down his veins. His mortal body had some interesting sensations he mused; the expectation of confrontation was exhilarating in this form. The thought of Daniel being helpless was something he'd thought he would never witness. He was the most powerful among them, but Samayaza had figured out a way to render him powerless.

Boria walked out of the garden, looking discontented. Not what he wanted to see right now, but it was somewhat entertaining to see her walk back and forth in frustration. It took no effort to read her thoughts; she was furious. She held up no walls and was practically shouting in her mind for anyone to hear.

"Where is she?" demanded a forceful voice belonging to no other than Daniel. He appeared in front of Boria so suddenly that she almost walked right into him.

She gave him a look of displeasure. Azazzel grinned from ear to ear at Boria's aversion to Daniel. This encounter was turning out to be more exciting than he had anticipated.

"What matter is it to you?" she spat out. She despised him and all the others who continued to take her time away from her lord.

"Answer, and I will take her from his attention."

Azazzel saw the turmoil in her head, frantically trying to rid her kin of Samayaza's attention. Mortals were interesting creatures indeed, so quick to satisfy their selfish desires that they were quick to sacrifice their own blood. And just as he expected, she told Daniel where Iris was and how Samayaza had ordered her out of her garden.

How endearing, Azazzel thought; she believed the garden was hers.

"Enter and get her out now," he demanded, gentle but fierce.

Boria looked at him incredulously; as much as she disliked Daniel, she would have obeyed him this one time, but her fear of what Samyaza would do held her in place.

He reveled over Daniel's helplessness and inability to reach his guarded. He had been fooled, and now he knew of the one place she could go, but he could not. Though Daniel did well in protecting his thoughts, he had yet to master the emotions his mortal face displayed.

"Enter and demand I request his audience," he offered another, less damaging way for her to retrieve Iris.

"I will do no such thing!" she answered, though Azazzel could see how badly she wanted to but feared the repercussions of disobeying Samayaza.

Azazzel continued to smile at Boria's defiance toward Daniel. Persistence was indeed a strong trait between these two sisters.

"Are you not the Seer of this Temple? Why do you fear?" Daniel tried another angle now, trying to persuade instead of overriding her will. "It is your garden, is it not?"

Interesting approach, thought Azazzel, as he continued to watch how Daniel maneuvered around her. She had no clue as to what he was doing as her face twisted with emotions at what he had said. Her belief that the Temple and garden were hers was pompous but amusing. Just the thought of them alone in her garden brought a rage of emotion deep within her belly. She had believed in the stars for an escape from a horrible fate, and Samayaza had appeared. He was made for her, the Seer, not her younger sister.

Leaning farther behind the pillar, Azazzel couldn't help but relish the moment. She was practically yelling out these thoughts without even realizing it. He knew Daniel heard everything just as he had. No doubt he would use it against her to reach his guarded.

"His favor is upon you, not Iris."

Ah, clever. Daniel continued to spur her confidence in her

mortal role. It was working as Boria's thoughts of fear were melting away quickly. Defiance took its place. Though her thoughts of Daniel were unpleasant, she believed in what he said. To Azazzel's fascination, she began to walk back toward the garden believing that Samayaza belonged to her and no one else!

Although Azazzel stayed hidden he knew Daniel had sensed his presence when he had appeared. He was making his thoughts easily known to him, which was questionable for Azazzel. He had to be plotting something to be so easily read. He saw half a smile embrace Daniels face at the thought of how Boria's defiant act would irritate Samayaza. Even going as far as saying how Samayaza should be grateful that he had resorted to a peaceful interruption rather than his wrath raining down upon this whole Temple.

Boria walked forth towards the garden with set determination.

That was Azazzels cue to come forward and call Daniel's bluff. "What a sight that would be." Azazzel announced as he emerged from the pillars, "Dramatic fireballs raining from the heavens, turning everything they touched into ash."

Daniel casually turned toward him, knowing he was there all along. "Your devotion is impressive." Looking straight at Azazzel. "I wonder what it is you are promised in return for your obedience."

Azazzel's nostrils flared in annoyance. He knew what Daniel was trying to do, yet he could not hide all his animosity toward his brother within this human form.

"My devotion is to rule among these weak mortals, not protect as you continue to do. Your purpose no longer exists as it did above," he spat out. "Adapt as a new creation or die trying to be the old."

Azazzel's words came out sharp, ready to hurt, to cut deep into Daniel's soul. He wanted to remind him of his disobedience and fall from his holy post. He was no one special anymore; like the rest of them, he would have to fight for power. Swirls of fire overtook his beguiling honey eyes as he stared at Daniel with the intent of challenging his authority.

Daniel was no fool. He would not dare take the challenge while his guarded was with Samayaza, but he wanted Azazzel to know that his powers were no match to his. He began to call energy around him purposefully.

Azazzel mirrored his actions; crackling and whipping sounds echoed as Azazzel merely touched upon his powers. Though Daniel did not flinch, he became curious at how strong his powers had become. He wanted to see more, but Samayaza called Azazzel through the consciousness of the angels.

"Your master calls," said Daniel as he stepped back to allow passage.

Azazzel fumed at the interruption but obeyed as he was bound by oath. Without breaking eye contact, Azazzel walked past him and into the garden.

# AMONG ANGELS 7

D aniel patiently stood waiting, eyes upon the door. He might have underestimated Samayaza's knowledge of the stones deep within the Earth. How could he have come across such knowledge? Only those allowed in all realms were gifted such enlightenment. This was troubling indeed. He would have to confer with Gabril soon. Something was amiss.

He felt a pang of guilt he should not have felt about using Boria to get Iris out. But he quickly disregarded it as she wasn't his guarded, and since she had already given her will freely to Samayaza, he had no authority over her wellbeing. She was Samayaza's now, and any guilt Daniel felt would be the knowledge that this truth would eventually bring sorrow to Iris, as she was her kin.

The garden door opened, and an admonished-looking Boria came with Azazzel behind her. Neither said a word as they passed by and continued down the hall. He had no doubt she was to be escorted to her quarters until Samayaza decided her fate for disrupting his failed attempt to ensnare Iris.

*"Soon enough, there will be no barrier of restraint between us, Daniel the Admirable."* Azazzel's contemptuous voice entered his mind, reminding him that their little spat was far from over.

His threat was nothing new and in no way a surprise. Daniel already knew the extent of what he was capable of. He learned quickly and rarely ever made the same mistake twice. Upon entering this realm, he understood why Samayaza had made him second in command. His hunger for power and recognition was ferocious, as was his pride.

Daniel did not have to wait long after they left. Samayaza emerged from the garden, looking straight into the eyes of his rival, his steps calculated and his eyes swirling with blue rage. Samayaza raised his hand without a word, and at once, they were transported to a realm between Earth and the one where they presided before. The domain was void of any other life other than themselves. Clouds of white were beneath their feet; light illuminated the vast nothingness of white all around them. They stood silently, each looking at the other with disdain and malice. If one could destroy the other, they would. But that would defeat the purpose of their fall.

"You want what you cannot have," stated Daniel.

"Free will is not yours to tamper with, Daniel. I thought you would know that by now," Samayaza teasingly reminded.

"You should do well to remember that the next time you deceive her into your garden," retorted Daniel.

"She came of her own free will; deception was absent."

"Using her kin to force her will is exactly that!" Daniel spat out as he was losing patience with him.

Suddenly the void and calm began to fill with energy that sent sharp shooting rays of light underneath their feet. White clouds above them began to turn dark, and lightning flowed through the darkness that started to engulf the realm.

"We are of equal strength, and you will only bring down His wrath before it is time!" warned Samayaza as he shot a bolt of energy toward him.

Daniel didn't flinch, nor did it cast any doubt in Daniel's mind of who was the more vital being.

Daniel held a deep secret that he would not even allow himself to ponder. He knew they were not equal; the one thing preventing him from destroying Samayaza right now was that his fall would be in vain and destroy a creation meant to bring about the new age. He was not going to allow one of the seven most deadly traits within mortals to ruin his plans; his pride would not triumph over his will. He would stay the course until the heavens above were ordered to rain down upon them for their transgressions.

"We are indeed," Daniel answered calmly, allowing Samayaza to believe they were equal. He collected himself and permitted the calm to extend into the void, returning it to its original state.

Samayaza's smirk was impudent, thinking he had done well with his show of power. Though gathering energy in a place that held nothing was as impressive as Daniel bringing forth darkness into it. Samayaza chuckled at how quickly Daniel had resorted to darkness as a form of power.

"Daniel, you are sinking into sin faster than I had ever imagined." He laughed, and it echoed throughout the realm. "It's almost too perfect."

Daniel held his pose; his jesting would not succeed in receiving a response.

"Let us return and continue our..." Samayaza paused, trying to find the right word, "subduing of Earth, shall we?" Samayaza's invitation was sickening. He considered this a game, a mere rivalry of wits and power. He knew not the dangers of what he was doing, of how he was invoking a punishment that he could never even fathom. Daniel knew of a darker force that had entered Samayaza, so he trod cautiously. For now, he would allow him to continue to believe what he wanted. Soon enough, Samayaza would see the error of his ways, and if he did not, then may the Creator have mercy on them all.

With a simple nod, they descended to Earth. Samayaza made his way to Boria for her disobedience, and Daniel found his guarded by the fountain again with thoughts of betrayal spinning in her mind, of none other than him.

He knew he had failed her, but he had not abandoned her or what she cared for in this realm. His choices were few, and his powers were limited on Earth. It was the cost he paid upon his dissension. He watched her as she allowed the deceptive seed Samayaza had planted within her heart to take root slowly. His soul retracted at the notion, and though he wanted to burst forth and show her everything for what it was, he knew it would completely overwhelm her human senses, and she would close herself off to him and everyone else. Her soul would wither for a time, and that would give the darkness precisely what it wanted.

He continued to watch as she realized the flower behind her ear wasn't the same as the flower he had gifted her long ago. She could tell by what he had purposely allowed for that flower to have that Samayaza had not permitted; the scent of this beautiful Earth and the elements that gave it that unique and precise beauty. He allowed the formula to manifest to that unique essence only her senses could covet.

He was pleased to see her question the flower and the intentions under which it was given. She knew something felt wrong, but her overtired mind allowed the simple and least admired emotions to fill her thoughts. She was allowing herself to believe what was simple and pleasing while beginning to lose faith in herself. Her continued questions were an attack on herself and her strength of will. Again, he felt the urge to intervene but pulled himself back and allowed her to gain discernment on her own. She may be wise enough to notice how quickly temptation and deception had taken root within her.

*"He had lied and denied my calls to him when I needed him the most."*

He heard what he had never wanted to hear coming from her, whether aloud or in her thoughts. She believed he had left her and allowed harm to come to her. She felt he had not even thought of her during the brief time he'd lost connection with her. He winced as he could now hear that she had called out to him not once but many times.

He searched her mind knowing it was intrusive, but he needed to know all that had transpired within the garden. He felt her fascination with seeing the majestic vegetation and animals within and the hurt she felt upon seeing Boria's jealousy. He saw the moment of lust that came upon her, the fear and pain she had endured. Daniel scowled at a memory; a residue of darkness lingered; it was not from any of his brethren that fell but a more ancient being he now realized was making his presence known more freely.

Yes, he had misjudged his enemy and failed her in what she believed to have been a moment of life or death. But he had not denied or forsaken her in the way she presumed; his entire being of fire and clay flooded in a fury of what she had just thought. He could no longer hide anymore. She was questioning everything about him and herself.

He burst forth from hiding, loudly proclaiming, "I did not deny you!" his voice etched with the frustration of his failure.

# CHAPTER THIRTEEN

**D**aniel's booming voice broke my thoughts as I abruptly turned around toward him, releasing the flower into the fountain.

Standing between the pillars, majestic and imposing as ever. His eyes held both fury and pain. Though his presence had always brought a sense of safety and power, the air between us held tension this time. Something felt lost between us, and at the moment, I did not care nor want to know what it was.

"Then where were you when I called for you?" I could not hide the disappointment in my voice, and he winced at my accusation as though I had cast a blow across his face. But I did not care how harsh I might have sounded; I was left alone in a place with a being that I'd never wanted to be alone with.

"There are reasons to my absence, none of which I can reveal to you." He took a step forward. "Nor would you be able to discern my plight or yours."

I could not believe my ears. Did he believe me to be daft? Did he think I could not grasp what life had become for me here?

"If that is your only reason not to speak truth, then you know nothing about me." My voice quivered as I felt inner anguish at his misconception. Yes, I felt betrayed by almost everyone around me. I felt tired and weak to the point where I wished to escape somewhere far away and never be found. I felt confused, too curious for my own sanity, and cautious over everything and everyone I encountered, and it was draining to my being. But I was of sound mind!

He began to walk toward me.

"Do not." I motioned with my hand.

I did not want to be lost and captured in his beguilement. Nor did I want to forget what I had just experienced with Samayaza or Daniel's lie. I ensured he heard my thoughts clearly as if I had said them aloud. His face instantly saddened and almost mirrored the same hurt within mine at my rejection of him.

I needed space from them, some time to rest and decipher the truth in all that I had seen. I knew he could still hear me; I made sure of it as I did not look away from his sorrow ladened eyes. No swirls were within them, just the lush green that even the vegetation in the garden could not compare to.

I needed to go.

"*As you wish,*" he whispered, stepping aside to allow me to leave.

Without a word, I walked past him, knowing that even though he allowed me to leave, he would follow and stand guard at my quarters. But what good was that now when the time I needed him the most, he was not there? How could I believe his words if he did not want to speak the truth or offer it like Samayaza?

I walked by several servants that bowed as I passed them, knowing they were bowing because Daniel was behind and not because of me. They only bent that low when they were in the presence of these beings. Whether they bowed out of fear or favor, I did not care to understand anymore. I had to make sense of more urgent matters.

I entered my quarters and headed straight to my room. I did not look back to check if he stood by the door; I just wanted to be alone without anyone telling me what to think, say, and do. I needed time to myself.

To my great surprise, I was left alone for the rest of the day and evening. Every now and then, I would peer out through the window and hear everyone going about their daily lives. At times it was deafening; other times, it was deadly quiet. All would hush and bow low as these beings would walk past. Some would throw flowers before their feet as they continued to bow in reverence.

I was surprised to see so many of these beings, something I had not considered before. I counted about seventy-seven, each carrying different staff-like objects in their hands or on their person. Some items were short and shined as the sun reflected upon them, while others were longer and clung to their sides. Though I could not see their faces directly, I could tell by their stature that they were all perfectly designed in appearance, like Samayaza and Daniel.

All the people were in awe even after they had passed by. It was odd witnessing the effect these beings had on everyone, including myself. They indeed held some power, beguilement, or trickery that was hard to deny. The closer they stood, the stronger one felt it. Their imposing will overcome the senses and indulge whatever they want someone to feel. I wondered how many times Daniel had done the same. How was he any different from the rest of them?

*"In time, you will know."* His calm voice gently entered my mind.

Daniel's voice fell like a feather in my mind, delicately responding to my question yet not answering it. *Please let me be within my own thoughts*, I pleaded.

Instantly, I felt the same void I had felt in the garden and knew he was no longer listening. It felt soothing yet lonely now that he had let me be.

The drastic change of what my life had once been and now was no more seemed unreal. It was as though the sun had turned into the moon, and the moon was now called the sun! I felt furious, hurt, confused, ashamed, and alone. One moment, I was reunited with my entire family, and within a few breaths, each one was taken away from me. And the only kin I had left had become someone completely different, unrecognizable from who she used to be. The few glimpses I caught within her eyes of remembrance quickly faded. Something deep within her fought to keep whomever she was now dominant.

Father and Mother were gone. But I knew they were safe. Grandfather Enok's word was always faithful and solid. If he said they were safe, then they were as he spoke. I missed them and longed for their comfort. How incongruous to know Boria was a short distance away, yet she was as foreign to me as the other villagers here. Tears rolled down my face as I wondered which circumstance hurt more.

If only Grandfather were here now to confide in and help me resolve the conflicts within my mind. Even though he was not forthcoming with the truth of what was happening either, I knew he would have given me words to guide me out of this emotional turmoil.

I needed to heed what he had told me and practice; it was a better option than allowing my thoughts to overtake me. So I closed my eyes and tried to imagine my quaint, humble home deep within my mind. I pushed all my feelings, thoughts, and secrets into it as I imagined the magnificent wall surrounding and protecting it. Though my home might have looked weak in structure, the wall encompassing it was as solid as the temple walls I was in. Which would be more helpful, my home or the wall? I probably should work harder on the little dwelling I had created, but I could not keep everything contained; my mind kept wandering.

I knew Grandfather Enok would be glad I followed through on this task and at least continued to practice, though I did not have much success this time. It was toilsome, but I had accomplished something today, and with that thought, I allowed slumber to take over. The sun was still high, and people were busy with daily chores and worries, but I slept deeply.

I awakened hoping it was still day but noticed the sun was lower than when I had slumbered, meaning I had slept the day away.

The calm and peace I had felt upon waking up diminished as I realized I was still within the Temple. My worries returned, flooding my mind like an overflowing river. Though the river was not raging and engulfing everything as before, it still raged with rough waters; I needed more time to rest.

I stayed within my quarters for a few days and nights alone. I only came out occasionally to some nourishment and water that was left daily. They always brought more than I could ever consume in a day. I would see Daniel standing by the door with his back turned to me as he had been days ago. I wondered how he did not tire of standing guard or if he hungered or felt thirst. I wanted to be kind to him, as he had been to me, but I needed to think of a course that would lead me out of this place safely or at least find peace to help me survive within this world; without his influence or that of any others.

I knew my choice was simple. I needed to either wade through these rough waters or yield to them. There was no other option. I needed to learn everything about these beings and their powers. How else would I get the truth if I did not go out and find it myself? My stone had proven to be useless against them; the being that had promised to be my guardian had failed, and my kin was too lost within her fear to see that what she had immersed herself in was a much worse fate than the one she almost had before.

Or was it? As much as I wanted to block doubt, I needed to question everything. What if, in my quest, I found the truth, and it was nothing like I would expect? What if all that was happening was for the better, and I could find peace, rest, joy, and maybe reunite with my family? I had to begin somewhere in this journey, and the only place I knew I could take that first step was within Boria's circle of priestesses. If I allowed her to show me whom she had become, she could lead me to the truth of these beings, her place within this Temple, and possibly a way to escape.

With new intentions, I refreshed myself with new garments I found in the central area of my quarters. I knew the temple servants had to have brought them in while I had slumbered. They were pretty in color, with beautiful hues of purple and green etched with unique, sun-colored stitching. They brightened my mood and brought a smile to my face.

Daniel was at the door as I had expected, standing protectively with his back toward me while facing the hallway. I felt conflicted about him again. Just when I believed he would be the one to guide me through these trials I was facing, he was nowhere in sight. I would leave these thoughts of him alone for now and tuck them behind the wall I had erected within my mind. If I were to practice what Grandfather Enok had advised, I needed to start now, not later. The rest would be easy if I could learn to keep him out of my head.

"I hope you succeed," he said with his back still to me.

My first attempt had obviously failed upon his remark. This was starting differently than I had planned. I wanted to ask him why he could not teach me, why he was here, or why any of them were here. But I already felt his presence leave my mind. He knew my wishes and honored them partially. He sometimes tended to interject a thought or two but never honestly answered my questions. I would need to solve this unaided to get to the truth, but I needed to get past him for now.

"I would like to see my sister. If you know where she is, please guide me to her." I tried to be firm, but I knew it came out as a plea rather than a demand.

He did not say a word for a moment, and I thought that would be my answer, but he slowly stepped out and stood to one side, "I will guide you as you wish, princess."

I paused and looked down; he had never addressed me as a princess or refused to look at me when speaking. Hesitantly, I walked forward as he began to lead the way. As we walked, I tried many times to say something, anything to take away this cold and awkward moment we found ourselves in. But I could not; I just stayed the course, silently following him like a sheep to her shepherd.

We walked past the fountains and hallways with grand pillars, realizing how small and insignificant it made me feel. Was I being overzealous in my ambitions to seek the truth? Would they figure out what I was doing before I had a chance to find the truth? I shook my head and tried to push thoughts of doubt away. I could not change my course because I had no other to follow. I needed to continue whether I doubted myself or not. Whether I succeeded or failed.

We passed many more servants than usual. They placed vessels of something throughout the Temple or at least the areas we passed. One accidentally dropped a jar and stood frozen, staring at Daniel, waiting for his inevitable punishment. But Daniel kept walking past him and the others. He did not even turn his head in their direction. I could see the relief wash over their faces as they quickly picked up the broken pieces from a puddle of what looked to be water. Strange. Why were vessels of water being placed throughout the Temple?

Naturally, I waited for an answer within my mind from Daniel but remembered I had exiled him from my thoughts. I felt bereft of his companionship. It saddened me, yet it was what I had asked for. I clearly said it openly in my mind, so I hoped he had heard. And if he had, he chose not to answer.

We reached my sister's throne room, and he stepped aside to allow me entrance. "I will be here if you need my guidance."

He spoke without even a glance in my direction again. I nodded and walked past him into Boria's throne room. I felt it once more, deep within my mind—the emptiness instead of his reassuring voice. A rapid rush of fear swept over me. What was I supposed to do if I needed him to protect me? Then I remembered how he had not been there the last time I needed him to guard me, yet I had survived.

Not wholly confident in that thought, I had no other course to take, so I continued looking for Boria. I was going to accomplish what I had set out to do; I just had to focus.

I saw the priestesses here and there and servants preparing what looked to be their morning meal. I saw fresh fruits and delicate dates placed perfectly on beautiful vessels. I could smell freshly made bread, and my mouth watered as my stomach ached in hunger. I should eat something, but what if it was against protocol? I should find Boria first.

I finally spotted her. She stood close to the balcony with her back toward everyone. She stood off to the side, somewhat leaning on a pillar.

I reached where she stood. "Greetings, Boria."

She did not move.

"Why have you come?" her voice was strained and quiet.

I was surprised at her response and did not know what to say. Should I ask what was the matter or pretend to have not heard the hurt in her voice? I decided on the first since she would remind me that was not what she asked of me now.

"I would like to abide by your practice if you will have me?" I requested in what I hoped was a genuine enough plea for her to believe and accept me.

"You know not what you ask," she replied nonchalantly, still not turning to look at me but staring off toward her garden.

I knew something was wrong, yet I had no understanding of how to approach her. She was a different person. Any time I tried to rekindle our past, she would seal the conversation before I could fully speak my thoughts. And the encounter with Samayaza in the garden created a much larger mess as she now thought I wanted him the way she did.

Remembering how she had looked at me with such bitter jealousy poked at the sore within my heart. Our bond never had a wound like this before. I wondered if it would ever heal.

Perhaps I needed to apologize. "Forgive me for my trespass upon that which is yours, sister. It is not my intention nor my wish for how things occurred that day in your garden."

She straightened slightly upon my mention of her garden and apology but stood facing away.

"You know it is not what you or I wish, but what they wish and will." Her voice was uncaring and tinged with hurt.

"As you say, sister, hence my plea to be under your direction and learn."

She finally turned around, and I saw the dried trail of tears from her beautiful eyes. She looked so hurt, more so than that night on the roof of our home. My heart ached for her again, and even though I wanted to reach out and comfort her, I knew the new Boria would not allow it.

"Fine. Let it be as you ask, but you enter into a world you know nothing of," tersely she answered as she walked away, leaving me to stare after her like a helpless child.

"I'm already in that world," I quietly whispered.

A moment later, one of the priestesses approached with a cloak and instructed me to wear it while we traveled to the bathhouse. Without question, I did as they directed. This was what I had planned and expected; to comply and learn as much as possible. I knew things would change, and I wasn't even surprised to see Daniel was gone when we walked out of the throne room. So much for slow changes, I thought to myself.

Three priestesses and four unearthly beings I did not recognize escorted us out. Each time their eyes met mine, there was an intense pull to go near them. To stay within their sight and allow their will; so I decided it best to keep my head down for now and avoid their gaze. It was startling, and I often had to hold back calling on Daniel—if he would even hear me.

We came out of the Temple through another passage I had not been through before. It was longer and smaller in width. The unearthly beings had to walk one ahead of another while we could continue walking two by two. The air was musky, and the stones around us were moist. The only light illuminating our way was a torch one of the unearthly beings held. As we approached a corner, I finally saw what looked to be sunlight peering in through an opening. The two unearthly beings before us were the first to step into the day. They stood on either side of the tunnel as we came out. The burst of fresh air was welcoming, as were the many aromas that lingered. We were in the marketplace again.

The villagers went about their day as usual but became silent upon seeing us and bowed as we walked past them. I saw the baker with many fresh round bread loaves, all beautifully laid out for hungry villagers. I, too, was tempted to grab one, but I knew better than to take something without being able to trade something in return.

My curiosity overtook my anxiousness for a little while as we traveled through the market. Though the people looked similar in what they wore and how they painted their faces, the things they created were not. From vessels, spices, baskets, and provisions, they all had a unique look, smell, and what I assumed would be taste had I been able to consume them.

I felt so out of place. Everyone continued to bow as we walked by; I heard their whispers and felt their gaze upon me as I looked back. I wished they could keep as they were in their tasks and disregard our intrusion. Who was I for them to think themselves lowlier and bow? Maybe they were bowing because of the unearthly beings rather than myself? Either way, it was uncomfortable. I tried to look for the stand that Gabril had been in when I first met him. I had no luck. Another tradesperson had replaced his table. Though I felt sad, I thought it was for the best since the last time my escort threatened him for just wanting to speak with me.

As we approached the bathhouse, my troubles doubled. Azazzel stood guard with other beings of his kind at the entrance. He stood in front as though waiting for us while the rest stood in a unison line behind him, blocking the entire front of the bathhouse. Immediately, I hid my face further into my hood, hoping I would get past without seeing his lecherous eyes.

I purposely fell a foot behind the priestesses around me, positioning myself in the middle. I prayed to the heavens that I could go unnoticed, but that did not happen. Suddenly, the three priestesses around me knelt on the ground. I now stood face to face with Azazzel. One of the priestesses on my right tugged on my cloak from her kneeling position. I paid her no attention as I would never bow to Azazzel. I will never forget his intent to harm my mother.

I could feel his scorching gaze upon me, demanding I look at him and kneel. I would not. All at once, I could feel the air thicken around me; an unfamiliar hum and a sudden ache entered my head like someone was tapping it continually from within. Each tap becomes more substantial and painful than the previous. The priestess on my right stopped tugging, and I knew why. I heard footsteps coming near, but the pain in my head distracted me from knowing which direction it came from; it had to be Azazzel.

"Let her pass," I was wrong as Daniel's threatening order came in loud and clear behind me.

I turned toward his voice in gratitude while thanking the heavens they had heard my plea.

"Now, why would I do that?" Azazzel asked cunningly.

I felt the air chill around us though we stood under direct sunlight. I knew something was not good when the air changed in such a manner. My head still ached, but a tingle of warmth came at me through my cloak behind me, slowly ridding the cold and pain away. Was Daniel pushing away what Azazzel was trying to assault me with?

Unfamiliar words came out of both beings. It was odd and rough to the ear, but somehow, each word ended in a smooth and finished manner. Almost like eating a honeycomb without the honey but being given a spoonful of the golden liquid at the end to help swallow it down. I tried my best to remember certain words I kept hearing coming from both of their mouths. After a final word from Daniel, I slowly looked up to see that the path to the bathhouse was clear. Although Azazzel's legs stood where they had been, the other unearthly beings moved and made way to pass.

The priestesses rose from their kneeling positions and escorted me in safely without any trouble or word from Azazzel again. I wanted to reach out to Daniel and thank him, but I held back from trying to connect with him. If I were to build strength within, I needed to do this alone, though I realized my success in this encounter was only successful because he had intervened. Without Daniel, I stood no chance against Azazzel. Any unearthly being would be able to dismantle me right now. I neither had the power nor strength of mind to deny them from knowing my thoughts. That slight fear made me wish Daniel would follow us into the bathhouse and stand guard. But only hearing the light footsteps of the priestesses, I knew I was on my own.

"You did well, my dear, as he had to peer into your mind instead of just reading it," praised the older woman Azazzel had tried to harm but could not.

"Come." She gestured and pointed toward the narrow paths that led to the perfumed waters. "I have been waiting for you for a while now," she said as she continued to walk in front of us.

"You have?" I asked curiously.

She turned to me with kindness in her eyes that was not there before. "I have much to tell you and little time to do so."

I nodded and followed her to the baths. I mused over how this encounter with her differed from the one I'd had before. Gone were the scolding eyes and the harsh voice. What had changed, or had I envisioned her wrong the first time?

As I entered the room with the large basin filled with water, steam rose as colorful petals steeped within its warmth. The fragrance that filled the air was sweet and delightful to the senses. I instantly felt my spirit lifted and at ease. Without resistance, I allowed the priestesses to help me undress and gather my hair above my head before I entered the bath. The water was pleasing, as were the petals that kissed my skin as I swam through them. I could already see the streaks of sweet oil the petals had released within the water. This bath was genuinely exquisite, something I had neglected to notice before.

After a time, once I had scrubbed myself clean, I wondered where the older woman had gone to. Had she not said she had much to discuss with me and little time to do so?

"I did," came her voice as she entered the room.

How did she do that? She read my thoughts as though she was like them! "How can you read my thoughts?" I asked, startled, as I sank lower into the water.

I must have looked frightened as she walked in slowly, explaining, "Your mind is the center of your being. You can open and close it at will, just as you open and close your eyes, mouth, and hand. As you learned these as a babe, you must now learn and control your thoughts according to your will."

I nodded as though I understood and continued to listen intently.

"When you speak in your mind or aloud, you have already sent out the energy needed to make the thoughts and words known to anyone or no one but yourself."

"Energy?" I inquired.

"Yes, energy, Iris. The energy that comes from within is where the spark of life resides. It is where you existed before you arrived in this world. This energy creates all, and all are able to connect if they choose."

She continued to speak as she walked around the bath. "The one knowledge lost to many is how to open and close that connection to one another." Stopping, she looked down at me, "This is the skill you must learn and where Enok should have explained instead of the fables he filled your mind with," she said sourly.

"You know of my grandfather?"

"Yes." She sighed. "I was the one to help your mother escape this place long ago."

I felt the excitement rush into me as this revelation. "You knew of my mother when she was a maiden here?" I needed to know everything from her past. "Please tell me what happened to her mother, my grandmother?"

Her eyes turned downward as her face mourned a past I wished to know.

"Please tell me. Everyone continues to hide the truth."

Without any further pleading, she finally told me her name—Hilanya. She told me how she helped my mother escape a fate that would have been the same as her mother's. "Your mother was fearful of her father, as most all were. She obeyed in fear and dared not question his authority, no matter how savage his rule had become." She paused as she sat down on a stool.

"It was in a fit of rage that Turian confessed to murdering her mother and that he should have done the same with her. Had it not been for your father and Enok, he would have had her sacrificed that night. They struck a bargain. At the time, Turian needed loads of dried grass that grew so easily in your village due to the river. They promised to yield whatever amount needed in exchange for your father being allowed to marry your mother." She rose again and started pacing.

"He agreed to this under the condition that their first-born child was to wed a suitor of Turian's choosing. Though hesitant, your parents agreed, thinking he would perish by the time they had a child old enough to wed.

"But that didn't happen," I muttered.

She looked in my direction. "Yes, that unfortunately did not happen. I blame your grandfather Enok for not instructing you girls about what would come."

"But how did you help if Father and Grandfather made the bargain? And how had they met before?" I asked curiously.

She smiled as she walked and sat back down. "I was the one who pushed the thought into Turian's mind. And your father and mother had met a season before while your father was trading in the marketplace. I was with her and noticed the sudden joy in her spirit at seeing him." She smiled as though remembering that day, "I arranged for them to meet several times after that to make sure your mother was certain of her fondness for your father. Once she confided in me that she was, I pushed the thought into Turian's mind."

"His mind?" How did she do that, I wondered.

"In time, you will learn to speak with the mind rather than the mouth." She went on about how we could connect to the path that led to each other and the heavens but stopped short of saying exactly how.

"How is this done, and where did you learn all this? Who taught you all that you say?" Had these beings counseled her, and if so, for how long had these beings been here?

"Iris, you ask too much too soon," she cautioned as she evaded the truth I sought. However, her voice was less harsh than before.

Negating my questions, she instead spoke of strengthening

the mind again. How was I supposed to understand what they continually said if they could not give me the cornerstone of what it rested on? Hiding pieces of information that I needed was not helping me reach the potential they thought I had.

*"I can give you all you seek," came a gnarled masculine voice that hissed out each word within my head.*

I gasped in fright at this new voice.

"What is it, child?" asked Hilanya as she noticed my fear.

I looked at her, knowing she knew and there was no way to hide it. "I heard someone in my mind just now."

Instinctively, she looked around, squinting at every corner of the large basin I was still in.

"What was said?" she asked as she continued eyeing the room.

"It promised what I seek." A chill went down my back, causing me to shiver even though I was in a steaming bath.

She looked at me for a while, trying to figure out who it was, but I remained silent, for it was a voice I had never heard. If one can even call it that. It sounded more like a hiss of a serpent.

Relenting, she sighed as she said, "Sometimes, there will be enemies who will seem like companions. Do not be fooled by their hollow words, lest your life be in vain," she stated ominously.

Without another word about what I had just heard, she got up and instructed me to prepare for more lessons in the coming days. I complied, as I did not want to dwell on that startling voice.

I was to practice all she advised and that she would be pushing into my thoughts to ensure I learned what I should have been taught long ago. Her grim demeanor returned as she left the room and sent in the priestesses.

I had barely a moment to think before being led to another room with a smaller bath and more flower petals than the previous one. I had never been in this small room. The scent of the petals was much more potent, and the steam rising from the water was very visible. Upon closer observation, I noticed the water was murky and had taken on the various hues of the flowers in it. Some flowers were fresh, while others had begun to wilt and sink to the bottom.

I placed a foot in the bath and felt the scorching heat of the water. How was I supposed to submerge my entire body in this? I felt the sting and breathed in as deeply as possible, trying to manage the discomfort.

"If you submerge yourself at once, it will be less painful, my princess," said one of the priestesses.

I looked at her incredulously. It was the one who had tugged at my side when we were outside the bathhouse when I refused to bow to Azazzel.

"What is your name?" I asked.

She looked down as she answered, "Calara, my princess."

I had not meant to make her uncomfortable. I just wanted to learn the names of those I would be around. "Calara," I repeated. "Tis a beautiful name."

She looked up and smiled.

"Have you been in these waters, Calara?"

Grinning, she looked at me and nodded.

I should follow her advice if she knew what it felt like since she had experienced these waters. So, I took her word and did what she said; I threw myself off the edge into the steaming floral stew.

I felt the sting of the heat, but as I bared down and touched the bottom, the waters below were cool. I opened my eyes and saw clear waters around me; how mystifying! I had never seen or imagined anything like it! I quickly rose to the milky warm top and felt heat on the upper part of my body and cool below. This was very peculiar indeed.

Calara and the other two priestesses noticed my awe upon surfacing. "It is odd but quite refreshing," she said as the other two chuckled.

"Yes, it is." I agreed, as it was invigorating to all my senses.

Once I had sated my fascination with the bath, I stepped out. I smelled lovely. The oils from the flower petals had absorbed into my skin. Each priestess took on the task of dressing me, coloring my face, and combing my hair. I was enjoying the lavish treatment until I remembered the voice I had heard while in the presence of Hilanya. Who was that voice, and why had it offered me something that only one other had offered? It was not Samayaza, as it carried a scratchy note that Samayaza's or Daniel's voice did not have. It was not Azazzel either; though his voice was harsh, it was not as sinister as the one I heard.

Those questions plagued me throughout the following days, during which I visited the bathhouse daily and went through the same path with the same priestesses and guards. Azazzel never attempted to block our entrance, and Daniel was only ever present when I was in my quarters at night. He stood with his back toward me, not saying a word, rarely turning to close or open the door. I had not seen his lush green eyes in days nor heard him in my mind. He always stood close when present but seemed so far away, untouchable. I felt regret seeping into my heart slowly, and I did not try to push it away. I came so close to asking him about the unfamiliar voice I had heard but held back every time. Deep within my heart, I knew that if I truly needed him again, he would not forsake me as he had before. Or at least that is what I told myself to comfort my fears.

Hilanya was the same every day, demanding that I practice everything she revealed and conduct her assessments by trying to break into my thoughts. I could feel the pressure in the front part of my head as she did so and imagined my wall each time. Sometimes, she could break through; other times, I could keep her out for a small amount of time before I would fail and allow my thoughts to wander. That would earn me a scolding that reminded me of my mother. Hilanya was similar to her in that way. That could be why I had the urge to see her every day and obeyed her instructions.

After the baths each day, I was taken back to the throne room, where Boria would instruct us all about protocol and how each unearthly being was gifted. How all had the power to alter our lives as they saw fit. And how each of us here could be chosen to become a Seer for their temples. She spoke about how we were to pray and worship them as the living gods among us, how we would only flourish under their guidance and protection. And more importantly, how we would usher in the age of enlightenment for all generations.

She spoke like I had never heard before, so confident in herself, not once wavering in anything she said. Gone was the Boria who flirted with dreams and shied away from assertiveness. She had developed, accepted, and believed the false foundation built beneath her feet. Though my heart ached, and doubt often came to visit, I knew I could not give up on her. If I were to be her silent guard, like I believed Daniel might be to me, I would take on that role for her. I would continue to do as she said and follow her ways, but my heart would never be in it as hers was. At least, that is what I planned.

On the eve of a full moon, I rose from sleep to the sound of my door opening. The moon's light shined through the window but not far enough to where I could see who had entered. Alarmed, I called out, "Daniel?" I hoped it was him.

"No, it is I, your sister."

I saw Boria's silhouette as she came forward into the moonlight. She wore a cloak and lowered her hood as she neared my side.

"Remember what you wished for?" she asked as she reached for my hand.

Still dazed, I answered no.

"You wished to be under my direction, my rule. So now you must be witness to what you have asked for."

I heard her words but barely understood what she said as the cloud of sleep was still over me. I decided to trust her word and follow. She helped me dress and quickly braided my hair. I followed her out of the room and past the door where Daniel usually stood guard. But he was not there; that struck me as odd. He was always there. Should I reach out to him, or did he know I was with Boria, hence his absence?

"Come quickly, as we need the moon's full light." She grabbed my hand, and we hurried down to the fountain where I had seen the first ritual she had personally performed with her priestesses. The moon was incredibly bright and lit the area of the fountain in a blue light as it shimmered upon the water.

She came near and whispered in my ear, "This is the blood I must spill for my disobedience." She kissed my cheek and continued, "Now you will witness my pain, sister." Her voice took on a vengeful tone.

Before I could comprehend what she said, numerous priestesses came forth from either side of the fountain. Some held vessels, while others had white clothes that lay across their hands and dropped to the floor as they encircled the fountain. Boria spoke words in a foreign tongue. I knew not of what she said, but I knew it was the same tongue the unearthly beings spoke.

"*Tekat, almanaye dilush maher,*" she shouted, standing at the fountain's edge and looking up toward the moon with her eyes closed and hands raised as though she was calling upon someone.

A shiver shook me as I looked on with alarm and fear. Two large unearthly beings appeared suddenly behind her. One had within its arms what appeared to be a small white animal. The water seemed to drip down, and something was hanging from it, possibly twine. I took a step closer to get a better view.

By the heavens, it was a newly born lamb with its cord still hanging off from its belly!

What were they doing with it? It should be with its mother, nursing while she cleaned it. What kind of cruel and barbaric act was this, to take it away from its mother? Boria knew all this as I did. Why was she allowing such a scene?

"*The price of disobedience is paid with blood,*" the scaly voice whispered again within my mind, multiplying my fears.

I tried to move, but I could not. Though I felt no fingers upon me anywhere, my feet and hands felt anchored like heavy stones. My heart leaped in panic, and I reached out for Daniel. This time, I held nothing back and demanded he stop whatever was happening!

The faint cries of the newborn lamb cut across my soul as I tried to reach it. I screamed to Boria, but she did not hear me or see my protest against this blasphemous ritual! The being with the newly born lamb neared Boria, who held an object that glistened in the moonlight. Before I could even figure out what it was, she brought it down so fast upon the lamb that I heard the painful cry escape. Tears rained down as everything around me seemed obsolete.

Boria looked toward me finally. "This is all because of you, Iris! You did this!" Her face was mangled with rage and pain as she showed me her bloodied hands.

"It's because of you, Iris."

I cried out my regrets, but she continued repeating that I was to blame.

"Iris! Awaken!" said a feminine voice.

I snapped open my eyes and sat straight up, breathing heavily on my bed. My mind tried to discern the dream from reality.

"What did you see while in slumber?" Boria asked, annoyed.

I thought she was concerned, but upon looking at her, I knew she was not.

"Nothing, just foolish things," I muttered, hoping it would deter her questions or curiosity.

"Well, foolishness brings about trouble, Iris," she chided. "Rise, and let us begin early. If you are to be within my faction, then we need to rid you of any obtuseness. You have caused enough friction within us as it is. Rise and be ready. My priestesses will help you prepare," she ordered. As she left the room, I saw her long, beautiful dress flowing behind her.

"If you may, princess, rise so we may dress you," said Calara.

I had not noticed her come in. Waking from a horrible dream to see Boria's sullen face only added to the distortion. As I rose and allowed them to help me dress, I could see the morning sun had just emerged, meaning I had slept the entire night away without waking. Even more curious was that I could not remember when I laid down and closed my eyes. It must be all these baths and oils; they had an effect I was enjoying. The scents were calming, and my skin carried them now always. Still, it was unusual for me not to remember such a simple thing.

"Oof, please, not so tight," I pleaded. The priestess braiding my hair was pulling so hard I could feel the hair being plucked out. She said nothing but gave a meager bow of the head. Her face was painted like the others, but she looked angry. She had a tight lip, her nostrils were flaring, and her eyebrows were pulled close together as though she was ready to yell at someone. I assumed she was not happy about attending to my needs. If only she knew that I did not care for her help and would be fine dressing and preparing myself for the day. I wondered if she had been taken from her family like Selah, hence her displeasure. It was possible if such a way of life was common here.

*Selah*. I prayed she was doing well now with her family and living the life she deserved. I hoped to see her sweet face soon. Maybe later, as the day progressed, I could inquire about her with Daniel. I felt so distant from him now. Almost every day since he'd stopped speaking directly to my mind, I had felt the cold void where his strong, warm, comforting voice once resided. I thought to myself, what an unusual reflection. How could someone live within your mind? And then, feeling as though I had lost a part of myself when he no longer invaded my thoughts. My fight against that pull he had on me was not waning as I looked for him more and more each day. Even a glimpse was enough to sate the yearning I felt. Though I should be ashamed of such thoughts, I could not lie to myself.

"You are ready, princess," Calara pleasantly chimed in. "Follow as we will lead you to the throne room."

The throne room, I pondered. "Am I summoned by him?" Why would I be going to the throne room?

She saw the look of concern on my face and knew I spoke of Samayaza.

"The Seer's throne room, my princess." she clarified.

My tension eased, and we began to walk toward Boria's throne room. This was different from the routine, but I knew things would change, as they always seemed to do here. Now was the time to start practicing what Hilanya had been teaching.

# AMONG ANGELS 8

"You were to keep her safe and away from his presence!" Daniel's tone took on a note of anger Gabril had not heard before. He knew it was his human emotions taking root within him.

"I cannot interfere with free will. You know that better than I do."

"Free will is not taken if it is for their protection!" he retorted.

Gabril looked at him with sadness. "That is not the truth, no matter how much goodwill you wish upon your guarded."

Daniel paced as he knew Gabril spoke the truth in everything. As much as he tried to keep Iris safe, the farther she strayed from him toward the fire. It was as though she yearned for things she could not comprehend nor withstand the weight of. She would refuse any guidance he would give and only seemed to succumb to his alluring nature when in close quarters. Something he noticed that was plaguing him, too.

"Her will cannot be changed by force, nor can her destiny. She was sent to be born for this time. She will learn as much as she will fail. Let it be." advised Gabril.

"I cannot stand by and watch her be dismantled and defiled by him."

Daniel shook his head as Gabril sighed at his brethren's frustrations. "Why would you believe she would allow him to defile her?"

Daniel understood what he was asking. He knew she was strong, but she was not prepared to fight against such principalities, visible or not, when she barely knew the strength of the spirit that resided within her. How was she supposed to overcome Samayaza's intense pull when she could scarcely keep herself sane around him? Daniel continually lowered his energy so as not to overwhelm her senses, and she still could not control her thoughts.

"Correct, she has much to learn, but she must learn on her own time and not yours." Gabril was always the voice of reason, and though Daniel agreed with everything just said, he could not help but feel the need to protect her and take her somewhere far away from here.

A small chuckle escaped Gabril. "That is what we all wish to do: protecting the light within is our most precious commodity. Those of darkness will never feel what you have felt, for the human form you have taken on is hindered by pride and ego."

"I fight this form every day, brother. The urge to crush him where he stands plagues my mind every moment within this human shell." His eyes swirled in anger as Gabril looked on. "Yet I fear the urge to make her mine will try to trump over all other needs upon this realm. I have not yet felt too weary to fight it, but I know that day will come." The swirls vanished as he looked at Gabril beseechingly.

Though he ached for his brother, Gabril could not help him in his inner turmoil. Daniel had chosen to take a path that was not ordained, and as such, the consequences would one day come. Gabril walked and placed his hand upon Daniel's broad shoulder. "The path to the light is in meekness and the humbling of oneself; remember that always."

As Gabril was about to take his leave, he mentioned something he knew Daniel would have already sensed. "If you have felt the darkness, you must be wary of everyone and anything. I fear it has visited her more than once."

Daniel's eyes swirled in defense at the mention of the evil Gabril spoke of. He knew how it lurked within the Temple, the people, and his fallen brethren. Without further words, both unearthly beings vanished. One ascended to his purpose, and the other remained below to become part of mortal history.

Samayaza stood with Azazzel at his right hand as he looked out from the highest balcony in the Temple. The city below him shined in wealth from the knowledge he had given and the gifts he'd bestowed on the humans. He understood now the importance of such comfort as the human body was fragile in every possible way. He wondered why there were such flaws in what was supposed to be the grand design of creation.

"Have the guide stones been prepared?" he asked as he continued to look out into the city.

Azazzel stepped forward as he raised his hand, gathering energy. He brought forth a satchel from within the air around him. It held the stones carved with knowledge from the heavens.

"I have contributed my own tale of events," he nonchalantly said as he pushed the satchel into the air. It floated directly toward Samayaza, who looked at him from the corner of his eye and raised a questioning brow.

Azazzel shrugged, "It creates a fascination these mortals will obsess about for ages," he explained.

Samayaza let out a chuckle as he expected nothing less from Azazzel. "Your need to be entertained by them is quite amusing. Like a lion toying with a field mouse before devouring it."

Azazzel shrugged, not denying his displeasure with the mortals. But Samayaza paid no attention as he knew all his brethren abided by the rule set within his Temple. He repeated this simple thought to Azazzel, reminding him of whom he served.

"Ah yes, speaking of temples and ruling them, my Temple is near completion. I will need to…" He paused as though trying to find the right words. "Embark on my journey."

Still looking out into the city, Samayaza smirked at his brother's impatience. "When Iris is mine, and your task has finished."

"Consider it already finished. She has made attachments to those already playing their part. It is only a matter of time."

Samayaza scoffed at him, repeating, "When Iris is mine, and your task is finished."

Azazzel scowled. He did not like his leader's doubt in his abilities but knew he must oblige to succeed with his plans of domination.

"As you say, My Liege." He yielded and bowed as he took his

leave.

Samayaza was no fool and knew of Azazael's ambitions and longing for power. In fact, he could sense all of his brethren's desires to rule over their portion of this Earth. They wanted their temples, mortals to enslave, and mortal women to defile. The temptation was greater now that they all had taken on human form. The desire to reign over the weak was great, but a more tempestuous emotion called them to couple with the daughters of Eve.

He mused and wondered why. He wanted to rule as a god as much as he felt that need. He wanted to be worshipped and feared as one.

A sinuous sound of scales across stone alerted Samayaza out of his thoughts. He turned to look upon a dark mass that lingered in the deep shadows of his throne room.

"You take upon yourself much before giving your share of our bargain."

Samayaza knew too well of the low hissing voice that emanated from the mass. He was not pleased. He bowed in submission as he said, "Nothing is mine, but all belongs to you, Master."

The black mass began to move toward him slowly. Samayaza furrowed his brows and held his head high. Fear was not an emotion that would infect him as it did the mortals.

"There is one hidden from us," hissed the mass as it stopped alongside Samayaza and began taking on a form of long ago.

Though the light was gone from his being, the black mass turned into the masterpiece that he once was. His design was extraordinary. He stood magnificently tall and stout with golden hair and unison facial features that would have brought peace to one's heart had the light not been diminished within his golden eyes. Though to any mortal, he would still be seen as such; mortals were easy to beguile as they denied the light within them to discern the truth.

"Hidden?" questioned Samayaza.

"Yes," he answered as he turned and looked straight into Samyaza's eyes.

Samyaza was in awe of his design, beautiful and beguiling indeed, but he was no mortal and knew not to be deceived by sight. He knew who stood before him and what he had done.

Through obedience, he had rejected this master during the first battle in the heavens, yet he felt the pull of all that was offered continue to draw him into agreement. So he took it when the temptation became too strong to deny. During the fall from the heavens onto this meek and lowly Earth, he felt the rush of power as promised and instant dominance over all those created from the dust of the Earth.

"Your inability to sense it is disappointing, Samayaza," scolded the lightless being. "Have the mortal women caused too much of a distraction for your mortal eyes?" He procured a deep red stone from within his robes. "The heart stone must be added to the rest. It bears the power to break barriers of the mortal mind with a simple sound."

The red stone glistened in the moonlight as it floated over to Samayaza with the wave of his hand. It hummed a vibration he had not heard before, high in frequency yet repetitive in rhythm.

"Weak minds are drawn to insistent sound," he advised as he spoke his final reminder to Samayaza. "Remember who is lord over you. Our bargain is not over."

Samayaza felt rage build within him but did not allow it to surface. Instead, he concentrated on the new stone that was given. It was indeed rare and not of this world. He knew what he held in his hand was none other than the heart of Lucifer. This stone would be very helpful in his conquest.

How ironic, he thought, the conductor of light to music had stolen so much fire from the heavens, yet he could not ignite his soul like it once had been. But that was the difference he saw between them—Samayaza did not seek that heavenly fire. The fire he could build upon the Earth was satisfying enough for him. He had time here to build upon and hierarchy over everything in his favor.

Though pity and disdain were in Samayaza's eyes, he dared not let it be known. So, a simple bow of his head in contrition was the solution.

The beguiling being arrogantly looked at him and instantly formed into a black mass as he hissed his orders out in the language of the realms.

"As you say, it will be done," answered Samayaza as he watched it disappear in a dark ripple, leaving behind a residue of smoke and sulfur.

# CHAPTER FOURTEEN

aniel escorted us to Boria's throne room and left as quickly as he guided us. The fast pace was unusual for him. I had never seen him walk so quickly that I had to sprint to keep pace behind him. Whether he was angry or irritated, I did not know. But asking about Selah was out of the question for now, as I felt reluctant when he seemed bothered by something. Maybe a small, subtle thought out to him. I took the chance while directly looking at the back of his head. I kindly sent my request and connected with him.

Instantly, I felt a powerful barrier. This was most strange and inconsistent with what I had experienced with him. Before I could try again, we were already in the throne room. His head held up high as I walked past, not even looking at me as I walked by. My heart sank, and without even realizing it, I gently swept my hand across the top of his. Within that exact moment, I felt the heat of his presence, and it was all I needed to know that he heard me. I do not know what it was or why I felt this connection to him, but I needed him to be my constant in this world of change. I left that thought, and a small part of my mind welcoming to him. My gesture was my apology, and I knew he was pleased as I felt his unique gentle warmth radiate within my mind.

As I neared my sister sitting upon her throne, the smell of sweet almond oil was being poured and brushed into her lustrous hair. She sat regally, almost arrogantly, and gazed down upon me as I neared.

"Welcome, sister," she said slowly.

It was surprising to hear her call me sister again; could it be she was coming out of her disillusion?

"Have you already forgotten protocol when approaching your Seer?" she reprimanded coldly. "Bow."

I should have known better than to believe she was sincere. I bowed as ordered while the priestesses around watched curiously.

"See, one bit of foolishness has already been remedied."

Her condescending tone was all about establishing her hierarchy over me. She was flexing her power and rule, letting it be known to all within her presence that she ruled. All expectations to see my sister return vanished.

She rose from her throne, smelling of sweet almonds as she came to stand next to me. "You have much to learn, Iris. Follow as I lead, and you will not stumble," she said dismissively, gesturing with her hand on where I should go. If only she could see that it was her that had stumbled, not I.

The day went on, learning about a ritual she called *Hashana*, the day of beautifying the skin. All the priestesses were preparing a thick dirt-like substance that smelled of raw Earth. Some were the color of grass, while others were red and black. They mixed and stirred until it reached a consistency that pleased them and then began using a thin, cleaned twig to draw upon their skin. They dipped it in their choice of color and began to draw intricately delicate designs upon one another's hands and feet. It was the most peculiar thing.

A smiling Calara approached and insisted I sit on a pillow as she drew upon my hands first. "You will look even lovelier with what I will draw."

She was so happy and eager to perform this task that I could not refuse. So, I sat and allowed her to do as she wished with my hands and feet. She was always kind and sought my interest at every opportunity. The least I could do was allow her this task she seemed to favor.

With a soft touch, she drew as I watched, astonished at her artistry. The large and small rounds she made and intertwined were beautiful. Even though she used only one color, the work she created on my skin was stunning. Her hand moved so fluently that, even though I could follow easily, it was impossible to repeat the patterns she continued to draw. It was amazing, almost as good as what I had seen Gabril stitch on the pillows and draw upon the vessels. I undoubtedly did not regret allowing her this task; she was gifted, and I was only too happy to watch her at her craft.

I noticed Boria look over at us now and then. I could not lie to myself as I yearned for it to be her and I trying our hand at this Hashana ritual. Alone, up on the roof of our humble home. As hard as I tried, and no matter how much I knew she had changed, my heart could not let go of her. She looked like my beautiful sister, yet the soul within her had shifted. Taking a deep breath, I held on to the promise of hope. If it was within me, then who was I to deny it?

"It is complete, princess," Calara said as she pointed to her finished work.

Looking down at my hands and feet, I smiled; It was as impressive as the stars at night and more beautiful than the wildflowers in the field. My hands held unique shapes; my pale skin and the red color she chose to draw made an unbelievably wonderful arrangement. The top of my feet had the same balance of images as my hands, but something caught my attention. Thereupon, my left foot was a familiar flower drawn out of place and directly upon the serpent's bite.

Was it just a coincidence, or did she know something? Before I could ask, she just smiled and backed away quickly. Boria was looking in our direction, and if I insisted on how she knew, Boria would sense something was amiss. So, I let it go for now, but it did not stop my mind from pondering about it. Why was it drawn on the ankle that carried the tiny scar left from the serpent's bite? Was it possible she knew from Boria?

As much I wanted to believe that it was because of Boria, my heart said otherwise. Boria had become cold and distant at each encounter and rarely spoke of her past or mine. I sighed, knowing this was just another riddle added to my long list since I arrived here. After all those years of Grandfather Enok speaking in riddles, it should have prepared me for all I have encountered. I suppose it would have, had I paid closer attention.

"Let us go forth to the fountain of the gods and cleanse ourselves in the blessed waters. May they be pleased by the work of your hands," she said as she looked up at Calara and some others.

I looked towards Boria's hands; there was so much red substance that it looked like her hands were wholly dipped in them rather than drawn upon. Her feet held small drawings, but her toenails had taken on the color of a dark red clay-like substance. It looked interestingly alluring.

A new unearthly being had arrived, one I had not seen before and one with features different from the rest. Though he was tall and as large as the rest, he had no hair on his head, and his eyes were the color of dark clouds that would come in winter. Boria called him by name, and it was just as unusual as his appearance—Haru.

His smile was only for her as he reached for her hand and brought it back to his lips while he spoke to her in that unfamiliar language. She smiled in return and allowed him to escort us all to our destination. How unusual, indeed, I pondered as I followed behind them and noticed how Daniel was not standing guard as I had assumed. I could not ignore it—my heart sank slightly at his absence. I heard no thoughts from him, and I sent none out.

Without further distraction, we proceeded to a fountain by her throne room. I had yet to notice this one, hidden behind a wall I'd never ventured around. It was significant in size, had shallow waters like most fountains, and had no waterfall. It had a large opening above it, more enormous than any I had seen. Most all the fountains here had an open ceiling to view the sky, as the sun and moon seemed to be critical in their rituals.

We began to dip our hands and brush off the clay residue. I thought the markings would surely fade, but they did not; they stayed vibrant in color. We did the same with our feet. Boria was, of course, washed first before any of us and perched herself on the fountain's edge as she watched over us. Once everyone had finished their task of washing, she spoke words of the foreign tongue and brought forth a light from within her hands that bounced from one hand to another. She blew upon it, and it burst into many small fragments of light that went all around the room and ascended through the opening above.

"A call of gratitude to our lords," she proclaimed as she began to speak about their vast knowledge and how we were blessed among all women to be within the great Temple of Enlightenment.

I listened and tried to discern what she said. Most were so foreign to me that all I could do was try to remember as much as possible and ask Grandfather Enok or Hilanya about them. How did Boria know all this so suddenly?

It had to be the ritual where Samayaza, Daniel, and Azazzel produced such unusual energy and gifted her with this knowledge. I wondered if she would speak to me about it and tell me what it felt like. Perhaps I should approach and ask. I waited for the right moment when the others were farther away.

I bowed slightly to show my willingness to her ways and asked, "How did you grow in the wisdom of the gods in so little time?"

Her expression softened, and to my surprise, she patted the area next to her, welcoming me to sit.

"My heart and mind have always been open to their wisdom," she proudly said as her gaze curiously looked over my hands.

"But how are you so familiar with who they are and what their will is for us?" If she could speak the truth, I might be closer to some of my answers. "Was it the night you wished upon all the stars in the night sky?"

She went still at the mention of that night and looked down towards her hands. She might be willing to speak if I remind her about the past.

"Yes, I suppose it was on that incredible night of their souls birthing into this world." She regained her composure and straightened her back.

"But how were they birthed into this world? Who was their mother? Or father?"

She laughed loudly as her demeanor relaxed. "Oh, Iris, you think like a mortal when, instead, you should think like they do! Like a God!" she exclaimed. "That is why you have so much to learn. You continue to rely upon your naïve understanding."

I tried not to feel inferior as she laughed, so I asked her another question, "Then explain, so I may understand and better serve you."

She liked what I said and smiled as she explained how they were from another realm, created of raw fire and power. They were never babes as we were, and they had no mother and father. They were deities and held the power of life and death within their hands.

"These deities you mention, is that another way to describe angelic beings that Grandfather spoke of when we were children?"

She sighed with annoyance. "No, Iris, they are gods. And not the fabled angel stories Grandfather has filled your head with. I had always warned you not to listen to him. They are real in every possible manner," she replied, irritated at my question. I knew I lost her interest as her stiff demeanor returned.

Whenever I tried to understand one thing, she spoke of other mysterious events. I could not keep up with her.

"Samayaza has shown me more than any other. His wisdom

is greater than all who walk upon this earth." Her voice went tender at the mention of Samayaza, and her cheeks flushed.

I was not waiting to hear this, but now that she had brought it up, I had to ask her again. "Have you been with him?"

For a moment, she looked hurt but quickly changed her expression. She got up and looked down at me. "Not the way I wanted, thanks to you, but yes, I have, and it was glorious."

My heart sank deep into sadness *at her admission*. I understood these beings' pull, but she did not resist once. Instead, she gave in to them freely. Could she truly be lost to them?

Days went by, and my interaction with Daniel began to heal. He would give me updates on Selah and her family and mine. I was happy to know they were safe and away from harm. Yet my conversations with Boria soured; the more questions I asked, the more irritated she became with me. I was to only listen and obey as the rest of the priestesses. Inwardly, I wanted to laugh at her because she knew I had always asked too many questions, so she should have been prepared, but this was not the old Boria. I needed to accept that I was no longer conversing with my sister but instead with the Seer of this Temple. I learned that too late as I inquired about Samayaza during our daily visit to the fountain of the gods.

"You ask too many questions about our lord. You realize I am bound to him, and he to me." Her tone was defensive, and I knew I neared a line she did not want me crossing.

"I have no desire to seek what you have." I ensured that she understood my intent was nowhere near what she was implying.

"You lie," she accused, "But I shall show you mercy as you are my kin. You are inexperienced and have proved how infantile your mind is. I will teach you even though you tried to betray me," she said as she began to walk away. Her hurtful claim lingered, but I'd grown accustomed to them the last few days.

I could not argue with her that I did not feel the pull from them every time they were near, for I remembered that one instance in the garden with Samayaza. Any rejection of her claim now would only push me further away from gaining her trust. So, I said nothing more and hoped she would continue teaching.

*"You will learn and know more than your kin. You may find me in the garden at your will."*

Samayaza's deep voice broke through my mind's barrier so quickly that it shook my senses, and I looked around in surprise. I thanked the heavens that Boria had already turned away. She would not take it too well to know the one she coveted was seeking my presence.

I stayed quiet the rest of the time at the fountain, thinking of all she had said and what Samayaza had whispered in my head. I felt my fight to win her back was futile, at least in the way I was planning. Every time I tried to speak and remind her of her past, she dismissed it and favored her present as though it was all she had ever known. She never mentioned Mother or Father, where or if they were safe.

My hope was slowly seeping out of my heart. I wondered if I should accept Samayaza's offer of knowledge to find a way to bring Boria back and return home. It was not as though he had no access to my mind; he had just proven he could break through whatever barrier I had. It was not much as I had not practiced as I should have, but why not let him have it all and find my way back home?

But what about Daniel? What if he could give me what Samayaza wanted to provide? Even though Daniel had failed to keep his promise, I still trusted him over Samayaza tenfold.

"I have a simpler solution. Allow me the honor, and I will tell you more than you ask for." Azazzel appeared beside me out of thin air.

I leaped to my feet in fright, alerting Boria and the priestesses to turn towards our direction.

"Lord Azazzel, you grace us with your presence," Boria said as she bowed. "But my priestesses are not prepared yet for your choosing," she concluded.

"I am not here for them." His smooth voice was as deceptive as his honey eyes, and his gaze remained fixed on me.

Without hesitation, I tried to reach out to Daniel but lost all concentration as Samayaza walked in with six of the most menacing beings I had seen yet. They were taller and broader than the rest. They carried weapons as big as I was, and each half of their faces were covered in the same ornamental material as their weapons. Their gazes held no warmth, and not one of them had eyes of blue, green, or honey.

"I believe the Seer said they are not ready," repeated Samayaza as he broke formation with the more menacing beings and drew closer to Azazzel and me.

"I claim my share," Azazzel simply replied.

"Admirable ambitions, brother. I expected nothing less." Samayaza took a calculated step to one side. Azazzel seemed unbothered.

"Since you are so generous with time, I claim her." He turned to Samayaza now. "You can have her once I am done." He winked at him, which only infuriated Samyaza.

"You claim nothing unless I allow it!" Samayaza's voice boomed throughout the room.

The priestesses shrieked in fright as they huddled near each other. I tried to move away slowly but caught Azazzel's attention. He leaped toward me in one stride and held me hard against his body. His arm wrapped tightly around my midsection as he pulled me against him; I could feel every stitch upon his garments. His fingers lingered on my side as I felt him release some pressure from his tight grip. When I thought I could breathe again, I felt his other hand slide up my arm in a caress.

Samayaza noticed, and his eyes began to swirl in crashing waves of blue. "You seek wrath rather than rule in due time?" Samyaza threatened.

The light shining through the opening above us suddenly dimmed as the air thickened.

"She is fair game, brother. As there is no claim on her," replied Azazzel as his fingers petted my side.

I pushed past my fear and reached out to Daniel, but each time I tried, I felt as though I was hitting a barrier. It was tiring, and my head began to ache deeply.

Seeing how Azazzel had no intention of letting me go, Samyaza responded, "Wrath it is," he quipped as the wind came rushing in out of nowhere.

Darkness suddenly came upon the Temple as the unearthly beings released blasts of power from within their hands. Blue streaks of light encircled us as I felt Azazzel's grip weaken and the heat that pulsated through the energy around us. It was as though the summer sun was blazing in the desert. Yet Samayaza seemed unfazed by it as he walked toward me, unharmed and undisturbed by the elements. The closer he came, the weaker Azazzel's grip became. The final step he took released me. I could barely stand; the heat was so intense that it had taken a toll on me. I had no strength left. Samayaza noticed and effortlessly picked me up as he began to walk away, disregarding Azazzel, who was suspended in the air with the four large beings circling him.

"My Lord, my priestesses and I will tend to her." Boria quickly interjected. Though my head ached, I knew she spoke out of jealousy and nothing more.

I wanted to tell her I did not intend to take Samyaza away from her, but I was too tired to open my eyes. I felt fatigued, and my head continued to ache.

"If I wished for you to tend to her, you would not be asking." His answer was similar to that in the garden. He must have sensed her jealousy as I did.

My eyes felt as heavy as my body, and my mind yearned for slumber. Whatever was blocking my call to Daniel had torn my strength from me. I tried to muster the energy to reach out to him one last time, but the fragrant aroma of cypress and musk that was Samayaza clouded my thoughts. Too exhausted to fight, I gave in as I heard him whisper the command *to sleep.*

# AMONG ANGELS 9

"We must ascend, now," ordered Gabril as Daniel continued to stall.

He knew Daniel heard him but could not break away from observing Iris in the company of her sister and the priestesses. A deep inclination from within his being begged him to stay and watch over her as he had been.

Daniel cursed in his mind on how time had become an enemy. He did not want to leave. He remembered this similar pull to stay once before, and when he had dismissed it, Iris had found herself in the forbidden garden. Unable to reach out to him, nor he to her.

"I know they will try what I fear the moment they feel my absence." Daniel's voice held concern and worry as he continued to observe Iris as she was casually speaking with one of the priestesses.

Gabril saw the surfacing of mortal emotion within his brother. A sentiment that was never meant to exist within him. But now, with his disobedience and human form, he knew what it was to have fear and doubt within his heart. Daniel saw the struggle deep within, fighting because he knew the truth, yet his discernment was clouded. And he knew who was obscuring it. She was sitting unaware and utterly oblivious to what Daniel was doing in order to protect her. It saddened Gabril greatly to see Daniel this way.

"Step back, brother. Breathe and allow the flawless design to render itself."

Daniel closed his eyes and allowed Gabril's words to sink deep into his heart. He should know better than to think that the power that wielded existence would not be absent at this time. He allowed what he knew to be true, and instantly, calm overtook him as he extended a final look toward Iris. She was smiling as she conversed with the women around her. He took that as confirmation and turned to Gabril, who joined him in ascending to the Fifth Realm of heaven to plead for his actions while Gabril stood witness.

"Well done," said Samayaza as he stood on the balcony overseeing his city.

Azazzel stood close with a grin on his face.

"Your performance was exceptional," he commended.

Azazzel nodded and winced as he felt a brief ache within his mortal shell.

Samayaza noticed. "You were slow to procure your shield, brother."

"I was not slow. I was authentic to the deception." Azazzel would not admit defeat in any way. Whether planned or not, he was not going to be made to look weak.

Samayaza ignored his arrogance as he moved along in his plans. He gave Azazzel new orders. "Burn it; let her see the illusion of her parent's death, but do not harm the sisters. Their disposition will become the catalyst for her obedience."

Azazzel smiled, anxiously anticipating the use of force and fear to dominate the sons and daughters of Adam. It was a pastime he was beginning to favor.

"And what shall you have me do with the mother and father?"

As much as Samayaza wanted to do away with them, he knew they might be needed later if Selah broke free of their deception. They could serve as much-needed leverage in order to keep her where he wanted and willed.

"Keep them alive and away from the city for now," he ordered as he heard Azazzel begin to walk away. "Azazzel," he called out after him. "Keep them alive and well. A breath away from death is of no use to me," he added.

Azazzel's smile shrank as the final order took away the joy he was about to have. He would obey and continue as ordered, but that did not mean he couldn't have a little fun with the uncle. Samayaza mentioned nothing about him or his well-being. A tenacious and crooked smile returned to his face as he walked away. Already, he called out to his squad of ten brethren, and they all appeared on the outskirts of Selah's humble home.

He gave orders about who was to be spared and who would be delivered to him at a designated location.

"Burn the home in a way where I can see them come out screaming and panicked. The fear in their eyes is exhilarating to witness." His vile pleasure in watching mortals suffer was becoming an addiction he enjoyed.

Perching himself upon a rock he'd conjured from within the Earth, he sat at a distance and watched his brethren descend upon the unsuspecting humans. They surrounded the home and assessed the location of all within it. Just as he had ordered them not to harm the ones mentioned, they began to send blasts of fire from their hands to one corner of the home where none were present.

"How exciting, indeed," he muttered as he timed how long it would take for these feeble humans to recognize they were in danger and come out stricken with panic.

"Twenty, twenty-one, twenty-two..." He counted.

The door burst open as the family came rushing out.

"Ahh, twenty-five. A bit slow but not surprisingly shocking."

His sordid motives were just getting started as he saw the weasel uncle run out of the door first. Squinting his eyes, Azazzel peered deep within his mind and noticed he did not care to look for the children but had residual perverse thoughts of them lingering in his head. Not that it mattered to him much what happened to any human, but now, he had an excuse to justify the torment he had planned for the insignificant mortal. He heard the cries of the children but cared not for their whimpers as they huddled near their mother. He rolled his eyes at the task at hand. He knew they would wail even louder once he inserted the image of their death into the yielding young minds. He looked over at Selah and decided to start with her. Maybe he would have her witness her uncle's demise. It might add that additional note of horror she might need to fulfill her duty in bringing down Daniel.

A formidable slithering serpent caught his attention as it came out from behind the rock he was perched upon. He looked down at the pitch-black creature as it made its way up the rock toward him. The sound of every scale on its long thick body rubbed against the stone as it swirled around and behind Azazzel, raising its head to face him.

"Yes, deception is such an easy feat with these mortals," he answered as he slid off the rock and bowed to the serpent. He heard the frightened family becoming aware of the unearthly beings surrounding them as the smell of fear made its way into his nostrils. He inhaled the scent deeply as though savoring it.

"Almost sweeter than torture," the serpent hissed as Azazzel casually walked away.

"No, torture is sweeter yet," answered Azazzel. His honey-colored eyes swirled in anticipation as he changed his mind and made his way toward the uncle first, who was now standing cowardly behind the father.

"Oh, ye of little faith, come forth so I may bask in your fear," Azazzel mocked and taunted the uncle as he drew near, forcing him to face his fate.

The serpent looked on as Azazzel took on his task with pleasure, making sure to go the extra length of adding terror and fear within the children as he inserted images of their parent's broken bodies into their susceptible minds. He impressed the dark serpent at every task he had been assigned, with the current job being the most efficient and creative thus far. And oh, what passion he had in delivering judgment upon his prey. No quarter given, no plea of mercy heard, only the wrath of his power and sheer will to destroy. His pleasure in suffocating the light within the mortals was just as intense as his own.

With the final curdling scream that came out of that lump of clay that was the uncle, the serpent was much satisfied. It was almost musical to hear their cries, but with the task complete, the serpent slithered away, enthralled by what it had witnessed.

Daniel and Gabril pleaded with the three giant guardian beings that stood watch of the Fifth Realm. Daniel kneeled in repentance as Gabril stood beside him with his hand upon his shoulder, hoping that standing witness for his fallen brethren would be enough for their plea to reach the footstool of the Creator. Daniel kept his head low and humbled himself as he genuinely prayed for atonement and guidance for his actions. His mind was solely focused on his petition and redemption. He allowed his mind to be open entirely to the realms as his regret and intentions were made bare for all to read. Intercession by Gabril was the bridge he hoped would take his plea to the Creator of all light.

"Your plea has been heard, Daniel of the First Realm, created by fire and light," said all three beings simultaneously.

Daniel lifted his head and acknowledged their announcement as Gabril raised his hand from Daniel, motioning him that it was done, at least for now.

The giant guards vanished, leaving them alone at the realm's edge.

"You must descend now and allow his will to reach you with an answer." Gabril had no other words of comfort for Daniel; he had done all he could for him.

Daniel rose and regained his composure as he collected his thoughts and probed what was happening in the world below. Instantly, he knew something was wrong as his eyes shot to Gabril.

"Yes, it is, and you must go now," Gabril acknowledged his foresight.

Without another word, Daniel descended upon Earth with the velocity of a fiery star. Gabril watched with concern as he knew his brother would be facing the worst temptations yet.

Iris stood before Samayaza's throne as he presented her with a crying and disheveled Selah. Her face was covered in soot, and her clothes looked battered and tinged by fire. Her beautiful big eyes were swollen and red from sobbing over the loss of her family.

"My guards alerted me of their peril," said Samayaza, sounding as concerned as possible. "Azazzel reached her in time, but unfortunately, all her kin are no longer alive."

He noticed Iris's fear at the mention of his brethren, hence his acknowledgment to Azazzel for the rescue, hoping this act might redeem him.

Since Selah was distraught by the horrors she had seen, she willingly allowed Samyaza into her mind. And he had wasted not a second before pushing the ordeal of her family's demise deep into her subconscious. It would take some time for her to remember, but he would not take any chances, so he quickly allowed and assisted Selah's sorrow to be the dominant energy in the room. All he needed was a bit of time for Iris to feel betrayed by Daniel and then willingly give herself to him both body and mind, just like her sister had so quickly.

Iris felt her deepest heartache yet. Selah had been left an orphan. Tears fell down her face in empathy for her little friend, who had to face life without the loving family she had just reunited with.

"She may stay here within the temple, in your quarters as your ward, if you wish." Samayaza made his grand offering to her as he hoped it would become the bridge to her heart and mind. Intently he watched as she held Selah tightly and wept in sorrow. He knew his plan had worked thus far; Selah was so fearful after witnessing the torturous death of her uncle that her mind was open to him. The images of her deceased parents would stay fresh in her mind forever, and the enslavement of her younger sisters would ensure her obedience to his will if she somehow remembered.

Full of emotion, Iris tearfully nodded to his offer as she continued to comfort poor little Selah in her arms. She was devastated at what she hoped would be a happy life for her little friend. How could this happen, and why? Who would want to cause such harm to this lowly family that hindered no one? Her sorrow was slowly turning into anger as she lost all barriers in thought.

Samayaza smirked as he saw her rage building. His plan was coming together perfectly.

"Who would do such a thing?" Iris asked as she choked back tears. Whoever committed this act was an evil beast that deserved no mercy. She wanted—no, she needed—to know who had done this to them. If ever she needed these unearthly beings to use their powers, it would be now!

She called out to Daniel in her mind, hoping he would come

as he had promised. Samayaza heard her thoughts and rejoiced inside. She called out for Daniel, and he would undoubtedly be here right on time.

Hatred had finally taken root within her. Who would have thought a mere village mortal would have been the seed to bring forth the rage he witnessed in her now. He regally rose from his throne and slowly walked down the steps toward Iris. He did not want to alarm her in any way, as he knew her hesitance toward him had not completely vanished. Though she was distracted with Selah, he knew his pull on her would quickly awaken her hidden memories.

"I am afraid it was one of my brethren who committed this atrocious act," he said sadly, placing a hand upon Selah's shoulder.

She shivered at his touch and pulled away. Iris took notice and frowned.

She grew impatient, waiting for his reply. "Who is it?" she asked again. This time her voice was louder as her anger began to boil over.

Doors thrust wide open as a cold burst of air rushed into the throne room.

"Ah, just in time," whispered Samayaza to himself.

Azazzel's grin was from ear to ear. He had been waiting for this moment for a long time. He took a wider stance and clenched his fists as he stood readily available upon command.

Daniel walked in with the fury of a thousand suns. He locked eyes with Samayaza and blasted him with energy that shot out from his hands and sent him flying into a pillar, cracking it as his body imprinted upon it.

Iris quickly picked up Selah and rushed behind the throne for shelter as the unearthly beings continued to quarrel.

"I warned you to stay away from my guarded!" Daniel seethed in anger as he watched Samayaza rise from the rubble.

Azazzel held steady as he impatiently waited for his orders from Samayaza. The rest of the fallen watched eagerly at the play of power that was taking place in front of them.

"Is this how you repay your brother and lord for watching over her while you were... Hm. Where were you exactly?" He stopped patting himself clean and looked toward Daniel, ready to frame him. "Oh yes, outside the city is what I was told. You wouldn't happen to have seen poor Selah's home or what was left of it out there, did you?" he asked sarcastically.

"Yes, I fully know what was left," answered Daniel.

Iris slowly came out from behind the throne. He saw the look in her eyes and instantly regretted his choice of words.

"Maybe you owe your guarded an explanation as to why you would do such a thing, Daniel. I was expecting better from you," Samayaza mildly chided as he looked at Iris.

Daniel saw the entire framework of Samayaza's deception and knew he had made a mistake. Ignoring Samayaza, he looked straight at Iris. "It was not I who committed such an act as this." He pushed images of where he had been and words of comfort but felt her mind impenetrable, just like when she was in the garden.

Iris felt the sting of betrayal. It hurt worse than the bite of the serpent. Her rage had turned into agony as she stepped forward. "Where were you then?"

Daniel furrowed his brows as he again tried to push through the barrier blocking his link to his guarded.

"Yes, Daniel, where were you?" Samayaza chimed in as he placed himself beside Iris, only further infuriating Daniel.

"I was not there," he repeated, hoping she would believe him. If he were to say aloud where he truly was, it would set off a series of chaos and destruction for them all. Samayaza and the rest of his brethren would cause such a war among themselves that it would bring upon their judgment before its appointed time, and all would be in vain.

"Why?" cried Iris as she felt crushed to the core. "You were to protect her and her family!" she yelled at Daniel, causing him to flinch in disbelief.

He sensed something was terribly off with her. She was quick to assume it was him and quick to anger. He felt he had no choice in what he was about to do but needed to get to her and take her out of the throne room immediately. Something was clouding their link, and he needed her away from what he suspected would be the cause.

Samayaza could see Daniel's suspicion and quickly ordered Azazzel to intervene lest he discover how he had manipulated her thoughts.

"Finally, my turn," said Azazzel as he lunged toward Daniel. Waves of energy burst forth from his hands, creating a translucent sphere trapping Daniel.

"This is not a war you wish to wage with me, Azazzel," Daniel warned, unharmed from within the sphere.

Azazzel laughed, "The war is already waged and is about to be won," he declared as he sent another burst toward him.

Samayaza looked on with delight as he ordered all his brethren to appear in the throne room and witness Daniel's downfall. They soon appeared one by one, filling the throne room within seconds. All clad in black robes and hoods, they stood silently and watched as the greatest among them was ensnared by his brethren. Some were weary, others looked on with delight, and some had no care if he were to survive or perish.

Iris looked all around in dread as she was now in the middle of more unearthly beings than she had ever imagined existed. She tightened her arms around Selah, trying to shelter her as best she could.

"Destroy him," ordered Samayaza to Azazzel as he joined forces with him. Together, they sent out streaks of blue and golden light that hit Daniel's sphere, trying to crush the orb with Daniel in it.

Iris screamed inside in protest at the given order and what she saw before her eyes. Yes, she wanted whoever had done such a thing to Selah and her family to be punished, but she was not expecting Daniel to be the beast who had committed such acts. She was not ready to accept the punishment she had wanted for such a being.

The current of power crackled and sent out spurts of light within the sphere, hitting Daniel in an all-around assault. He kneeled in a moment of weakness he knew they needed to see. He searched their minds without their knowledge, as they believed him to be weak and dying. One by one, he read all the thoughts of his brethren and knew who was for him and who was not. Then he peered into the mind of his guarded and felt the residue of Samayaza's energy. He looked in her direction and noticed something he blamed himself for not seeing; her stone was gone and replaced by a dark red jewel. Evil leeched from it, and he finally knew why their link was blocked.

He felt his entire being built up to what he was about to unleash upon his unsuspecting brethren. Pretending to be defeated was the only way to allow the perpetrators to make themselves known, and they did just that.

With a roar, Daniel stood, extending his arms on either side of him as a force so bright and great was released from within him. It sent almost every being in the throne room to the ground except for those who were for him, including Iris and Selah, who held his protection. They did not feel the pulse of energy that blasted everyone around them.

Only Samayaza was able to lessen the blow's impact with the serpent's help, but Azazzel was not as lucky. He flew back, hit his brethren, and took a row of them to the ground with him. Daniel now stood alone and idle in the middle of the throne room, staring at Iris as she cradled Selah's head in her chest. She locked eyes with him in a predicament she never imagined. He softly whispered aloud, asking her to investigate his mind and heart and find her desired answers.

Samayaza stood motionless, disturbed by what had just occurred within his throne room. His anger was building, and he wanted to pummel Daniel to the ground. But the serpent ordered him to stand down. The time for revenge would come soon enough. He stressed about Iris, but the serpent again silenced him into submission. Samayaza obeyed and watched the multitude of his brethren vanish one by one. They had seen enough for now.

Iris finally spoke and gave Daniel an answer. "You are no protector or guardian. I need not look for answers in your mind, as Selah has already given me the answers I seek." Selah lifted her head and looked at Daniel with guilt dripping from her eyes.

"Why did you destroy my family and home?" asked Selah, tears running down her face.

He searched her thoughts again and saw the seed of illusion

deep in her mind. She believed it true; Daniel had burned their home and killed her parents. Daniel was betrayed and ensnared in a great deception. He had to uproot that seed to gain their trust back. Time was no longer a friend to him, as he knew he could not accomplish that task right now.

"I believe you have your answer now," Samayaza broke the silence. "Your presence is no longer welcome in my temple." If Daniel stayed any longer, the deception would begin to deteriorate as he would connect with Iris even with the heart stone present.

"I will take my leave if she wishes it so." Paying no attention to Samyaza, Daniel kept his gaze focused on Iris. Hoping she would allow him a chance to come close.

Samayaza, again with the help of the serpent, sent the false image of Selah's parents burning alive within the home. Iris winced at the horror, and with a broken heart, mind, and soul, she whispered as tears fell down her face, "Leave and never show yourself to me again," she cried out.

Daniel's heart ached at her pain, but he knew she was not of sound mind; the influence of the heart stone was overtaking her senses. He was about to take a few steps towards Iris, when one of his brethren who had not left spoke out.

"Now, why would Daniel do such a treacherous act as you have accused him of when you are his guarded." He stepped forward with confidence as he presented the question to Iris.

Iris looked at him through teary eyes and quickly remembered seeing him before. It was Haru, the one who had escorted Boria recently and had eyes only for her. She did not know how to respond to him, as her thoughts were muddled with Selah's pain.

"Ahh, Haru," Samyaza said dryly. "I was wondering when

you would pick a side."

Haru chuckled at Samyaza's obvious irritation. "Anything to bring you joy, my lord." he answered as he mocked him by pretending to bow.

Azazzel had now steadied himself from Daniels's blow and had joined Samyaza. He looked at Haru disgustedly. "You chose the wrong side, brother."

Haru looked at Azazzel's disheveled state and then towards Daniel, who stood impeccably solid without a single strand of hair out of place. "Either your mortal body is blinding you, or you are just that stupid." he countered.

Daniel was thankful for Haru; he had caused enough disruption to get a few more steps closer to Iris. He had sensed Haru's distrust and dislike towards Samyaza the day of Boria's crowning of Seer. He had feelings towards her and knew it was only a matter of time before he would oppose Samyaza. This was well for Daniel as any brethren fighting against Samyaza was one less brethren fighting against him.

All the while, Azazzel was losing his temper with Haru. Daniel knew he would have to act quickly before his honor would force him to stay and defend Haru from any further attacks.

As if on cue, Azazzel readied himself to pounce toward Haru when Samyaza shouted, "Enough!" silencing everyone as he sent out an explosion of white light that illuminated the throne room.

And within that blink of an eye, Daniel was able to secure Selah and Iris within his arms and vanish.

# ACKNOWLEDGEMENTS

To my husband and parents, who provided financial stability in my life and made this dream reality. To my family & friends, who have patiently waited for the completion of this first book for years. It was not always easy to believe in me, but I genuinely appreciate the support and endless encouragement to continue and finish what I started. In an endeavor such as this, the comfort you all provided allowed me to release a bit of my imagination into the world.

To my wonderful children, who, without your constant unconditional love, I would not have overcome the common hurdles in life. You guys have had simple solutions to what I perceived as the most complicated situations. Thank you.

To the English college instructor for continually pushing me to go past the cliches in writing and fearlessly create my spin on any tale, thank you for making that class so tricky; it helped inspire my writing and gave me the confidence to pursue my dreams.

To Mary for helping me edit this book and providing the feedback necessary to deliver a story lost in time. To Kelly, who patiently waited for the manuscript to be finalized and provided the most fantastic cover to match the tale. Your expertise in this process is truly appreciated.

# ABOUT THE AUTHOR

As the first-born Armenian American in her family, the Author was raised with English being her second language. She grew up on the west coast of the United States of America, where culture and diversity helped establish her love for all people. Most of her time is spent with her ever-growing family and supportive friends. Apart from writing, she enjoys learning history, biblical history, and traveling. Though she majored in and graduated from college with a multi-media and production degree in science, she chose to follow her passion for writing. She is working on Book 2 of the fallen angel series and hopes to have a release date sometime in 2024.